Martin,

THE BUTLER REALLY DID IT

THE BUTLER

BOOK 2

Hope You Enjoy!☺

SEAN BUTLER

All the best,

Sean

Sean Joseph

THE BUTLER REALLY DID IT

SEAN JOSEPH

DEDICATION

I would like to dedicate this novel, 'The Butler Really Did It,' to my wonderful parents, John Albert and Vera Sophia. I would like to express my sincere gratitude and tell you how much I loved you while you were alive. I always think about both of you so much and often hear myself saying things you both said while you were alive, which makes me smile. Thank you so much from the bottom of my heart for the heart full of grateful memories of you and the experiences we shared, which are priceless. You live on in my heart and are always with me in spirit.

Sean Joseph

CONTENTS

PREFACE

Johnny Butler returns in this sequel to 'The Butler Did It'. The Butler Really Did It is a crime novel written by Sean Joseph. Certain events in this novel mirror and reflect some events which the author has been part of and witnessed. Specific facts and names have been changed. The central character is a recovered alcoholic and addict living in recovery one day at a time, seeking a life of purpose rather than pleasure.

He attends 12-step fellowship meetings regularly and has become a successful world-famous author due to his journey's many twists and turns. He has left his criminal life behind and become a law-abiding citizen trying to help others find purpose and meaning. He has found faith in a Higher Power of his understanding, which he calls God. He wants to get his novel made into a film. He likes that idea and wants to pursue that plan and dream.

His life will unravel in a way he could totally not see coming and change forever. Certain events from his past rear their ugly head again and make him the centre of a showpiece trial at the Old Bailey that will grip the nation and the world.

The only question on everyone's lips is, Did the Butler really do it?

CHAPTER 1
PUBLICATION

JOHNNY BUTLER HAD GONE from being the head of an organised crime racket to a published author, or as he preferred to say, 'from being Don Corleone to John Grisham,' that certainly had more 'Je Ne Sais Quoi' about it; he thought. It had certainly been an amazing journey. He had managed to write and publish his first novel. The most important life lesson he had learnt was that a life without a purpose is meaningless and very unsatisfying, or to use the words from the Big Book, irritable, restless and discontent. So, he had learnt that 'Being of Service to Others' was and could be the only meaningful life he could lead from now on. The hole in his soul could not be fixed with cigarettes, gambling, sex, drink or drugs. His own experience had shown him they were all very short-term fixes based on pleasure, which never compared to helping others. The book was not published just yet, but it had all been submitted to Amazon for publication with the editing completed, obtaining two ISBNs, the book cover, blurb and formatting all finally completed. It was now all about Amazon; when would they publish? There was no set answer, it was in their hands now. The novel was to be published in paperback, hard copy, and Kindle.

It had not been a straightforward journey. Once he had finished writing the novel, he knew he would need his manuscript to be proofread, edited, formatted and a book cover created before publishing. He went online and found a firm of academic editors that specialised in proofreading and editing. They seemed a highly efficient company. He realised they did not specialise in editing or publishing novels but more in academic and business projects and work. He had spoken to several firms about doing the work, but Ace Proofreading, trading from the website address www.aceproofreading.co.uk, agreed to lower their price and match other quotes he had received and promised the world in terms of service and quality. He felt really good. He had finished writing the crime novel and gave the finishing touches to a highly specialised proofreading and editing firm. What could go wrong? There was only one problem: he never realised they were bigger crooks than he had been. Nothing happened after talking to them, agreeing on the details, instructing them, and paying their fee.

After a few weeks, they just returned the first chapter and made it worse than it was initially. They had Americanised the chapter and used specific terms like gas and so on, which meant the person doing the editing did not speak English as a first language. Johnny quickly realised they were just giving the jobs to editors from countries like Africa who had no understanding of dialect or ability to do the work. He complained, and they said they would get someone else to do it properly. They did it again, but the result was no better. After one more attempt, Johnny said as they could not do the work, he would like a refund, and then he would get the job done elsewhere. Then it got worse. They said they could not process his refund until he hit the £5,000.00 threshold for refunds. They said they would refund the whole lot once he paid the additional £3,300.00 to hit the threshold, which was a joke and a made-up scam. The bare-faced front of these people. They now wanted more money to process a refund. That is when it hit home: they were crooks. So, he said there was no need to pay the additional top-up fee, just pretend and then refund. It just went on like this for a while. He knew what was going on. It was his first time dealing with them. He considered taking legal action. Then he realised there was no address on their website. The communications were done via the contact facility on their website, emails, and WhatsApp messages. He had been stitched up. The irony of the situation was that a criminal writing a novel about crime had been turned over by a bunch of criminals online. After getting over the initial disappointment and taking it on the chin, so to speak, he did, on one or two occasions, laugh about it.

After that complete disaster, he managed to find an author called Patricia, and she put him in touch with two ladies who were reputable and honest. They did the work and got the job done. He smiled and thought never again would he instruct anyone without a reference from someone he knew and trusted.

Johnny did manage to get a result shortly after that with a reference from a guy he knew from Deal called Bernie, but it was a different sort of deal. Johnny's teeth, by now, had seen the best days of their life, so to speak, and Johnny had been considering a completely new set of teeth for a while. He knew that what he needed to get done in England would cost about £25,000.00. He also realised that you could get a great job done in Turkey for about £7,000.00. He also knew he would not take a chance in Turkey with a dentist where he did not speak the language, understand the law or know anyone. You hear horror stories about surgery and dentists in Turkey, and he would not take potluck, although he knew his teeth were loose, missing, filled and had seen better days. Bernie had booked to fly to a dentist in Kusadasi because he knew several people who had been there, had the work done and was very happy with the service and the quality of the work. That was enough for Johnny. He got the contact details from Bernie, got in touch with the dentists directly in Kusadasi, and then booked the treatment at the next available appointment and booked the flights.

They did turn out to be a small dentist in Kusadasi and were great. The staff and service were very good. Johnny thought it was like being at an excellent dentist in the UK. They did realise after examining and doing an x-ray of his mouth that his sinus level needed to be raised, and he also needed bone transplants because of the condition of his gums as well as his teeth. Then they realised he needed more implants because he had many loose teeth. He knew everything they said was true because they showed him the x-ray and explained everything. He had already been told in England about his gums and gum disease before. He also knew many of his teeth were very loose because he could just touch them and wiggle them. In the last few years, he would often suffer from toothache because of lost teeth and air getting in, as well as gum disease. He agreed to have the extra work done, which would cost more, but at least he knew he would get a proper job done.

They started the work on Monday, doing a little every day, then on Friday when a dentist/surgeon who was the leading partner in the firm worked on his teeth, taking teeth out, putting stitching in, raising his sinus level and doing the bone transplants while he was continuously injecting Johnny with a local anaesthetic. After about two hours, Johnny had lost the will to live. It was as simple as that. He had never been in so much physical pain, even with all the injections that were continuously being put in the gums; he was lying in the chair and thought it would be easier to call it a day and die there and then. The surgeon realised Johnny was in such a state. He looked at Johnny and said, 'You are almost in a state of trauma; I am going to stop working on you now.' He could see Johhny was at his wit's end. He had not been able to complete all the work necessary but had got 90 per cent of it done.

The process for an entirely new set of teeth in Turkey normally takes two trips. The first trip is to do most of the work, lay all the foundations, and make implant insertions. Then, go home and allow the mouth and gums to heal for six months before they do the final work, implants and bridges as necessary and agreed in advance. The situation now Johnny faced was he was going to have to return in six months just to have a couple of insertions for additional implants, then allow for a further six months of healing before the work would be completed. After leaving the dentist on Friday with his flight booked back to England on Sunday morning from Izmir, he was given a piece of paper with a recommendation to nip up the chemist and get some strong painkillers. He was in so much pain he never took on board that information. He had just returned to the Carina Hotel and lay in bed. When he saw his face in the mirror, it was covered in bruising everywhere. He looked like he had just gone a couple of rounds with Mike Tyson and had the bruises to prove it. He went to the bar and got some painkillers. The guy would only give him two. Very quickly, he went back to the bar and managed to nick the whole packet from under the counter at the end of the bar. He had been tipping everyone well and knew the guy wouldn't let him have any more, so he helped himself. When he went back to his room, he realised there was blood all over the sheets and pillows from his mouth. It finally dawned on him the immensity of the work that had been done on him. His face had changed shape. He couldn't sleep at all but just kept drinking water, lying down, and praying for the pain to go. He couldn't eat anything, that was for sure. By about lunchtime the following day, most of the pain and the whole packet of painkillers had gone. He couldn't eat, but he was beginning to smile gain. He realised that he would never have opted to go through what he had been through if he had known, but the worst was over, and the vast majority of the work had now been done. The dentists were very professional, and he found a lot of comfort in that. He caught his flight home early Sunday morning. He now felt alive and a bit like 'the Colegate kid,' he smiled or at least tried. Even with the additional charges, he thought he would save about sixteen or seventeen thousand pounds, which more than made up for the loss with ace proofreading. You win some – you lose some, he thought. Maybe more to the point, remember you should never get involved with anyone without references, regardless of the business type.

Johnny had been told by a guy called Adam, whom he knew from the rooms, about a 12-step convention in Newport, Wales. Johnny misunderstood Adam and thought he had booked to go. Johnny decided to go and booked his place and room at The Celtic Manor Resort. He just saw it as a weekend away and always enjoyed weekend conventions. He often met many people he may not have seen for a long time and caught up, as well as the convention, the relaxation, and overall fun at these things.

When he booked, he had been seeing a young lady called Jemima from the rooms whom he was smitten with, so he booked a double and thought if that were working out, he would invite her along for the weekend. He liked her and thought she was like a doppelganger of Sandra Bullock. Once they started talking and getting to know each other, she told Johnny, 'We will be like the Gangster and the Princess.' What a strange thing to say, Johnny thought. No one had ever called him a Princess before. Still, there was a first time for everything, he smiled and laughed to himself. Jemima had been a fitness instructor for about twenty years. She always ate very well and looked after her body. When she was younger, she had been an ambassador for Great Ormond Street Hospital. She used to go on trips and climb and run up mountains, including Kilimanjaro, to raise money for Great Ormand Street Hospital. One night, they went to Boys Hall in Ashford, and both Jemima and Johnny had dressed for the occasion. Jemima had made a big effort and looked stunning. After a while, one of the waitresses approached the table and said, 'Do you mind if I say something to you?' Jemima says no, she says I just wanted to say to you, you look absolutely beautiful. What a wonderful compliment for Jemima to receive from an absolute stranger! As the waitress leaves the table, Johnny asks, 'Are you talking to me?'. She turns her head while walking away, smiles at Johnny, and replies, 'Yes, you as well.' Johnny laughs and thinks 'great answer!'

He thought if that were progressing and going well, her company would be the icing on the cake in Newport. That had not worked out well, really, because they both had such different ideas about relationships, and they didn't spend long getting to know each other; cracks started appearing on both sides. Johnny had told her, "Let's call it a day and wish each other well. She said I thought we were just getting to know each other. Johnny suddenly didn't like her attitude and couldn't understand her. It was a complicated situation, to say the least. After they agreed not to have an exclusive relationship, Johnny started moving on with his life, and she thought they were going to stay in touch and catch up daily. How strange! Johnny thought. She then said I think you are being funny with me; he didn't see it that way; he just thought you either want to know me or you don't. The romance had been too quick, and that was the problem, so it was kind of hard to know how to understand it all. The idea of a fling with such a young woman would have been very appealing to Johnny years ago, but Johnny wanted something real and of substance. She had her own family, and he had met them. He knew deep down that a friend like her in tow, whether that was with benefits or not, would hold him back from the chance of finding love with a decent woman in the future. Anyway, they didn't speak for a while, and then they started speaking again. Johnny didn't know the basis and still liked her company, so they started going out again and spending time together. He knew he liked her but thought we should see; they went out and had fun together doing different things. A good friend of Johnny's told him she was right and he was wrong; they should have tried to be friends, get to know each other and let it take its time. Johnny laughed and realised he had jumped the gun yet again. Johnny invited Jemima along, and she said she would try to get the Friday off work, but she didn't get back to him.

So, he travels down to Wales alone and turns up at The Celtic Manor Resort, a five-star hotel with a golf course. It turned out that it was at this venue when 'The Open' was played in Wales. As you would expect, everything at the place and about the place was tip-top! The staff were excellent, professional and friendly. His room was like a showroom from a palace. Everything is just in its place, just how it should be. The food was to die for. Johnny thought the hotel was full for the convention, and all its guests were attending the convention. He jumped in a lift, and there was a young couple in there, both dressed up; she looked elegant, and he looked like he was a male model out of a magazine shoot. Johnny says are you here for the convention? They both looked puzzled and said, 'What convention? Is it a work convention?' Johnny replies no, it is a CA convention, then he throws in for good measure; we are all here because we are learning how to live life, not drinking alcohol or taking drugs, but we only do it just for today and smiled at them. Their faces were a picture; he wished he had a picture of the expressions on their faces, and then they said to him, 'Well done to you.' It was so patronising, he realised, but they were not addicts or alcoholics, obviously, and they didn't understand, so really, they were just a bit shocked by his honesty. To be fair to them when most people who stay at five-star hotels and pay for the privilege don't expect to meet a guy in the lift shouting that the place is full of addicts and alcoholics who are all meeting there to have a convention. The image that may have conjured up in their minds did not sit with the idea all these people may have that would be staying at the hotel for the weekend.

In reality, addicts and alcoholics can be some of the most successful and talented people on the planet when they are not using or drinking. Some of them can be very rich people who could buy the hotel, let alone stay there for the weekend, but some alcoholics and addicts never seem to achieve success or get on their feet. Some remain homeless and die from addiction and alcoholism. They are just like any cross-section of society, really, very different in many ways; a lot of them are nothing like each other at all; they just share the one disease of alcoholism and or addiction. Johnny believed that the stigma attached to alcoholism and addiction years ago has subsided a lot today. Is that because many high-profile actors, musicians and celebrities openly share their periods of sobriety today and are proud of it? Is it because many people are touched by the disease today on a personal level? Is it because society is more tolerant today? Who knows but the only real difference between an alcoholic and a non-alcoholic person is the reaction in the brain when they drink alcohol. The alcoholic brain gets the phenomenon of craving, and that starts the reaction, which just craves more and more and more. Then, the behaviour and consequences follow. Alcohol and drugs just become a fix, and so the cycle of using begins.

In America, lots of companies like to employ alcoholics and addicts in recovery because they are aware that the solution is to live and lead a spiritual way of life, which makes them very attractive employees.

Then Johnny left the lift and looked around the reception and registration area. He realises many of the people he does not recognise, strange he thinks. He always met several people he knew from London or Kent at most of the conventions he had attended over the years previously. The more he looks, the more he realises he doesn't recognise anyone at all. Then, at the registration area, it became clear to him that it was a European Convention, and many of the people spoke in broken English and different European languages. He had not realised that at all when booking, so it would be a new and different convention experience. He had seen on social media earlier that day Richie was on his way to Wales for the weekend, so no doubt he would bump into or see him sometime over the weekend. Johnny headed into the main hall and saw a few halls and rooms being used for different purposes, which is how they all work, he thought.

So, after settling down and listening to a speaker or two, he became peckish, so he nipped up to the reception area and asked if he could book a table for dinner. He was then advised that there was a selection of restaurants. Still, because the hotel was fully booked and dinner had to be booked, there was no space available except in the dining area that was doing the buffet for the evening, which was the Olive Tree restaurant. That restaurant did have space available but in two hours. He didn't want to wait two hours for a table, so he paused for a minute and said he would have to consider it. He then entered the bar and had a Diet Coke and a coffee. After going back and listening to another speaker in the main hall, he went back to the Olive Tree restaurant opposite reception and just blagged a table straight away. He had forgotten after all the travelling that it was a five-star hotel. He had his joggers and trainers on. The food was amazing. The hotel advertised its restaurants as the ultimate dining experience, and that phrase said it all. The setting, the service, albeit it was in the buffet-style restaurant Johnny was in, and the food were all perfect. The selection was well chosen, cooked and displayed simply as well as possible. Johnny was settling in well, enjoying the convention, loving the food, and having a great experience. Then he asked for the bill for the buffet rather than charging it. They certainly knew how to charge, that was for sure. Perhaps Jemima not going with him wasn't as bad as he thought; he smiled and laughed to himself.

He went to bed Friday night in a beautiful bed after having a busy day. He had never been a natural early riser. He was more of a night owl and always had been. He was not going to worry about breakfast. When he got up Saturday morning, he received an email from Amazon. His book was published and available on Amazon. He felt like a child at Christmas. His face was lit up, and he was walking around his hotel room with a grin like a Cheshire Cat. 'The Butler Did It' was no longer an idea in his mind. It was completed and published. He felt a great sense of achievement and was feeling rather proud. Slowly, he bathed, picked up a few clothes to wear, and decided to go and join the conference again. He skipped out of his room, into the lift with his smile still there and went down to reception before walking through into the conference area and sitting outside drinking cups of coffee and eating croissants, like there was going to be a famine tomorrow.

A few hours later, after lunch, he bumped straight into Richie in the reception area. Richie explained he had been doing a chair and sharing his experience, strength, and hope in a workshop about steps 1, 2 & 3. That made total sense to Johnny. Richie always carried a good message for a newcomer. The committee had invited him to speak. Johnny had not seen Richie for a long while, which was nice because they had a lot to catch up on really, and they had the time to do it. They both praised the hotel and laughed, caught up, put the world to rights, metaphorically speaking, and, of course, had a few photos taken together to put on social media. The time seemed to fly; next thing they both agreed, they were going to get ready for the banquet dinner and entertainment that evening. Johnny went back to his room, had a bit of time to spare, got changed into his best suit and went down to the room for the banquet dinner. The table Richie was on had a couple of spare seats, so Johnny sat on that table. It was all guys, many of them on their own, as Johnny and Richie were. The food came out and was exceptional. Then, after dinner, they had an auction, raffles and entertainment before the main speaker from America for the evening. The MC introduced a woman as our own Bonnie Tyler before singing onstage. Johnny did not quite hear 'our very own' and looked at Richie and said, 'Did he say Bonnie Tyler?' Wow, what an unexpected treat, Johnny thought. She certainly looked like Bonnie Tyler may look now, Johnny thought. She started singing and had a great voice. Could it be her? Then it became apparent she was good but not that good. Johnny said to Richie, 'I thought it was her.' Richie laughed and said she was 'Connie Tyler!' Johnny smiled and laughed at that. After listening to the main speaker from America and saying good night to all the lads at the table, Johnny went up to his room on his own and simply thought, wow, what a great day to be alive, yet again. Johnny felt like he had won the lottery but had not cashed the cheque yet. It was certainly the beginning of a new experience and what may prove to be his best adventure yet!

On Sunday morning, Johnny and Richie spoke a little, and Johnny talked to many different people before deciding he would leave early after lunch. It was a long drive back, and he now wanted to try and think about promoting his novel and getting home. So, it was official now, he had now become a published author. He now had to promote the novel. That was food for thought. His new life was going to be based on helping others where he could, or at least not harming anyone and for now, it felt like he was best positioned to help other alcoholics and addicts see what they struggled with and from by going through the 12 steps together and helping them recover from the hopeless state of mind and body. Johnny realised he was a recovered alcoholic and addict now, and he had been for many years now. He knew it was just a daily reprieve based on a daily spiritual way of life. He decided until he felt like he had a new calling or purpose, he would try to help addicts and alcoholics using the 12-step program, but he was a realist and knew he could only help addicts and alcoholics recover from their addictions if they were truly willing to put in the work one day at a time. His experience had also taught and shown him lots of people simply choose not to do the work. It was as simple as that. The twelve-step process of self-examination, healing and living a spiritual way of life was not for all, and he respected that. He always said to people if you change your mind once we start going through the work, just let me know. Johnny was aware that some people would rather live in the lie of blaming others and see themselves as victims of circumstances. Johnny did know that about one-third of alcoholics and addicts had not suffered actual abuse in their childhood, and about two-thirds had, so he always encouraged people to get outside help from specialists if needed. Even the best specialists in the world can only tell people to forgive people for the wrongs they did to them and understand that leaving the trauma in the past is the best thing they can do. The idea of reliving traumas or negative experiences had to be overcome, and living in the present moment and being grateful for the present moment is a good way to live if you can.

However, Johnny could see in some people that they simply could not overcome certain traumas. He was also fully aware of Winston Churchill's quote, 'Most people go through life, discover the truth and ignore it.'

Maybe the best lesson Johnny had also realised on his journey was that his wealth was not in things; most things were just an inconvenience almost; his true wealth was in the profoundness of his experience of this life, and for that, he was certainly very grateful. It had been an interesting journey packed with many experiences. He occasionally met up with Sophia and grabbed lunch or dinner with her, as they now lived only a few miles apart. She was probably the one living person on the planet who knew more about Johnny than anyone else, even though he had hidden a lot from her or tried to. He had made his amends to her about his behaviour towards her, she had accepted the amends, and now they had become really good friends. The irony of his now friendship with Sophia was he would enjoy catching up with her maybe once or twice per month, depending on each other's lives. She has a long-term partner now, and Johnny is grateful for that. Was she truly happy with him? Johnny thought they had their fair share of ups and downs, but he did sound like a decent bloke all around, and they both had their own home, which gave them a lot of freedom and space on an individual basis. The man was a retired police officer, which always made Johnny smile. The irony of her now in a relationship with a retired police officer was not lost on Johnny. Johnny thought now he probably had far more respect and a better relationship with Sophia because it was just a very healthy platonic friendship and he still enjoyed spending time with her. The intelligent, educated brain, wicked sarcasm, sense of humour, and woman with great life experiences to draw on were still alive and well, making the friendship enjoyable. She would often ask Johnny to look after her pets when she travelled as she often did, and Johnny quite liked sitting in her house talking to all her pets and feeding them.

Johnny even asked her advice from time to time when he met new ladies, and inevitably, when Johnny asked for her opinion on them or things, she would tell him they were right, and Johnny was wrong, which made him smile. In truth, he couldn't believe he had the type of relationship with her today where he could discuss such matters. When she discussed her relationship, he could also give her a perspective on where her partner may be coming from. Still, whatever it was, it was probably the closest and best true friendship he had. There was no pretence or fear on either side, and there were often lots of laughs as well.

CHAPTER 2
MARKETING A BOOK AND RELEASING THE AUDIOBOOK

JOHNNY RETURNED HOME to Canterbury from Wales and started seriously thinking about marketing his new novel. Johnny was happy with what he had written. So now he thought it would be helpful if he got some feedback from other people about what they thought. He knew he needed some reviews for Amazon and to at least get some honest feedback from the general public.

Johnny was up early one morning waiting for B & Q to open. He decided he wanted to get a wallpaper table to go to a boot fair and try offering copies of his novel to the general public in return for an honest review after they had finished it. He pulled up in Asda car park opposite B & Q as he had about fifteen minutes to spare before B & Q opened. He was going to nip into Asda, get something to nibble on, and then drive over to B & Q.

As he jumped out of his car and started walking towards the entrance, he was approached by a man in his twenties with a puffer jacket on. He asked Johnny for some money to get something to eat and drink. Johnny was confused by beggars or, at least, people asking for money. Canterbury is full of them seven days per week. No doubt some of them are genuine, and of course, it's nice to contribute from time to time, but the idea of giving someone cash who is just pretending and has a Porsche hidden around the corner to nip home in later didn't sit well with him.

He knew a few people who said Canterbury attracted many people asking for money because it was an affluent area and filled with tourists. So, he would try and pick what appeared to be a genuinely good cause occasionally and stick his hand in his pocket. Johnny was in a good mood – he stuck his hand in his pocket, pulled out some coins and gave the guy three £1 coins, although he didn't look hungry or in bad shape, in all honesty. Then the guy says to Johnny well, I can get breakfast for £9.50, and I need a haircut cut, which is about £12.00 as he was trying to show Johnny the line at the bottom of the back of his hair was not straight. So, no thanks or cheers for the £3 but more of a request for £21.50. Johnny looked at the guy and almost said to him, any chance of the £3 back, mate? Johnny walked off smiling, thinking I do my hair with clippers at home, and a coffee and cereal at home was going to cost about £1. Still, it's a free world – perhaps Johnny would be happier setting up a regular contribution to an animal charity every month or maybe just putting more in the pot in certain meetings he attended.

So, after leaving Asda, he nipped into B & Q and got a suitable wallpaper table. He found a boot fair or market, which was on each Sunday in Ashford. He then ordered some author's copies and waited for them to arrive. He then advertised on social media effectively the same deal. The books arrived, and he went to the boot fair and offered the novel for free to some readers who would leave a review. He then sent the copies to people who responded on social media and gave some copies to people in meetings he attended. He did not have an unlimited budget for advertising or promoting the novel; it was more of a let's see what people think and see what happens approach. Johnny could read the book from start to finish in two days if he just curled up on the sofa, turned his phone off and had an unlimited supply of coffee and fizzy pop in the kitchen to keep him fully alert. It was a long book, he realised, and it would take time for people to read through it at their speed, and of course, maybe the book would just go in a pile of books they had to read. Still, that was out of his hands now. The book was published for sale, and some people agreed to read it and leave a review.

Then, a friend asked if it was available as an audiobook. No, Johnny thought. He hadn't thought of that possibility or thought that through previously, but it made sense. Who could Johnny get to narrate the audiobook? Well, Morgan Freeman was the first thought; apart from the fact Johnny didn't know him, couldn't afford him or didn't know how to contact him, he would have been the ideal candidate. Johnny thought the job would have been done if he had read the book and been the narrator; that would have been perfection. Still, then, Stephen Fry and Ray Winstone came to mind, but the same applied, so it was going to come down to a relatively unknown narrator, or maybe Johnny could do it himself. Johhny didn't have the recording equipment or the experience, so he approached a recording studio in London with the idea that he would narrate the book, and they would edit, produce and upload it. The quote seemed expensive to Johnny. It was one book, and Johnny thought the recording studio and production company thought he was perhaps Prince Harry with a bottomless pit of money for the project.

So, Johnny found a narrator who would narrate the book and also edit, produce and upload the completed version. His voice was clear, and Johnny had previously dealt with him over video clips. He was a genuinely nice guy who did what he said he would do, so by employing him to do the job, at least Johnny knew he would have peace of mind. He contacted Christian Neale; they spent a few days haggling over the fee and all the details. Johnny asked him to do it once all the details had been agreed upon, including a time frame. It was going to take a while as Christian had other work on the go already, and a realistic time scale was agreed upon to allow for Christian's up-and-coming holiday plans as well. Still, it had now started, and the whole process was just one big learning curve for Johnny. He had chosen him because he believed he could and would do the job to a decent standard and would not change the price. Time would tell if Johnny was right or not.

Once the process started, it was Christian doing one chapter at a time, sending Johnny a copy and Johnny listening and reading the book at the same time, and sending his views back together with any corrections. Mistakes were few and far between, in all honesty, but there were genuinely just a few, maybe words skipped or mispronounced on the odd occasion. Reading and flying through a book was one thing, but repeating it word for word with all the words pronounced correctly, tapping it, and getting it spot on was a much slower and lengthier process. Johnny was happy overall that it was ongoing and progress was being made. Then Christian had his holiday for a couple of weeks, came back, and it all got finished and agreed. It had taken longer than anticipated, but it was all now complete, and Christian had not come up with any reasons for additional charges, so it was finished and done, then uploaded to Audible. Johnny was pleased and listened to it on Audible with a big smile on his face. A few people suggested to Johnny he could have done it himself, but that was in the past now. Christian had tried to inject some humour occasionally, and Johnny was quite impressed by his accents for some characters, not because they were perfect. Still, maybe because they were so obviously a narrator trying to replicate local accents and people from different countries, it made him smile, and of course, books and audiobooks need to entertain, or what was the point?

So, another celebration was in order now; celebrations nowadays tend to be with food and Diet Coke. Johnny remembered reading an article in the paper about when Roman Abramovich purchased Chelsea many years earlier, which said he celebrated with a Diet Coke once the purchase was completed. At the time, Johnny thought how strange; that's not a way to celebrate, but today, he would do the same thing. Be grateful for the achievement and completion of a project or an experience, and celebrate the moment with a can or bottle of fizzy pop, or Diet Coke, to be exact.

So, the book was available in all possible formats, and time would tell if the sales would match J K Rowling. Reviews were a bit thin on the ground, but they were just starting to come in, and Johnny was very pleased with what he was reading overall. Of course, it was apparent everyone reads a novel and has their own experience and views about it, but that was healthy and good to read a variety of opinions. Johnny liked the book, and that was all that mattered to him, but seeing how other people related to it and viewed it was interesting, to say the least.

Johnny had recently bumped into a few people he knew who he had worked with previously, and there were characters in the book that were based on them. A few people just started telling him I bought your book, which was nice to hear. Apart from an author's reputation, word of mouth and people's ratings and reviews were always the best advertising; Johnny knew that. Then, a few people he knew started asking if they could be in the film when it was made, which made Johnny smile, there would be people playing parts or characters that were based on them in reality. The massive upside to that was they wouldn't need any acting skills, more turn up and be themselves with a different name. A few reviews and strangers also told Johnny they couldn't wait to watch the film. Johnny sat with the idea of a feature film or series based on the book, and that seemed quite appealing, to say the least. Of course, it is probably every author's dream to have a book turned into a film. It was an idea for now!

Still, good progress had been made to date, and Johnny started receiving royalties every month, which were way above his expectations. The book was certainly selling quicker and faster than Johnny had expected. Some months, Johnny received eye-watering amounts of money from the publishers, which was very pleasing.

Johnny was attending regular meetings still and enjoying life again. People were calling him a published author; of course, it was true. Johnny Butler was now a published author. He had taken the idea and made it happen with no previous or real writing or publishing experience. Later that year, he was fortunate enough to attend a Bruce Springsteen concert at Hyde Park and sat in the Vodafone charging area for mobile phones when he struck up a conversation with a delightful Scottish lady in her late forties, he guessed. She was sitting beside him in the Vodafone area, charging her phone and telling Johhny all about her life. She lived a good life, was involved in many different businesses and ideas, and was a happily married mother. She confessed to Johnny that she dreamed of writing and publishing a book. She had lots of ideas and experiences, and she wanted to get it on paper and printed. It was on her bucket list to do. Johnny smiled at her and said sounds like a great idea – you should do it. Then, he casually slipped into the conversation that he had already done it. She was so impressed and, at that moment, Johhny felt very proud. Johnny thought about his bucket list and realised that apart from visiting a few countries he had not been to and helping others, there was not much for him to do, or at least it appeared that way to him then. That was a satisfying feeling. The Scottish lady who was Glenda went online on her phone and ordered a copy of The Butler Did It. She said she was going to read his book and write her book. She felt she was inspired enough to start her book by talking to Johnny.

More reviews started to appear from time to time, which was pleasing, and Johnny was taking time to feel good at that moment and appreciate and be grateful for the experience. Johhny set off one Wednesday evening to a 12-step meeting in the local Baptist Church. Maybe Johhny would be able to share a message about recovery, or even better, maybe some poor lost soul might ask Johnny to sponsor them and take them through the 12 steps as laid out in the Big Book. Johnny generally enjoyed the meetings a lot, he tended to know a lot of people locally in meetings. There was a lot of fun to be had in meetings. There were so many characters from different backgrounds and professions that you would never know who they were. From time to time, Johnny would see people who were famous or from the TV, which he recognised. Over the years, Johnny was fortunate enough to be asked by a variety of men and women to sponsor them. He had always been sponsoring people, apart from through the COVID period in which he had been trying to help a girl he knew called Louise. They had also started going out, but it never went past friendship. Johnny would often bump into her over the years in meetings. They had certainly been to many places together in a short time, mainly during COVID-19.

Johhny doesn't sponsor women much now. He had done it in the past, and it never seemed to work out particularly well. He had no bad experiences with it, but he seemed to attract women who had had women sponsors who they would not have done the work with and then just changed sponsors. As far as Johnny could tell, and believed the only reason to sponsor an addict or alcoholic was to go through the 12 steps. Johnny knew many fellows in the rooms but had made just a few friends. Johnny defined a fellow as a colleague at work or somewhere he would go, pass the time of day, and enjoy conversation with. His definition of a friend was based on whether he would let them sleep on his sofa at 3 am and whether he could sleep on theirs if needed. Those people were a lot fewer on the ground. Over the years, Johnny had let two people from the rooms detox and stay at his place. At the time, they had both been wonderful experiences, and both people left clean and sober, but both later relapsed. Nowadays, Johnny probably would not do that anymore, but maybe he would reserve his position just in case, he thought.

Upon arrival at the meeting, a few friendly faces were smoking and greeting outside the meeting. Johnny stopped and started chatting to a few lads, then out popped Leonard from the hall. He seemed strange that evening. Johnny and Leonard knew each other from the meetings. They were not particularly close, and Johnny did not want to be closer to him. Johnny never realised Leonard had relapsed and was on drugs again. It was certainly an eye-opener again. His appearance and voice had changed. Generally, he seemed to be quite happy for the most part. So, Johnny enters the meeting, grabs a coffee, and sits at the table. It was a busy meeting, with maybe 25 people in the room. Johnny sat between Matt, who he knew, on his right and a guy called Steve on his left. He took his coat and cap off and made himself comfortable. As the meeting went on, Johnny felt a hand on his right leg, and it shocked him initially. he turned and looked at Matt, who smiled at him – which made it worse because his initial interpretation had been that Matt had just touched him up or was making a sexual advance towards him. So, Johnny quietly sat there and wondered what he could do in such a situation. It happened again, and he turned towards Matt; Matt was smiling but had both his hands in front of him and was reading the book. So very quickly Johnny realised it had not been Matt's hand at all, he looked over his shoulder and saw Leonard sitting there smiling and realised the truth was that Leonard was trying to go through the pockets in his coat to steal some money from him. He then picked up his jacket and put it on the other side of where he was sitting so Leonard couldn't reach his jacket anymore, which he thought would solve the problem. He had never realised until then that Leonard was sitting behind him. People didn't tend to sit behind people in meetings.

So, as the meeting goes on, next thing Leonard has moved himself around behind Johnny so he can now get into his jacket again. But Johnny was unaware of this. Then suddenly, Johnny felt his coat being pulled and realised Leonard was at it again. Then Leonard ran quickly towards the door, and Johnny looked at him and realised he was carrying his wallet, which he had lifted from the inside of the pocket of his jacket. This was a new experience for Johnny – he had never been robbed in a meeting before! As Leonard gets to the door, he turns and pauses. Johnny was up on his feet in a flash – he wasn't going to have that. Then Leonard ran out of the door, and Johnny set off in pursuit. Leonard ran straight down towards the city, and Johnny was quite impressed at how quickly he could run after him. At this time, Johnny was unaware that several lads from the meeting had run out after Johnny to help resolve the matter. So, Leonard is running flat out down the street, Johnny is in after him, and a few lads are running behind Johnny. As Leonard got to the bottom of the street, approaching the city, he stopped and looked around and still had Johnny's wallet in his hand. As Johnny was chasing him, he realised there was very little cash in the wallet at all, but his driving licence, bank cards, and other very important documents and details were in the wallet, which he couldn't afford to lose in reality. Lenoard is now on the railings looking at Johnny down behind him, and Johnny shouts at him, 'Take the cash, just give me the wallet back.' As Johnny shouted this, Bernie came running past Johnny and grabbed the wallet from Leonard's hand. He looked at Johnny and said, 'Don't give him anything.' Lenoard's face was an absolute picture – Johnny could see he was resentful about returning the wallet he had just stolen. Johnny thought, what a bloody liberty taker! Then, some other lads arrived at the railings. The whole matter had been resolved. Leonard went off with his tail between his legs into the city. Johnny, Bernie, and the other lads returned to the meeting.

Later in the week, Johnny saw that Al Pacino was in England for a few days, and there was an opportunity to meet him in London in a few weeks. Johnny thought surely all the tickets would be gone by now but decided to check in any case, and it turned out there were some tickets left. Johnny was able to get one, which he was astonished about. Later that day, he spoke to Jemima as he realised there were other tickets left for the event, and asked her if she wanted to go as well, but explained that she wouldn't be sitting with Johnny; she would be sitting on a different table as there were only single tickets left. She decided, on balance, that the idea of seeing Al Pacino sitting at a table with strangers wasn't that appealing to her and said to leave it. Johnny was made up that he had his ticket and wanted to try to give Al Pacino a signed copy of his book and ask for a review.

The event was being held at the Intercontinental, the hotel attached to the O2 in London. It was Sunday, 23rd April, and Johnny decided to arrive early as different tickets were being granted entrance at different times. He sat at the bar of the Intercontinental hotel, drinking Diet Coke and taking in the atmosphere with a selection of very well-dressed, affluent and famous faces. After a couple of hours, Johnny could enter the hall where the auction was on, and Al Pacino would later be interviewed on stage. He had his book to give to Al Pacino and soon realised his best opportunity to present the book would be afterwards when he had his photo taken with him. Johnny's seat was at the rear of the ballroom and nowhere near the stage in reality.

It was a wonderful evening. Johnny loved listening to Al

Pacino talking about his life honestly, the highs and lows, including touching on his addiction issues throughout his career. Johnny was recording certain moments of the interview on his phone, and they would be interesting memories to watch back on from time to time, no doubt in the future. The time seemed to fly – as it always does – when you're enjoying yourself, and very quickly, it seemed the whole experience with Al Pacino being interviewed was over. Then, there was a break for time to allow Al Pacino to move from the ballroom upstairs to where the photos would be taken. When Johnny got in the queue, he was astonished at how many people were queuing to get a photo, and he ended up talking to some Dutch women who had flown from Holland and stayed at the hotel for the whole weekend just to meet and listen to Al Pacino. By this time, everyone was beginning to get a little restless at the length of the queues and the time it was taking for them to move. The time seemed to pass slowly, and suddenly, Johnny was nearer the front of the queue than the back. He managed to slip the book in without permission and gave it to Al Pacino when he met him, who kindly put it to one side and said he would read it with interest. Johnny smiled back and said, 'I would love a review,' and he said it would be 'an absolute pleasure.' A photo was taken of Johnny with his arm around Al Pacino, and as quick as a flash, it was all over. Johnny left the room by the exit and waited for his photo in a queue, which surprisingly only took a few minutes to retrieve. He then went back down to the entrance. It was very late now – gone midnight. He paid the parking charge in the hotel, jumped in his car and drove home. The whole experience had certainly lived up to his expectations.

Financially, Johnny seemed to be getting back on his feet. Life was good again. He went down to Marks and Spencer in Canterbury one day just to browse around the menswear section and maybe pick up the odd item or two, if he found anything he liked. Before he got to the men's section, he bumped into a guy he knew named Chris from the rooms, whom he had not seen for at least five years. They stood and chatted in Marks and Spencer for about half an hour, just catching up and talking about life. Chris shared with Johnny some moments when he had enjoyed really good fortune and could help others financially, which he had found very beneficial. He felt like it was the right thing to do, as life had been good to him in so many unexpected ways. It was a really interesting chat. They parted company, and Johnny continued to browse around the menswear section without buying anything before he went home.

The next day, he received a message on social media from a woman called Lola, whom he had met about a year previously in an AA meeting. When they met at that first meeting, there were no women in the meeting, and Johnny took her for coffee afterwards and laid out what he thought was in her best interests. They had coffee and a chat, and Johnny suggested that it would be a good idea for her to get to as many meetings as possible, grab a big book, get a female sponsor, get some service, and do the steps.

The message Johnny got on social media said that she had remained sober ever since, and she just wanted to thank Johnny for the conversation and chat they had at the first meeting. Johnny was pleased to receive the message, and they started chatting about life, particularly that she had over a year's sobriety and was attending regular meetings in Thanet, where she lived. He realised you never knew who was doing well and who wasn't, just because you didn't see them in the meetings. As they started talking, she was telling Johnny where she was at that time and that she had very serious health conditions, which had been made worse with other complications around her health. She was effectively lying in bed every day at home, couldn't go out, and was waiting for a serious operation on the NHS. Johnny was surprised that she was on an NHS waiting list when she had lost all of her mobility. Johnny asked her why she didn't just pay and go private. After all, her health was the most important thing she would ever have. She said she had never considered it, and she was skint. Johnny said to her, 'I will lend you the money for the operation if you promise to pay me back when you can'. She said she didn't have any money and couldn't offer any sensible repayment options. Johnny took a deep, deep breath and realised she was being honest, realised she was desperate, and said, 'I will pay the cost of operation off for you privately if you just promise me that you will make every effort to repay it in the future, when you can, without any conditions attached.' She was overjoyed and said she would find out the cost of the operation and get back to him. Within a few days, she found out that the operation could be done at a local private hospital for a cost of £9,0000, and it could be done in a couple of weeks. They sent her the invoice for the operation, and Johnny paid the bill for her. She got her date for the operation. He did it due to the earlier conversation with Chris, and it seemed like the right thing to do.

The operation was a great success. Lola was over the moon and told Johnny how grateful she was and would never forget it. She said she would do her best to pay back the money as soon as possible. To Johnny's surprise, she contacted him within about two or three weeks and said she had the money to repay him. He couldn't believe it. She had no money at all a few weeks earlier, and now she could repay the money in full. Johnny never really found out the full story, but she did say that her ex-husband had given her the money to repay the debt.

Johnny had been speaking to some guys in the rooms who were working at a homeless shelter in Canterbury, and Johnny thought this could be a very rewarding way of trying to give back and help other people less fortunate than himself. He applied at the homeless shelter for a position as a kitchen assistant to help cook and prepare meals for homeless people.

He went for an interview and was offered a start date. They decided between them that he could work every Thursday at the shelter, and they would see how it went. Johnny had felt before going there his past criminal convictions may pose a problem to working for a charity. It didn't seem to be an issue and never got brought up! Johnny started the work and found it very rewarding. He looked forward to it immensely – it was certainly an eye-opener to see men and women who were homeless – coming into a day shelter for maybe a wash and a change, as well as a warm meal. It certainly gave him a lot more perspective about different people's lives. In the kitchen, generally speaking, there was a team of about three or four people preparing breakfast and lunch for the clients at the shelter. There were lots of different characters, and people who were trying to give something back to society. Johnny generally got along well with most of them. Some of them thought they were Michelin chefs, and others just thought they could cook to a high standard. Johnny said he had cooked and cooked at home from time to time but let the other people lead the way, and he was happy to take guidance and do the washing-up and preparation of vegetables rather than create the menus. It was a very light-hearted environment to work in, and Johnny enjoyed the experience on the whole.

Very quickly, after a few weeks, he got into the swing of it and became part of the furniture, so to speak. He even got to know some of the clients, or at least chatted with them, as it was advised to everyone not to get friendly or too close to the clients, which could lead to misunderstandings in the future. He had settled in well and could remember many of the clients' Christian names and at least enjoy a light-hearted conversation with them.

One day, Johnny was asked to make the custard for the dessert after lunch. It brought back lots of childhood memories for him when he made cakes or custard at home with his mum, and he enjoyed licking the cake and the custard out of the bowl. He forgot where he was for a moment and was licking custard with a spoon, really enjoying that moment, then doing it again, when suddenly one of the clients shouted, 'he's licking the custard and putting the spoon back in the bowl, and we have to eat that!' Of course, he was right, Johnny realised. Still, Johnny felt like saying to him why don't you stop moaning? It's free, after all, then he realised that was so inappropriate, and the guy was right! So, Johnny walked round the corner and finished eating the custard with the spoon out of sight.

Johnny had recently felt some pain at the top of his right leg, near the groin area, and on occasion, he had to sit down as it had become too painful. A couple of weeks later, when he was at the shelter, he was working with Eddie and Sheila preparing the lunch, and he couldn't stand up. He was in agony. Eddie told him to sit down, which he did for a while, and he then thought he could continue. The job in the kitchen meant he was on his feet for hours. After a couple of attempts of sitting down and resting, then standing up and trying to work again, it became apparent that he couldn't stand. He didn't want to leave Eddie and Sheila in the lurch, so to speak, but he had no choice. Everyone advised him to go to the local hospital and get it checked out. He attended the accident and emergency centre on Thursday morning around 10.30 am and was told he would be seen as soon as possible, to sit in the waiting area, and to be placed in a queue. After about an hour, he was then assessed by a nurse in the room, to whom he explained his symptoms and what had happened. She thought it might be a hernia, but he would need to see a doctor as it was just her opinion. Within about 20 minutes, Johnny went into a room and was met by a lady doctor who asked him about his condition and then made him strip off to examine him. She confirmed after a physical examination that she believed he did have a hernia after listening to what he said. She said he would be referred by his doctor for a scan to confirm what she believed. Johnny returned home and let Kayleigh know at the shelter that he couldn't continue with his voluntary position until after he had the appropriate operation. She wished him all the best and said that as soon as Johnny was able to get back in touch in the future, they would be delighted to have him back on board again.

CHAPTER 3
JEMIMA

One Friday evening, Johnny walked into an AA meeting in Canterbury, grabbed himself a cup of coffee and started chatting to a group of fellows who were hovering around the tea counter and a few outside. He had not been to that particular meeting for quite a while and was enjoying catching up with some old faces. Then, in walks a woman he recognised, Mia, to whom he said hello. After about ten minutes, he decided to grab a seat and wait for the meeting to start. It was a speaker meeting, where generally, a member would share their experience, strength and hope for about twenty minutes before the floor would open up for other members to share where they were back to the chair. On this particular evening, a guy called Benny was doing the chair. Johnny sat back with his coffee, and Benny was the funniest guy he had ever heard in any meeting he had been to. Johnny was in bits the whole time he was speaking. It wasn't particularly what he was saying that was funny, it was how he was saying it. Johnny spoke to him after the meeting and found out that he had come from London and moved down to the Kent coast quite recently with his wife, who had unfortunately just passed away, and he was considering moving back to London. Johnny thought that evening that he had never been better entertained in his life, although at the same time, he had shared a serious message of recovery. Johnny later regretted not exchanging numbers with Benny and keeping in contact, or at least having his number and being able to come and share his experience, strength, and hope at future meetings. He has never seen him since.

After Benny finished speaking, the meeting was opened for general sharing, and Johnny was sitting next to a guy he knew called Alan. Someone shared for a few minutes, then Johnny nudged Alan and asked him if he would share, as Alan would often not share, and Johnny was just curious about whether he intended to share. The first share back had concentrated on sharing a message for the newcomer. After Johnny had nudged Alan, Alan introduced himself to the meeting as an alcoholic and began to share. He was not in the best of moods and was struggling with his recovery. He pipes up and says, 'fuck the newcomer, what about me. I come to these meetings, and I am sick to death of hearing about newcomers. I want people to help me!' Johnny couldn't believe what he had heard. He was laughing his head off again. A lot of people in the meeting, clearly from their body language, felt that what Alan had said was inappropriate. So, Johnny was left in this meeting sitting in his seat, laughing his head off – the more he tried to stop laughing, the more he couldn't stop, so now everyone was looking at Johnny! He was going to try to adjust his focus and keep a straight face, but he couldn't. So, Johnny walked out of the meeting and sat outside for ten minutes on his own. He never got to hear the end of Alan's share but as he was leaving the meeting, he did think to himself Alan's selfishness and self-centredness had certainly got the better of him that evening.

After going back into the meeting, Johnny had managed to compose himself a little by now. His fits of laughter were under control! The meeting continued with various people sharing, and very quickly, the end of the meeting was upon them. After the meeting, Johnny started talking to Mia, and she asked him if he fancied grabbing a coffee together at the Chocolate Café and having a chat. Johnny liked that idea; he agreed and said, 'Can we have five or ten minutes to chat in the meeting after the meeting, and then we will?'. She then says, 'I want to go home and get changed. I will grab a cab and meet you up there in twenty minutes.' That sounded like a good idea, so Johnny agreed. Next thing, Johnny left the meeting, walked up to the Chocolate Café, grabbed a table and ordered a hot chocolate. He had Mia's number but knew what she was doing, so he thought he would just sit and wait. Quite a bit of time had passed, and Johnny sent her a text asking if she was OK and if she was on her way. After about five minutes, he got a reply saying she was struggling to get a cab back because the firms were busy but that she did have one on the way. Johnny said no worries, and whenever you can and asked if she wanted him to order it for him. He didn't get a reply, and about fifteen minutes later, the cab turned up with Mia in it, and she looked like a million dollars. She came in, Johnny ordered her a coffee, and they sat down and started chatting. Johnny knew from previous conversations with her that she had been a pole dancer for many years. She had often joked about her boob job with Johnny, which made sense to Johnny as a lot of pole dancers have boob jobs from an aesthetic point of view and a confidence booster for low self-esteem. Then she says to Johnny, do you fancy going dancing? Johnny asked her where they would go, and she said it didn't matter and, 'Let's just go and find somewhere.' Johnny thought there was no harm in that, as Johnny had always enjoyed his dancing and liked the idea of going with Mia because of how she looked. Within twenty minutes, they were ordering drinks in a nightclub at the bar in Canterbury city centre. Johnny ordered a Diet Coke and asked her what she wanted. She said a large gin and tonic –

Johnny looked at her and said, 'You can have whatever you want, but I am not buying you alcohol.' She then says, 'I will buy it myself!' Now, the situation has drastically changed. Johnny liked the idea of going dancing with Mia and drinking non-alcoholic drinks. He genuinely had no interest in drinking alcohol or buying her alcoholic drinks. So, Mia ordered herself a large gin and tonic and, after one, was dancing all around the bar and all over Johnny, which, in all honestly, he enjoyed. Then they got talking, and she had another large gin and tonic and the club was beginning to fill up, and her dancing had become very erotic and sensual. Johnny remembered looking at a table of women near the bar, and all over their faces was written, 'That is disgusting and inappropriate behaviour at the bar.' About twenty minutes later, she decided to have another one and had now lost the plot. The security approached Johnny and Mia and asked them to change their behaviour, or they would need to leave. Mia had gone too far and now couldn't stand up properly. They were asked to go out in the courtyard, compose themselves, and after that, they could come back in. When they got outside in the courtyard, the fresh air hit Mia, and she was lying on the floor within a couple of minutes. At this point, her demeanour and appearance had changed totally; her language was terrible, and Johnny realised she was a total mess. Johnny decided he just wanted to get her home and get rid of her. They managed to get to the club entrance, and Johnny stopped a taxi coming down the high street. She asked him if he was coming back to her place – he smiled to himself – and said, 'No, you just need to get home safe.' He put her in the back of a taxi, told the driver where she lived and asked him to take her home and please at least see her to the front door. Johnny paid the cab, which, because of his previous experience in the taxi business, he knew was probably at least double the right price, but he was grateful that the experience was over. Johnny made his own way home and realised he hadn't done anything wrong, and there was no harm done. How Mia decided to carry on had nothing to do with him.

A few days later, Johnny changed some of his profile pictures on social media platforms and his WhatsApp. He had found an image he liked which said, 'I am an author; anything you say or do may appear in my next novel.' The next day, he never received several suggestions from some people he knew and reminders about certain events and people in his life. Some of them certainly would tick the box, that was for sure.

Sales of the book had continued to pick up at an alarming rate, and Johnny was very grateful for the royalties he was receiving every month. He remembered a conversation he had with his mother many years previously about buying an Aston Martin and realised he could now afford to buy and run an Aston Martin. He made a short list to view after looking at cars for sale in the Kent area on Autotrader. He contacted a guy who lived in Sarre. He was an estate agent and had listed his silver Aston Martin for sale. Johnny made an appointment to view the car, and when he turned up at the address, it turned out to be up a private lane and was a large, beautiful residence. Johnny introduced himself to George, and they viewed the car together in one of the garages. The condition of the car took Johnny aback as George had the full-service history of the vehicle and was just genuinely showing him the car, talking him through, and presenting the car in its best light. Johnny realised the best advert for the car was the car itself rather than George's presentation. Johnny felt like he had fallen in love at first sight. Next thing, George's wife turns up in a Porsche convertible, introduces herself and then enters the property. George then says, 'Let me take you out in the car and see what you think.' Johnny realised by now he wanted the car. He agreed to the test drive and jumped in the passenger seat. George seemed hellbent on pointing out everything about the car and was very thorough from start to finish. He drove the car down the private lane onto the main road, which led to Margate. They turned left, headed towards Margate, and as they got about half a mile out of the residential area, the road opened up, and George put his foot down! The car took off, and Johnny had seen and heard enough. After a few miles, George turned around and drove back. Upon arriving at the house, Johnny was honest with George about the fact he had a short list to view of three Aston Martins. In truth, he could have bought the car there and then, but he wanted to get at least a decent discount on the car as he was a cash buyer. He thought it would be better to leave and explain to George that he may well like to be back or ring him and discuss the car rather than being too keen! This was his preferred strategy. Johnny gets back home after around fifteen minutes and has lost his phone. In slight panic mode, he searched high and low. Then he grabbed George's number from the advert and called him from his landline. Johnny had been ringing his mobile constantly, and he couldn't hear it anywhere – maybe he had left there by mistake. George said, 'Give me five minutes. I will nip back out and look for it. If you ring the phone in three minutes, I will see if I can hear it or find it.' The next thing George answered, the phone had fallen out of Johnny's pocket and was on the passenger side floor. Johnny was very happy and grateful and asked if he could nip back and get the phone, which George agreed to. Johnny shoots straight back to Sarre to collect his phone, and when he gets back, he grabs the phone, and they start talking again. Johnny said, 'I do like the car; would you be open to an offer?' to which George replied, 'Only a small one because I've only just started marketing the car, and it is fairly priced.' Johnny immediately thought that's just classic estate agents' language and realised at least he could have a deal with George, it was just a matter of getting the best deal he could. Johnny asked for £4,000 off the car, and George said no! Johnny said he would leave it, but George came back and said, 'I don't expect to get the full asking price, but £4,000 off is a lot.' After about five minutes of haggling, Johnny agreed to a price reduction of £2,500, and they shook hands. It was agreed that Johnny could pay by bank transfer, and once it had been made, he could collect the car, although there may be a slight delay due to George having a private number plate on the car, which he had to take off first, and put the original plate back on. They started chatting about private number plates, and George said to Johnny, 'Why not get one for yourself and stick it on the car?' Johnny hadn't thought about that idea but took it on board. Johnny and George agreed on the finer details, and Johnny left with a big smile on his face. George was happy as well.

Over the weekend, Johnny started looking at private number plates that might suit the car. He also started to transfer the money to George's wife's account, using the details George had given him. Johnny's bank had a daily limit of £20,000 per transfer to the same person, so the transaction took place over several days. George managed to change the number plate to the original with the DVLA within five days. Johnny started looking at number plates online and realised number plates are like cars. There are some nice cheap ones and some wonderful expensive ones. Once Johnny started looking, he realised he wanted to get one to suit him and the car. He had always been a big Bond fan. He found a number plate with his exact initials followed by 107. That was the one he wanted and liked. He thought it would look good on the car. The price was very high – you could buy a lovely car for the asking price of the number plate, but you only live once, he thought. He tried to haggle with the owner and get a deal. The owner told Johnny it was part of his pension and he would not reduce the price at all. Johnny realised he was telling the truth and paid the asking price. Next, he nipped on to Amazon and bought a CD with all the James Bond tracks. He thought that was or should be a compulsory purchase for all Aston Martin owners, but each to their own. Everything was agreed upon, and Johnny went to collect the car Johnny had first viewed on a Saturday afternoon. it was the following Friday, and it was now his car. He took his new CD with him, loaded that up in the CD player, drove back into Canterbury, and was ecstatic with his purchase. The car simply glided along, and because it was a 6-litre, it had so much acceleration at the touch of a peddle. He pulled into the Esso garage on Sturry Road to fill the car up with petrol. As he pulled up at the pump, jumped out of the car and released the fuel cap, a guy came running up to Johnny, an Aston Martin enthusiast who was nearly more excited about the car than Johnny was. He knew all about Aston Martin; Johnny explained to him he had just bought the car, and it would be the first of many conversations Johnny would have with strangers about the car.

It still had the original number plate on, and it would take Johnny a couple of weeks to get his new private number plate transferred to the car. Johnny realised there was a bonus to having the private plate on the Aston. Every time he went shopping at Asda's, it would make it easier to find his car when he came out with his shopping. That would avoid confusion about getting into someone else's by mistake. It was similar to having his name tag sewn in his school jumper. If he took his jumper off in the Summer or for PE, he would always know which one was his.

Life was finally looking up for Johnny. Over the next few days and weeks, he realised that the book was now available to buy worldwide in countries such as America, Brazil, Poland, and New Zealand, as well as others.

Johnny and Jemima had been getting on well recently and spending some time together. It was an unusual relationship – it was nice to see each other, but because of their busy lifestyles, they hardly got to see each other. One Tuesday evening, they had a wonderful time watching Derren Brown at the Apollo in his new show 'Showman' and returning to her country cottage for the night afterwards, as the girls stayed at their father's place that evening. It was such a wonderful night for so many reasons. Jemima had candles scattered all over the cottage, which she lit. She preferred natural lighting to electric, and some of the candles were also scented. It was a beautiful cottage in the middle of nowhere, just a few miles outside Ashford. It was the first time Johnny had met Pistachio, who was the man of the house and wanted Johnny to know that. Jemima had bought him from Romania. He was a rescue dog who was a mixed breed, so playful and lots of fun. Jemima said that both her daughters loved Pistachio, as she did. He used to act as a guard dog for Jemima and always looked out for her best interests when they would go for and enjoy country walks together. He never ran off, could be trusted off a lead and never left her side. Pistachio was used to sharing Jemima's bed with her. When Johnny and Jemima went to bed, he was not amused at Johnny being in his bed as he saw it and made that clear. After a while, everything calmed down, and he seemed relatively happy at the bottom of the mattress. Johnny liked dogs on the whole, and their first meeting had gone relatively well, all things considered. Johnny and Jemima quickly became passionate, as they always had when sharing a bed. Johnny always remembered the first time they shared a bed for the evening. He had said to her after about an hour, 'If you kill me tonight, please tell everyone in the morning. He went with a smile on his face.' That made her smile and added a certain 'Je ne sais quoi' to the occasion. On this particular night, everything seemed to be going well. Johnny was having the time of his life, and Jemima seemed to be enjoying the experience; they were laughing and joking a lot, which made the moment far more intimate. So, as the passion grew, both of them were nearly naked at this time, and deep into the lovemaking, when Johnny had an amazing sensation and feeling. It seemed very odd. What was Jemima doing or up to? he wondered. Then, very quickly, it registered with him that Pistachio was licking him from behind in totally the most inappropriate place possible. He was on top of Jemima, and perhaps the temptation of seeing Johnny's naked backside moving about was too much for Pistachio. Johnny told Jemima what he was doing, and they both ended up in bits, laughing their heads off. A bit later, the passion was reignited when they stopped making love. All went well for a while. Then Pistachio just stuck his nose in between the cheeks of Johnny's backside this time. So, that killed the passion for a while again. Johnny had never experienced anything like it at all.

The only previous memorable experience he had with a dog in the bedroom was when he met a single woman in the rooms after he was about three years clean and sober. Johnny had asked her out for dinner one Saturday evening, and she agreed. They had been chatting and getting to know each other on social media for some time. Her name was Bernice, and she lived in Gillingham. There is only one small problem. Johnny realised he had double booked himself for the Saturday evening. He had agreed to do the chair at Age Concern in Canterbury. Cancelling the chair didn't sit well with him. He never liked doing that. His recovery had to be the most important thing in his life. He let Bernice know that he was doing a chair at a meeting. He told her he would shoot straight over to Gillingham after the meeting. He then suggested they could grab an Indian or Chinese together. She agreed this would be ok. So, he was relieved. At the time, he cared for his mum and had a friend who agreed to stay over for the evening and keep her company. After Johnny had done his chair and was listening to people share back, he received a message on WhatsApp saying she didn't fancy a Chinese or Indian later and was just letting him know. Johnny was disappointed as he was looking forward to meeting her. Then he received another message saying why not just come to my place, and we can stay in instead. So, he thought she was cancelling originally. It turned out she was just amending the arrangements. Johnny had gone to her place; they got a takeaway and watched a movie in the lounge. She had got out her photo album and was showing Johnny many pictures of herself in various jobs and trips abroad as well as other memories. Johnny was tired by now and was yawning. She asked if he was tired. He said, 'Yes.' He asked if she had got a television in her bedroom. She said 'no'. She then said, 'Do you want to stay?' Johnny was naturally delighted.

As they got into bed, Johnny thought maybe passion would follow. She said no, I don't know you well enough for that, which was understandable. She then started talking about her life and recovery. Johnny listened with interest. She then said to Johnny, 'If you do your chair for me, then I will know you well enough that we can make love together.' What a result, Johnny thought. He had not thought through properly what she had just shared. Do a chair, and you can have a nibble. Anyway, he did his chair while lying next to her in bed. It lasted about half an hour, and she loved it. Then she said now I feel I know you well enough. Johnny got his nibble, so to speak, and afterwards, they kept talking; she shared about her ex-partner, whom she had been separated from for years. They still owned the house together. He had served a seven-year prison sentence for Grievous Bodily Harm and sounded very violent to Johnny. It was at this point Johnny heard a person waking up the stairs. The only thing going through his mind was that it was her ex-partner. He realised he was naked and there was only one door in and out of the bedroom. It was a two-storey property, and Johnny decided in that split moment he would jump from the window naked, taking his car keys with him and run for his life to the car and get away. The person was approaching the bedroom, and the door slowly opened. Her dog had walked up the stairs and pushed the door open with his nose. Johnny had never been so relieved to see a dog. He had nearly had a panic attack and heart attack as the process unfolded. What a relief. Johnny's heart calmed down. He couldn't get dressed quickly enough. Within a few minutes, he had dressed himself then made his excuses, flew down the stairs and straight out of the front door. He got home, his heart was pounding, and he struggled to calm down and sleep for a while. His fear and imagination had got the better of him in the heat of the moment. On Sunday, about lunchtime, Johnny was chatting to his sponsor Arthur, and he said, 'How did you get on last night?' Johnny's mind went blank, and at that moment, he panicked. it took him a few moments to realise that Arthur was asking how the chair went. He had forgotten about the chair earlier in the evening. Johnny replies to Arthur, 'Yes, the chair went well, I think; it was a great meeting, and I grabbed a Kentucky Fried Chicken on the way home.' That was the end of that conversation and the end of Bernice and Johnny.

Johnny's two experiences with the dogs were different but not bad at all. On balance, Johnny was very grateful Pistachio had not bitten him. He was, after all, just playing, he thought, not being aggressive or attacking Johnny, which could have been a horror story for Johnny. Anyway, Johnny and Jemima were almost being entertained by Pistachio at this point. Derren Brown had been great to watch earlier and was a very accomplished magician, really pulling some great tricks out of the hat, so to speak. He finished his show by saying his late Father had told him that whatever you do in life, don't rush through life, missing life as it unfolds. Johnny remembered those words and realised he had, on occasions, been too busy and rushed through life and missed it unfolding in the moment. So, later the following morning, Johnny leaves Jemima's place. Jemima had told Johnny it was her birthday soon, and her girls were planning to take her to the Theatre for her big day. Johnny had met both her girls, and they all seemed to get along quite well. Johnny suggested he would take Jemima and her girls to see Dirty Dancing for her birthday. He managed to get four tickets at relatively short notice. Johnny had thought that Patrick

Swayze would be taking the lead role as he had in the movie until it was pointed out to him by Jemima's eldest daughter that Patrick Swayze was dead. Still live and learn, Johnny thought! It was a great show, and they all had a cracking evening. A bit later on, Johnny asked Jemima if she would like to go and see Mickey Flannigan in a few weeks at the O2 arena. Johnny had booked two tickets ages before for his new sellout concert. She said she loved Mickey Flannigan and would look forward to it.

Johnny had now received his scan appointment date for confirmation it was a hernia. Luckily, it was local in Canterbury, and he nipped in the clinic one afternoon and was seen by two nurses who did the scan and confirmed to Johnny it was a hernia as he had told them that was what he was being told from day one in the hospital. Otherwise, they would have sent the results to the doctor and let the doctor confirm the diagnosis.

Later that evening Johnny went to an AA meeting in Canterbury and was chatting to a guy he knew called Phillip. Phillip seemed to be in and out of the rooms a bit. His sobriety was not continuous, and he seemed to be taking more of a break from drinking rather than trying to live in sobriety. Still, it's really clear that anyone is always welcome, and they did away with the honest desire to give up drinking and changed that to a desire to give up drinking. In reality, anyone is welcome at a meeting. It seemed to Johnny the only requirement for a man or a woman to attend a meeting was a pulse. That was how he viewed it.

Johnny knew a guy called Pete in the meetings who had in the region of 30 years of continuous sobriety, and he told Johnny when he first came into the rooms it was in the fishing port of Hull. Many fishermen working on the boats would always be legless, and when they returned to dry land, they would head for a meeting. In those days, if anyone in the meeting was sober, they would be secretary of the meeting. Wow, what an incredible insight into alcoholism. Johnny always enjoyed talking to Pete.

Pete was not a big talker in the meetings, but when he did say something, Johnny always listened with fascination and a willingness to take on board what he had said because he had heard Pete's chair, which was brutal. Yet, Pete had turned it all around and became a loving father for his children from what can only be described as a horror story of an early life. He was indeed positive proof people can grow and change if they want to.

So, Johnny and Phillip chatted in the meeting, and Phillip asked Johnny if there was any chance of a lift home. Johnny didn't think too much of it and agreed he would be happy to drop him home after the meeting. Then Phillip asked Johnny if he fancied a coffee. How nice, Johnny thought. Phillip sticks the kettle on and makes the coffee. They started chatting about AA and meetings in general. Then Phillip pops up with this chestnut. He said, 'Of course you know I am gay.' How on earth did he think Johnny could tell who was gay or not? In truth, Johnny never considered who was gay or not, whether they were a man or a woman. Johnny had met a few very camp men in his life and thought they might well be gay but, in truth, was not interested in people's sexuality unless he was involved with them. Then Phillip looks at Johnny and says to him, 'I go to meetings looking for lads to pick up and bring back home, quickly followed by Don't worry, you are ok. I don't fancy you.' At that point, Johnny thought to himself, well, perhaps it is fortunate for you that I am not your cup of tea because one of us would be going through the window in a minute if you did, and you thought I was going to be your entertainment for the evening! Johnny realised he was perhaps asking new lads back to his place for a drink after the meetings. Johnny finished his coffee and left. That was the end of their conversations and lifts. Maybe it explained why Phillip was never sober. You can't go around meetings offering newcomers booze and sex, but in the real world, men and women do exactly what they want to do, Johnny realised. Still, it was another learning curve for Johnny.

There was a guy in the rooms who Johnny liked listening to and talking to. His name was Howard. He was a barrister, and Johnny would often strike up conversations about the law, crime and recovery. He knew Johnny had lived on the wrong side of the law. Howard often explained changes in the law in recent years which did not apply to the legal system when Johnny had been in trouble with the law. He would often share that in the legal profession with solicitors and barristers, drinking and alcoholism are rife. It is one of those professions where it seems to be very prevalent. Johnny also liked listening to some of the cases he had acted in and heard how deals were done and how cases collapsed, and he shared some of the barrister's secrets and tricks of the trade, which Johnny had noted and taken on board. When Howard spoke in meetings, you could always tell he was being honest and real, with no pretence or front, which Johnny admired. Johnny had realised that the secret of recovery and sharing was to be real about who you were, where you are, and how recovery has worked for you and is working in your life today. There is no point in following the crowd or being dishonest in meetings. The real flex was and always will be 'To Thine Own Self Be True.' Johnny said to Howard one day, can you give us a card, please, Howard, just in case I need your services in future? Howard laughed at Johnny and said you will not need my services in the future. That remark made Johnny smile!

A few weeks later, Johnny reminded Jemima about the event, and she said that she'd forgotten all about it but was looking forward to it. They agreed Johnny would pick her up from work in Ashford at 5 pm on the day of the event. He wasn't doing anything that day, so he drove over to Ashford a little earlier and decided to have a bite to eat in the Bybrook Barn Harvester to kill a couple of hours. He was just about to leave the restaurant at 4.40 pm when he got a text from Jemima saying her friend had problems, needed to go to the hospital and that she needed to leave work early to help her, and needed to cancel. Johnny was gutted and not impressed, to say the least. Johnny's real mistake was not talking to Jemima about it. He knew her friend, and she always had problems, real or not. He didn't like the idea of being looked over in favour of her and said so in a text. He knew it was the wrong text to send but had not seen her for a while and was expressing how he felt in a not particularly kind or sympathetic text. He knew she was a caring girl and he was just thinking about himself in that moment, but there you go; after it is sent, you can't change it. He did make the mistake and knew it, but he was honest. Very quickly, that situation got out of control. Anyway, it was what it was and it just was another misunderstanding and interpretation of a precarious situation.

So now Johnny has just finished having a bite to eat and has two tickets for Micky Flannigan. He decided he would go on his own and enjoy the evening. So, he had now composed himself and got a reply to his text from Jemima, which he didn't enjoy reading, but there you are.

He was just about to ask for his bill when he noticed a blast from the past walking through the restaurant. Was he imagining it, or was it Lucy, whom he had known many years ago when he was smuggling tobacco through Dover? He looked at her, and his first instinct was that it was her, but he decided not to talk to her because he didn't know who she was with. Next thing, she was looking at him, and they both started smiling at each other from across the room. So, Johnny gestured to Lucy to come over to his table as she appeared alone. She gets up and comes to sit down with Johnny; after a brief conversation, Johnny offers to buy her something to eat, which she accepts. Now Johnny was sitting talking to Lucy about the old times and what they had both been up to since. Johnny was quick to tell her he had just written a book which had been published. She seemed over the moon for him and asked for a copy. He nipped out to his car, grabbed a copy out of the boot, went back and wrote a message for her and signed the book. Very quickly, they were laughing and joking about the book and life.

Johnny had always had a soft spot for her many years ago, and they got along well. At the time when Johnny knew Lucy, she had met a guy called Zac. Zac had been a small-time tobacco smuggler, and Lucy worked for him then. Zac's life changed dramatically when he found out one of his relations used to deliver the daily newspapers to the P&O Ferries at Dover docks from a newspaper wholesaler in Canterbury. His cousin's name was Patrick, and it was his job to fill up his van with all the daily newspapers, then go down the docks early in the morning as different ferries arrived. He would drive onto the ferries and deliver the newspapers to the duty-free shops for passengers to pick up a copy. After the two started chatting, Zac quickly realised that Patrick was trusted and was never checked by customs or security when leaving the docks. Very quickly, he realised Patrick could carry off tobacco and cigarettes in his van with the guarantee of not being stopped or checked.

So, Zac and Patrick worked out that if Zac went over to France very early in the morning and came back on a certain ferry that Patrick was aware of, Zac could leave the tobacco and cigarettes in holdalls on a particular level of the ferry which meant after Patrick had boarded, they could be transferred into the back of his van. They had been doing this three times a week for many months, and both were doing very well financially from it. Zac had worked out quite quickly that if he replaced the cigarettes and tobacco with cocaine instead, the possibilities were mind-blowing. Zac didn't have any knowledge or contacts that he knew of that were importing cocaine or wanted a safe passage for their product. Zac was a regular user of cocaine, and he had been using and buying large amounts of cocaine from his new level of income. He let his biggest supplier know he has guaranteed safe passage from France to England for cocaine if the guy needs it or knows anyone who does.

Within a few weeks, Zac's phone rings one day, and an Albanian-sounding man suggests they may be able to do business together, and clearly, it wasn't something they could discuss on the phone. He had been informed that Zac could provide a potentially very interesting service. The guy told Zac where he would be at a certain time and told him not to be late and to come on his own. Zac was suddenly very excited, knowing this could be a life-changing opportunity. Two days later, Zac is in a lay-by down a country lane where he was told to be, ten minutes before the agreed time. He sat there listening to his music and looking for the lights of a car coming down the lane; who might be the guy on the other end of the phone? It was now five to two in the morning, and Zac thought he would be here soon when both rear doors of his BMW opened simultaneously. Two men in black jeans and jumpers jumped in wearing balaclavas and gloves.

Zac did think they were Albanian but wasn't sure – it was a heavy accent, and they spoke broken English, which he could just about understand. They made it clear to Zac that he didn't need to turn around and look at them to talk to them and to turn the music off. One of them then scanned the car from top to bottom for listening devices and asked him to turn his phone off. After this had happened, the larger of the two guys said to him, 'How can you guarantee safe passage for any product from France to England?'

Zac realised he didn't want to share that information. By sharing that information, he would effectively give up all his value to the men. He then replied that he had a contact who worked in Dover docks who could take stuff through security and customs in his vehicle without being checked. He suggested his contact worked for customs and excise and was a very trusted employee. They asked him how much he could transport and the frequency at which he could do this. He told them he could get between eight and fourteen kilos of cocaine safely through to England from France three times a week. They didn't say much. He knew from talking to other people that the rate for this piece of transport was £2,000 per kilo. He also thought for larger amounts, it would be less. They then made it clear to him that if they trusted him with the cocaine, and he either ran off with the cocaine or did not get it through the Port of Dover, they would kill him. They made it clear they wanted his home address and his parents' address in the UK if they were going to do business with him. He hadn't realised the seriousness of the people he was dealing with and the possible consequences for him and his family. He didn't have any children of his own – he and Lucy were seeing each other, but that was a new thing. He sat silently in the car for a while and said he was prepared to provide that information and do business with the guys if the price was right. He knew he didn't currently have other options that he could explore. As usual, in these matters, it was all going to come down to the money. They told him they would pay £1,500 per kilo and could let him have 14 kilos three times a week in France. Zac knew he had no other offers on the table at all and agreed to their offer. He then provided them with the information they required, which they said they would check out and get back to him. It had not been a long meeting; they jumped out of his BMW and disappeared into the darkness of the night.

A few days later, they had checked Zac out. He got a call from a different number and he knew exactly who he was talking to. The voice just said, 'We need to meet once more', and Zac was given the instructions to be at a new location at 3 am the following morning. Zac arrived ten minutes early, and five minutes later, his rear doors opened again, and they were back in the car. A location in France is agreed upon as a time and a date for Zac to pick up the first ten kilos of cocaine. They ask him when it will be in England and tell him where to deliver it. They made it clear that this was a trial run, which would continue once they were satisfied with the results. Everyone is clear about what will happen and then they leave the car and disappear again. Zac drives off in the middle of the night, and the only thing to cross his mind is that he hasn't discussed this with Patrick. Greed takes over, and he realises Patrick doesn't need to know. Patrick never looks in the holdalls; he just drops them off in a location just outside of Dover after leaving the docks, where he meets Zac, who transfers them to his car and takes them home.

Zac travels to France, picks up the cocaine as agreed, stays in a local hotel, and books his ticket for the P&O ferry home, which he knows Patrick will meet him on. Zac also knew from previous experience that the French were too lazy to check vehicles travelling to England. They pretended to be more interested in looking for stowaways. The first trip went exactly according to plan, and everyone was happy. After dropping the drugs to Wingham, a small village in Kent, Zac goes home. The next day, £15,000 in £50 notes appeared in two envelopes on his mat at the front door. More phone calls would follow, and it became his new line of work. He felt guilty about not telling Patrick but knew he couldn't do it if Patrick didn't want to do it. If Patrick wanted to do it, he would have to share the money with him, whereby paying Patrick for his share of the cigarette and tobacco smuggling was a lot cheaper.

Within a few months, he had more money than sense. He had hundreds of thousands of pounds hidden all over the place in £50 notes. He even told Lucy what he was doing as he had now fallen in love with Lucy and wanted them to be a couple.

Laundering the money was now Zac's biggest problem – he knew he couldn't walk into banks with that amount of cash without setting off alarm bells all over the place. He needed to figure a way out to make his money legal. Lucy said she knew that lots of Turkish barber shops were not barbers, but opened, owned and operated by people laundering money by owning a large chain of shops, for which they could pay large amounts of cash into the bank as earnings from the barber's shops. Of course, it would mean paying taxes, but it would clean all the money up. Lucy then says to Zac, 'Let's open a chain of nail bars and beauty salons, as well as hairdressers, and we can launder the cash through every week.' What a great idea, Zac thought; he knew that he and Lucy were tied up together in every way possible. Very quickly, Zac and Lucy had a million-pound dream home; Lucy was driving a brand-new Range Rover, and Zac had a Lamborghini on the drive. They told their neighbours the truth as they saw it – they had and were making a fortune from the beauty industry.

Johnny lets Lucy know he has a spare ticket for Mickey Flannigan, and if she is free, he'd love to take her for the evening to catch up. She had already let him know that she and Zac were only a distant memory now, and she was single.

CHAPTER 4
A TWIST OF FATE (BUBBA)

LUCY SEEMED happy to bump into Johnny again; as luck would have it, she had no plans for the evening. She also liked Mickey Flannigan. Johnny asked 'do you want to skip dinner, and we can grab something when we get to the O2 because of the time?' She replied, 'That would be great; let's go.'

How quickly life can change, Johnny thought. It was less than half an hour ago he was expecting to go to the show on his own, and now he was going with Lucy, whose nickname had always been Bubba. They laughed and joked on the way, catching up on the past. The show was brilliant – Johnny hadn't seen Mickey Flannigan live before. Still, he lived up to all the expectations and was very entertaining, particularly in his analysis of Boris Johnson and his jokes about the times we live in today. Lucy seemed to enjoy the evening. Johnny didn't ask about Zac much. After the show, getting out of the car park took ages. Bubba asked if Johnny could drop her back to Deal as she had been visiting her sister in Ashford when she wanted to grab a bite to eat in the Harvester before making her way home, and she didn't have her car with her. Johnny drove her back to Deal. They exchanged numbers and agreed to keep in touch.

Within a few days, she had got in touch with Johnny on social media. Bubba then started texting Johnny to say that she had listened to the book on audio, loved it, and wanted to be the leading lady when the film was made. Johnny said that she would make a great leading lady and agreed for the wrong reasons (when the film was made!) He was a little smitten with Bubba at that time.

Johnny and Bubba were contacting each other regularly and texting more than anything else, chatting about everyday stuff and how their lives were going at the moment. Then Bubba said she would be so grateful if Johnny could get her in the film, and the obvious implications of the conversation were that she thought it would be a good idea that she and Johnny started seeing each other. After all, they got on and were both single. Johnny had let her know Jemima and him were going their separate ways. It sounded like a nice idea, Johnny thought, and what followed was Bubba sharing all her sexual fantasies with him on social media and the type of relationship she wanted with him, which he found very stimulating and wanted to pursue with her. By now, Johnny was seriously thinking about how to make the film. The messaging on social media became very explicit very quickly. In reality, they were both sharing all their sexual fantasies, including what they wanted to do to each other and how.

Johnny realised he had to nip back to the dentist in Kusadasi to have a couple of implants fitted, which he couldn't have done on his first trip. The dentist had said to allow two days for treatment in Turkey so that the flight would be one day and the flight would be on the fourth day – allowing Johnny two spare days to have the treatment. Johnny flew from Stansted as he did on his first trip. He arranged with a local taxi guy from Kusadasi to pick him up from the airport at Izmir and take him to Kusadasi as this time, he was staying in a different hotel, which was the Ilayda Avantgarde Hotel on the seafront – about half a mile from the dentist. He arrived on a Sunday evening, and his appointment was at 11 o'clock the following morning. He walked from the hotel to the dentist for his appointment, spent another hour and a half having the work done, then it was explained to him that his last appointment would be six months from now as it needed that time for the gums to heal, where the implants had been inserted. He realised that he now had Tuesday as a spare day to relax and enjoy the local scenery and culture. In reality, he had his hair cut, his head, shoulders, and fingers massaged, and he did think to himself it was probably the best experience he had ever had in a barber's shop, including the Turkish coffee, still water, and friendly service. He then found a nice place to have lunch before walking around the beach in the afternoon, returning to his hotel, and putting his things together for the taxi to take him back to Izmir early the following morning. When he arrived at Stansted about lunchtime on Wednesday, it seemed the last few days had just flown by, and at least he could get back on track and start thinking about the process of how best to get the film made. He had also received some very complimentary reviews from strangers who said they couldn't wait to read his second book. He liked the idea of a second book and thought, what better than writing a sequel to his first novel, 'The Butler Did It.' He toyed with various names for the sequel. Would it be 'The Butler Did It II? No, he liked the title 'The Butler Really Did It.' That was his preferred choice.

One evening, Johnny walked into a meeting in Herne Bay on a Sunday evening, and a guy called Paul, whom Johnny had known for a few years, whom he had got off with on the wrong foot when he first met him in the rooms, waved at him and said 'I loved your book. I think it would be great if you shortened the book to a short story, and it got inserted into the stories at the rear of the Big Book.' Johnny loved that remark for certain.

It became clear to Johnny that Bubba wanted the sequel based on her and her life as well as the possibility of being in the movie. She had gone on a girls' holiday with a couple of friends to Tenerife and was constantly sending Johnny pictures of herself in a bikini on the beach. Johnny noted that she had a great tan and was in really good shape. She was certainly a temptation. That he could not deny.

Johnny realised more and more that he was enjoying life for being clean and sober, and the real meaning of life was to enjoy all the experiences in his life and have purpose at the same time. Perhaps the meaning of life was to give life meaning, to turn up in every situation as if you're meant to be there, and to make the most of it. He did think that through the perspective of gratitude for what he had, his recovery, and his new career, he was certainly able to do this and was enjoying the journey. Deep down, he knew the journey was the most important part because every event he got involved in lasted longer than reaching the destination would. He knew a guy called Lester from the rooms. Lester had always told him, 'The fireworks always tend to disappoint', and Johnny could relate to that in so many ways in his experience – the chase and the journey – were far more important.

One Friday evening, Johnny went to the AA meeting in Canterbury and bumped into Shaun and Dan, two fellows he had spent much time talking to in the rooms. He had spent weekend retreats with them and always listened to their experience and strength around recovery. However, they always decided they were on separate journeys and had totally separate lives. There was a new guy at the meeting, a lecturer at the University of Kent in Canterbury named David. He was probably in his forties, very well educated and articulate, and it was his first time at a meeting. Johnny and David started chatting about recovery, and Dan also got involved in the conversation. Dan, Shaun and Johnny asked David if he wanted to go for a coffee after the meeting and would talk further about recovery. What that meant in Johnny's mind would be that they would try to put him on the right track and talk about what AA was all about and if he wanted to engage in AA and recovery. The meeting that evening had a powerful chair and lots of good sharing, and at least a message of recovery was being shared that evening. After the meeting, they headed to the Chocolate Café, which was very busy. They went upstairs, sat down and ordered what they fancied. Shaun was in a particularly childish mood. Shaun was helpful around rough and ready characters but was not well-educated and liked to be the centre of attention. They were sitting, having their drinks, eating their food and chatting about recovery, it was a grown-up, serious conversation. Thirty minutes into the conversation, Shaun acted like a child with his cream on top of his hot chocolate and started smearing it all around his face and lips in front of David. Johnny and Dan looked at each other, totally embarrassed by his behaviour. Johnny was speechless, and they tried to ignore him. The more they tried to ignore him and talk to David, the more childish Shaun's behaviour and attention-seeking became. In the end, they all looked at Shaun and clearly, David had never seen anything like this before – he was shocked and embarrassed. Johnny and Dan knew Shaun did like to make things about himself. David politely excused himself and was never seen again.

His love affair with his Aston Martin was amazing – he had realised it was not an everyday car, and he felt he couldn't and didn't want to use it just to nip to the shops and back. He wanted to save it for special occasions, maybe Sunday best, as it were. The royalties from the book now meant he could buy another car, too. He had previously owned very nice vehicles but never a Range Rover, so he decided he would like the Range Rover as an everyday car to compliment his Aston Martin. He went down the same route to look for vehicles, searching on

Autotrader at Range Rovers for sale with the specs and colour he wanted in the local Kent area. He found an absolute gem near Borough Green. He rang and spoke to the guy and checked if the vehicle was in the condition it appeared to be in the photos. he discussed the service history, previous owners, and vehicle in general, and he knew it was the one he wanted. It was a Friday afternoon, and Johnny explained he would be over on Monday and that he was serious about the car, and if it all stacked up, he would have it. The salesman told Johnny, 'Great, please just give us a ring before you set out to check we haven't sold it.' Monday morning came around, and Johnny was up bright and early. He set off to the garage near Borough Green to view and buy the Range Rover. The satellite navigation took him up two or three wrong turns, but 45 minutes later, he arrived at the road and saw the garage on the left. He parked and was looking at the vehicles as he walked up to the office, looking at all of the cars while looking for the Range Rover, which he couldn't see. A salesman came out of the office, and they started talking. Johnny explained who he was and that he came to look at the Range Rover. The guy said, 'You said you would ring before you set out.' As soon as he said that, Johnny knew he had sold the car. He explained to Johnny that a guy had turned up and bought the Range Rover the next morning after their conversation. He then tried to sell Johnny a few other cars, including another Range Rover, but it wasn't the colour or spec that Johnny wanted. Johnny decided to leave it, go home and start his search again. He started searching online, and the one he found that fit all his requirements was in Swindon. He had the same conversation with a salesman who happened to be the garage owner in Swindon about the condition, the service history and the vehicle in general. They agreed to the deal on the phone, subject to the vehicle being in the condition it appeared to be, rather than trying for a discount; Johnny got many extras thrown in. He was offered a new service, a new

MOT, and a longer warranty package, included in the asking price.

Two days later, he jumped on the train at Canterbury West heading for Swindon. The journey took about three and a half hours after changing trains in London. The garage was quite close to the train station in Swindon. When arriving at the garage, Johnny saw the car outside, and everything was how he had expected it to be. He went into the office and purchased the Range Rover; the paperwork took about an hour, and shortly after that, he was leaving the garage on his way back to Canterbury in the Range Rover he had wanted. He had already been searching online for a private number plate for the car and found one he loved. It would have to break the bank to get the plate, so he took a chance with quite a hard offer and thought he would see what the guy said. To his amazement, the guy accepted his offer after a brief conversation, and Johnny was over the moon that he had saved £7,000 on the asking price of the number plate.

Johnny walked into a meeting one evening and met a guy he had known about 15 years ago. His name was Steve, and he lived in the Medway towns. Johnny and Steve had a few conversations in the past, and Steve lived with a girl called Rebecca, whom Johnny had known before Steve. Rebecca had phoned Johnny one evening and asked him if he would collect her from Medway. At the time, Rebecca had been chatting with Johnny regularly and had denied that she had been seeing Steve or was in a relationship with him. She had tried to convey the picture that she was more a friend of Steve's parents and that Steve's mum had offered to put her up. But Johnny knew that Steve and Rebecca were in a relationship and that they were living together with his parents. Rebecca was a lovely girl but a lost soul who had worked for Johnny previously. This evening in question, she had simply had enough of Steve and his behaviour and rang Johnny and asked if she could stay with him at his flat.

It was late, about 1 am, and Johnny said no. After that, they kept chatting – Johnny changed his mind and said he would pick her up, but she had to stop lying and being honest. So off Johnny went to Medway to pick Rebecca up at Tesco Rainham. Steve was a lot younger than Johnny, a tall, stocky guy, and had done a lot of kickboxing; Johnny knew he was a proper handful from his reputation. The reality was that Steve and Rebecca had met in rehab and hooked up after leaving the treatment centre. Johnny arrived at Tesco near the petrol station and parked up as he couldn't see anyone. It's now nearly 2 am. It was very well-lit, and there wasn't anyone around. After sitting there for a while, he thought he'd give her a little longer, and if she didn't turn up, he would call it a night and go back home. The next thing in the light was that there was no sign of Rebecca, but he could see Steve striding up the road towards him, waving a phone. 'My god', Johnny thought, 'this is not going to end well.' He was probably about 70 metres away and closing in quickly. He appeared clearly to not be in the mood to have a civil conversation, more of a proper tear-up, was Johnny's initial thought. Johnny started the car, started driving towards him and decided he would rather run him over than have a tear-up with him. Johnny would be pleased if he just moved out of the way, and then Johnny could go, but that was a decision for Steve. Johnny accelerated as quickly as he could towards Steve and, in fear, decided he wasn't going to swerve or divert from driving directly towards him. Steve realised what Johnny was up to and quickly got out of the way and onto the pavement, which was the best option for everyone. As Johnny turned onto the main road and drove off, he realised it was all unnecessary drama that Rebecca was creating and was never honest with anyone, including Steve, as it would turn out.

Within a few minutes, Johnny was now back on the M2, heading towards Canterbury and relieved, to say the least. Then, his phone rang, and it appeared it was Rebecca calling. He answered the phone just after the services headed towards Canterbury, but before Johnny could speak, Steve was shouting down the phone at him. He seemed more rational than Johnny thought he would be. He said, 'I know she called you, and you didn't call her. I think there's something wrong with her. She never tells me the truth about anything.' Johnny listened intently and thought that was probably true based on his knowledge of Rebecca. Steve said he had spoken to her, and she told him she was going to meet Johnny at Tesco, and that was why he turned up with her phone. She was still at his place. The conversation then became more civil, and Johnny realised, as he had known all along, that as far as Steve was concerned, they were a couple and shared the same bed. At this point, Johnny wondered if Steve was being coercive against Rebecca, but she had the freedom to leave him if she wanted to. Johnny decided it was more a matter for them to sort out than for him to get involved.

When he met Steve at the meeting, they recognised each other instantly. Johnny walked up to him, and they spoke, Steve said that Rebecca and he had split up shortly after that night and that she had moved on with her life. He hadn't seen her since. Both Steve and Johnny realised there had been a lot of deceit and dishonesty around the whole situation, with people being told different versions of the truth. They shook hands and wished each other all the best.

Johnny met Shaun for dinner one evening in Canterbury, chatting about life. Shaun had read Johnny's novel. He was very complimentary and talked about making it into a film. His opinion was that it would make a great film. They started talking about options for making the film a reality. Johnny thought crowdfunding might be an option. Shaun had no film experience and thought the best way forward would be to get copies of the book to film producers and directors like Guy Ritchie. Johnny knew nothing about the film business – the only thing he knew for certain – was he just needed the right person to say yes.

He started exploring his options with film production companies, suitable directors and producers in the UK, as well as media streaming companies. He researched all the addresses of the companies in the UK. He then decided he would approach all of them individually, offering a copy of his novel, explaining it was available on Audible and inviting them to read or listen to the book, to make a film or series based on it. Most of them were in a small area in London. He typed up letters, which were his best pitch, enclosed copies of the novel, went to London for the day, and grabbed a taxi to run around all of the offices of the companies he had found online. It was a really interesting day, and he fully understood that he was not going to be talking to the decision-makers in reception or at the entrance point of the offices. After Johnny had finished delivering his last pitch letter, he felt it was a good start as at some of the offices, he had received a warm welcome and wishes from the ladies in reception. They had explained they could pass it on, and that was all they could guarantee. He was happy with that – he didn't know individuals at these companies – and the fact he had attended the premises and delivered them personally, he believed maybe some of them would end up in the right hands, or at least in the hands of people that worked for the decision-makers at the top.

He decided he would grab dinner at his favourite restaurant in London, which had always been Langan's. He made a reservation online and thought it would be a nice way to end the day on his own, deep in thought about the possibilities of what could come from today's efforts. Langan's had changed an awful lot since he had last been in, and he now didn't know any of the staff at all. As always, the food was very tasty, but it didn't seem the same anymore. Maybe eating out was more about the company than the restaurant he wondered. He grabbed a cab from outside Langan's to take him back to the station so that he could get the next train back home to Canterbury.

Johnny's eyesight was slowly getting worse. He had attended Specsavers to renew his glasses and have an eye test at their invitation. Upon having the test, the woman advised him that his eyesight had become weaker and, as a result, he would need stronger reading glasses, and she also made it clear to him that he was on the cusp of needing glasses to drive. Johnny didn't particularly like what she said, but he had realised lately that driving one of his cars at night, his eyesight wasn't what it had been. He also realised that his view of the TV at home was not as clear as it was in recent years. His close-up reading had got to a stage where he simply couldn't read most text of a normal size without glasses. Although the eye test results were not welcome in his view at the time, he knew they did honestly reflect his weakening eyesight. As a result, he decided it might be a good idea to spend less time on his PC and write the sequel himself, using the dictation software. So, he bought himself an online dictation software package to translate his voice into text. That would surely help him with writing the sequel. He then realised, after testing the dictation software, that although it could pick up some words, and it did appear to work, an awful lot of the time, it couldn't make sense of his voice and was typing gobbledygook rather than what he was saying. He decided he would get someone to help him type the manuscript for the sequel. He didn't know anyone who could type and would type on a part-time basis. He decided he would ask on social media if anyone he knew who could type would be available to help. A young lady he knew called Emma from being in the rooms, who he is friends with on social media and had chatted to several times, dropped him a line to say she could do it. So, they chatted briefly about the hours and details, and she agreed she would help. That would make it a lot easier for Johnny to get the draft manuscript finished, he thought.

Johnny's attention was turned back to the making of the film, and he decided he would leave his pitch and novel in the hands of the film companies for four months before deciding if there was any possibility of a reply. He was now attending film events in London regularly. They were varied and full of people trying to get a break in the film business, often filled with actors, actresses, writers, people looking into film production, and people working at all levels in the film industry. The events were really interesting, very helpful and informative for Johnny to point him in the right direction, as well as at the same time to how difficult the task may be.

One Monday evening, Johnny headed to North London for an event hosted in the Bubba Oasis Bar and Restaurant. That made him smile as he thought he was in the right place because of the name! That evening, he met a lovely woman called Susan at the bar. Susan was a writer trying to get some breaks in the film industry. He also met some actors and actresses who were full of ego in themselves and desperate to get a break in the business. Johnny spoke to Susan, the woman in the bar, for some time. She had given him such a lot of good advice and tips for going forward. Next thing, Johnny was sitting on a table full of strangers. Everyone was introducing themselves. This young black guy called Winston appeared on Johnny's left with a drink in his hand. Johnny and Winston started chatting, and Winston introduced himself as an actor. He was young and thought he was very good-looking, probably in his early twenties. He was talking about acting work that he had done and wanted to become a full-time actor. Johnny had asked him what he had been doing, and it turned out that he hadn't played any major parts in any films, but he didn't view or fancy himself as an extra, but to date, he had done nothing more than extra work. Johnny smiled at him and said, 'You remind me of Luther,' because he couldn't remember Idris Elba's name. Winston was over the moon with that remark and said he would take that as a compliment. Johnny smiled to himself and thought he was nothing like him, but at least it would put a smile on his face. Johnny quickly realised in the film business, everyone wants to be flattered, more than most, he thought.

At the same table of people was a young woman on Johnny's right-hand side, who described herself as an actress. He asked her what work she had done, and she explained that she had none to date and that she was looking to be discovered in the business. She had come down that day from Wolverhampton for a photo shoot as she was a model. Straight away, Johnny wondered what type of photoshoot it was as he had never met a Brazilian girl before who was living in Wolverhampton. She introduced herself as Nunes. She asked Johnny what he was doing at the event, and Johnny replied, 'I'm in the process of making a blockbuster movie, based on a character who was born in London in the 1960s, with an addictive personality, which explores the connection between addiction and organised crime. It covers areas such as drugs, prostitution, drug and financial crimes.' Her face lit up, and she asked if she could be in his film. Johnny realised he suddenly appeared a great proposition to her, which made him smile. He then said, 'I do need some young models to play parts in the film, but I'm not in a rush to decide, and I've got a lot to choose from.' She then pulled out her new Apple iPhone and asked him to take her number. He declined and said he didn't need it at the moment, which made her more and more persistent. Johnny then said he would take her number and keep in touch, but he wasn't promising anything. At that point, she told Johnny, 'I promise I won't let you down. I'd be so grateful if you give me a chance, and I can show you some of my previous work.' They swapped numbers, and she sent him a WhatsApp message so they were sure they had the correct details.

Later that evening, Johnny bumped into two Indian guys at the event who described themselves as filmmakers. Johnny thought he had hit the jackpot, and they started chatting, but very quickly, it became obvious that they wanted to make Bollywood films. At that point, Johnny asked if they knew filmmakers in England who may be interested in his project. After continuing to talk to them for a while, Johnny realised that they sounded like they had no idea what they were doing. They weren't currently making films, but they liked the idea of making a Bollywood film to get shown in India, which was probably a far more accurate description of where they were.

After leaving the event that evening, Johnny reminisced that it was less than a mile away from the Bubba Oasis where his parent's greengrocers shop and Highbury Stadium had been many moons ago. That evening, he had managed to get free parking in a petrol station, which he was quite pleased about. He had gone into the petrol station just up the road from the venue and asked where there was some local parking. The cashier behind the till said he could park on the corner of the forecourt for the evening for nothing, which Johnny was grateful for. He picked up a can of Diet Coke to walk to the venue with. He got back to his car, pleased with how the evening had gone. No deals were signed, but he was beginning to understand at least the nature of the film industry a little, and the more people he talked to, the more he began to understand some of the language, which may help him with future presentations and pitches. He had, after all, enjoyed the evening, and there had been a lot of laughter and jokes at the event, and he would be driving home with a smile on his face once again, feeling that some progress had been made.

Bubba had returned home from her holiday a few weeks ago, and although Johnny and Bubba were talking and texting a lot, at this point, they had not met up. Most of his conversations with her seemed to be about her part in the book and film. Her imagination seemed to be running riot about her appearance and how men perceived her, as men fell at her feet she believed and were always lusting after her. Johnny thought she seemed to think she was the new Cameron Diaz. Although Johnny had to admit he did have a thing for her, as many men would. They had agreed to have lunch and catch up.

They meet up at a beautiful seafood restaurant in Deal called Dunkerley's, and when she turns up, Johnny is speechless. She told Johnny she was now Lady Bubba since he first met her in that random chance meeting in the Harvester. Her appearance had changed beyond belief. Her tan was amazing. She was one of those very fortunate people who just goes golden brown. She wore a short denim skirt; her hair had just been done, and so had her nails and lips. She had a very summery top on, and that complimented her denim skirt. Her perfectly chosen pair of heels and sunglasses nestled nicely in her hair. The waiter did a double take and looked at Johnny, then started laughing and running up and down the restaurant like a schoolboy. Johnny thought to himself, calm down, mate, you will give the game away. Lady Bubba had certainly made her mark with her entrance. Johnny felt like the waiter was behaving but tried to play it cool. She looked like a glamorous film star on holiday in the sun already.

Johnny had first gone to Dunkerley's about twenty years earlier. It had expanded over the years. They bought the property next door. It was now a restaurant and hotel. It was owned and run by Ian Dunkerley and his family and now employs many additional staff as well. Ian Dunkerley was a great chef and a whizz in the kitchen. Johnny liked the restaurant and had never had a bad meal in there at all. This occasion was no different; the food was great. The company was very enjoyable, and Lady Bubba and Johnny seemed to bounce off each other with the conversation flowing all afternoon. Everything had gone well, Johhny felt; maybe meeting her had been a twist of fate. He and Bubba were both happy about how it had all gone.

She told Johnny that Zac's life came a total cropper with his drug importation business a few months after the cash was rolling in. He knew the guys he was involved with were serious players in the drug importation business but never realised they were working directly for and taking orders from a drug cartel. It made sense, allowing for the amount of cocaine they were importing. One morning, Zac boarded the ferry from Calais to Dover as always. Patrick left his phone at home that day because he got up late and just shot off to work as he didn't want to be late. Then, his van broke down while driving out of the yard. The office called out the AA, but they were going to be about an hour or so before they could attend. The manager knew the ferries had to be met at certain times – that was part of the contract where, if shop deliveries were a little late, that was never a problem and could be covered. Straight away, he got Patrick and another driver to swap loads and rounds for the day. They could switch the newspapers in about ten minutes, which meant the papers would be on time for the ferries. Patrick didn't even have Zac's mobile to hand. It was just logged and stored in his phone. Patrick didn't get too carried away. He realised both Zac and him had earned an awful lot over the previous months. It meant, in reality, that Zac would leave the two holdalls in the agreed place on the right deck full of tobacco and cigarettes. The other driver would not pick them up, and P & O would, in time, discover them and either destroy them or give them to Customs officers, depending on who found them, maybe a better scenario would be if they took them for themselves. That would be the end of the matter. Zac and Patrick would just have to chalk up the experience as a loss and take it on the chin. Patrick thought the total loss was going to be about £1,200. Zac did leave the holdalls in the agreed place, and they had, on this occasion, contained 14 kilos of cocaine, not that Patrick knew anything about that. Once Zac had left the docks and driven to the regular meeting place, he would normally have had to wait about an hour for Patrick to arrive. After Patrick did not arrive, Zac rang him on his mobile, and Patrick's wife answered and explained Patrick had forgotten his phone when going to work that morning. Zac didn't want to say anything to her and just said OK. Patrick had forgotten his phone, but it was no big deal; it didn't change the plan or arrangement. After about another hour, Zac was in a complete meltdown; he knew something was wrong but couldn't put his finger on it. Please, God, Patrick had not been checked for some unknown reason. That was all he kept thinking.

About another half an hour later, Patrick nipped back home from the round he was doing, grabbed his phone, and just wanted to let Zac know what had happened. Of course, Patrick never knew and was relatively calm and unconcerned about the day's events, thinking Zac would get over the day's events quite quickly in the circumstances. Zac knew he couldn't even tell Patrick. What on earth was he going to do? He had to explain to his foreign employers that 14 kilos were now vanishing into thin air. Zac was already under pressure because he was late delivering. He thought it best to go and explain where he used to drop the drugs off. They didn't seem overly concerned. He said the shipment never made it across, and he wanted to make that right. That was the message he left. The next night, the discovery of drugs on the ferry was all over the local and national news channels. The following day, a guy taps on Zac's front door and says, 'Put your shoes on, jump in the motor, we need to have a chat'. He tells him to empty his pockets and leave his phone indoors. The motor outside was a blacked-out seven-seater. As Zac got in the rear, a guy scanned him all over for electronic devices. Then told Zac it was a simple mathematical sum: 14 kilos in England would net them 1.4 million pounds. £21,000 was deducted for transport. He owed them just under 1.38 million pounds. He had guaranteed delivery, so he was responsible for honouring that guarantee. They were not interested in excuses or losses. He explained he had the cars, partly on finance, the house had a mortgage on it and the business never actually made any money. It was just a money laundering operation, which he subsidised but cleaned up the money. There were two guys in the back of the seven-seater. One of them says to sign everything over to our colleague, and we will work out what it is worth, and you need to get back to work to clear up the balance. Zac didn't know what to say. He knew he couldn't argue and agreed. He did know after what had happened, he couldn't go back to work with Patrick. Patrick had quickly worked out what had gone down from the news. They had fallen out and didn't even speak anymore. A few weeks later, Zac and Lucy found a one-bedroom flat to rent and moved out, their house and all other assets had now been transferred. Zac went out to grab some fish and chips one evening and never returned. The following day, his body had been discovered at the bottom of the cliffs at Dover. The police said they thought it was a probable suicide. He had just jumped. Had he jumped, or was he pushed? Maybe Bubba would never find out, but the police did start investigating his death as suspicious and started looking into his background after a while. The case was eventually left with an open verdict. There was no evidence of foul play, although the investigation into his business dealings continued for a few years. Bubba decided on balance to say nothing and distance herself from the financial affairs, although the company had employed her. Wow, what a drama and change of fortune, to say the least!

The afternoon had flown by. Just before Johnny left, he was telling Bubba a funny story about his Aston Martin, an experience he had with a policeman when Johnny had parked on double yellow lines; as he returned, a policeman was waiting by the car. Johnny automatically assumed he was going to get a parking ticket. What could he say? It was a fair cop, so to speak. As he returned to the car, he unlocked the car with the key fob and looked rather sheepishly at the police officer. When the doors unlocked, the police officer looked at Johnny, smiled and said if I had one of those, I would also park it anywhere as well - then walked off laughing. That had surprised Johnny at that moment. Bubba did a double take and said, 'You have got an Aston Martin.' That had not been the story's point, but she had certainly noted that – for sure! Johnny thanked her for a wonderful afternoon, hugged and kissed her on the cheek, and let her know he was working on the film deal, and she was already featuring more and more in the sequel. They both agreed to meet up soon.

Life was jogging along nicely for Johnny, and he attended meetings quite regularly, tried to work his 12 steps, sponsored people, and shared the message about recovery and how it is possible. The following week, he went to a CA meeting in Canterbury, and after the meeting, everyone agreed to go across the road for coffee and food. Johnny was sitting next to a young lady called Nalani, who he thought looked like Naomi Campbell and was joking with her about it. She started sharing with Johnny in the restaurant about her life, her recovery, and where she was at the moment. Johnny kept joking with her about the fur coat she had on, saying she looked like a supermodel. The next thing, it turns out, is she had been a model previously, led an amazing life while living in London and been around the film industry, with some of her ex-partners having worked in the film business. One of them had made films in Hollywood, and Johnny's eyes were beginning to light up. Maybe she would be a good contact who could put Johnny directly in touch with people who were capable, or knew people who were capable, of getting his novel turned into a film – or maybe that was just wishful thinking? Time will tell. He realised maybe a lucky break would play a major part in finding someone keen to make the film. To Johnny's amazement, Nalani shared with him that she had a great sponsor, but she had a large family and work, and sometimes, it was difficult for them to meet up and keep in touch. She shared she was thinking about keeping her as a friend and finding a new sponsor. Johnny made one or two gentle suggestions about possible candidates. She looked at Johnny and said, 'What about you?' Johnny was taken aback. He had certainly not seen that coming. Johnny said he thought it might work and be possible. He suggested the two of them meet for a coffee on their own, continue their interesting conversation and discuss the sponsorship deal honestly and openly so they both knew what they agreed to. She liked that idea and they agreed to meet up in Canterbury for a coffee one evening a couple of hours before a meeting started that they both attended on occasions.

CHAPTER 5
LIVING THE DREAM

JOHNNY ARRIVED back home from Deal and realised he was literally 'Living the Dream'. Wow, what a journey he was now on. It had all happened so quickly, and he seemed to be gliding along in life. He had now received his referral appointment for his hernia operation. He had to pick his preferred hospital to see a consultant and arrange to be put on the waiting list for the surgery to be performed. He had researched online that the waiting list for the NHS was about 6-9 months. He selected the Chaucer Hospital based on location and time to see the consultant from a whole host of options available. He couldn't exercise or walk on certain days without feeling pain, so he decided when he saw the consultant, he would ask how much to have it private and just pay privately to have the operation. He figured that way; he would probably have the operation within a couple of weeks after seeing the consultant.

Nalani and Johnny met up for a coffee in Canterbury on a Friday evening to discuss the idea of sponsorship. Johnny found her interesting and was fascinated by some of the stories she shared about her life and background. In the back of his mind, he still hadn't forgotten that she did, at least in the past, have contacts in the film industry. She was an interesting character. She had been a very accomplished horse rider and had competed at the highest level, as many addicts do. Johnny realised that many people he had met in the rooms had reached massive highs in their chosen fields or industries. As a rule, they are just people who don't know when to stop in anything they do, which, on the one hand, makes them great achievers, but on the other hand, can be very painful indeed. When she was younger, she was also a gymnast and represented England in the 1996 Olympics hosted in Atlanta, America. After retiring as a gymnast, she became a model and was often seen strutting the catwalk in the latest Versace designs.

Johnny and Nalani shared a lot about their backgrounds at Costa Coffee before turning to the serious business of sponsorship and going through the 12 steps. They had met face to face as it was in both their best interests on how their relationship could develop in the future, and in particular, it was better for both to know what was expected from each other. Johnny couldn't speak for Nalani, but he could tell her and show her what he had done in his recovery and ask if she wanted to do the same or not. Of course, Johnny knew he could only shine the torch and let her do the digging. Johnny was always up for trying to take someone through the 12 steps if they were a willing participant. The conversation ended with Johnny saying he would email her everything that evening or the next day. He thought she should sit with the idea for two days to decide if it was something she wanted to commit to. Nalani never actually got back to Johnny, and shortly afterwards, when they bumped into each other one evening, she explained that she changed her mind.

One evening, Emma went round to Johnny's to type, and they started to talk about Johnny's original novel, 'The Butler Did It.' Emma's mother was good friends with the manager of a large independent bookstore in Canterbury. Emma suggested that it might be a good idea if Johnny approached the manager and asked if they wanted to do a book signing evening. Emma had previously trained as a journalist, and when Emma was at university studied for a degree in journalism and got a first. When she left university, she worked for the local newspapers all over Kent and had lots of contacts in the local media. She suggested getting reporters to go to the book signing evening and report on the event in the local newspapers. This may prove to be a great opportunity for publicity. What a great idea, Johnny thought. He would go into the bookshop, speak to the manager to see if it was possible, and go from there.

The day of Johnny's appointment at the hospital arrived, and he was looking forward to seeing the consultant to make the necessary arrangements to pay for the operation privately. He attended the Chaucer hospital one afternoon, waited in the reception area, filled in a couple of health questionnaires, and waited his turn. After a short time, he was directed to a private room where he met Doctor Harjeet. He was a small Indian man, very polite and knowledgeable, and he started speaking to Johnny about his current health condition. He asked Johnny to strip off and lay on the bed to examine the groin area. He confirmed exactly what had been suggested to him in the reports. He asked Johnny how he was coping in daily life with the situation. It was a tricky one for Johnny to explain as the pain could come and go at any time, and Johnny never knew how much physical assertion he could apply before the pain would come. Or, at other times, he would have long periods of grace. Then came the bombshell; Doctor Harjeet explained to him that he could not do the operation at the Chaucer Hospital on the NHS because of Johnny's health records and history. He asked Johnny about his heart problems and thoroughly reviewed his medical history with him. He explained to Johnny that Johnny could not have the operation at the hospital because if there were any complications with his heart, they didn't have the necessary resources to save his life at that moment.

In an NHS hospital, if there were any complications, they had all the resources at the drop of a hat to save Johnny's life. At that point, Johnny realised his idea of paying privately and jumping the NHS waiting list was a total non-starter. To make matters worse, Doctor Harjeet then explained that he would refer Johnny back to his General Practitioner, who would then refer Johnny back to see a consultant at an NHS hospital to be put on a list for the operation. He then told Johnny he would probably see him again at either the Kent and Canterbury Hospital or the William Harvey Hospital in Ashford. A few days later, Johnny received a copy of the letter that Dr Harjeet had sent back to his General Practitioner and would now wait for an appointment on the NHS to see a consultant.

Ever since Johnny was a child, he was always a big fan of Billy Joel and, in particular, always had fond memories of the track 'Uptown Girl' and was fascinated by the fact that Billy Joel had met Christie Brinkley while making the video for that track, they had started dating and later married. Shortly after, a friend of Johnny's called Gary bought a Billy Joel cassette of his greatest hits, which Johnny would play driving with Gary in his Ford Cortina listening to the tape. Now Johnny had the opportunity to see Billy Joel live at Hyde Park. He bought two tickets for the event around six months earlier and was looking forward to it. When he told Sophia about it, she said she would love to go with him. A couple of weeks before the concert, he reminded Sophia about the day, and she apologised and told him she couldn't make it. Then Sophia told Johnny that her partner David had a ticket to Bruce Springsteen on Saturday after Billy Joel was playing at Hyde Park on Friday. She asked Johnny if he wanted to buy the ticket from David, who couldn't attend the Saturday concert. Johnny decided to sell the second Billy Joel ticket online if he could, and he would go on his own to see Billy

Joel. He wasn't exactly sure about Bruce Springsteen but did decide he would buy the ticket from David and go along. Johnny sold the Billy Joel ticket to a woman called Bella from Liverpool. He asked her for the same amount of money he had paid for the ticket, and she was over the moon. Johnny received a message after the concert from her to say it was the best day of her life. On Friday, Johnny set off early to get to the event. He hadn't been to a concert in Hyde Park before. He drove to London, found some parking a few miles from Hyde Park and decided to jump on the tube to get to the park. It was a beautiful sunny Friday afternoon. After leaving his car in a secure car park, he was walking down the road looking for Pimlico Tube Station. Instead of putting it on Google Maps on his phone, he figured he knew the general direction when he came across three young lads who, for some reason, he thought lived locally. They all appeared to be around 15 or 16 to Johnny. Johnny asked them if they knew where Pimlico Tube Station was, and they all pulled out their phones to look at Google Maps. Johnny felt a little embarrassed because he could've done this! They seemed like nice lads, a bit rough and ready round the edges, and one of them had explained to Johnny that it was just around the corner, on the right-hand side. He apologised as he thought they were local, and they explained they were from Dartford. Johnny wondered what they were up to in London, thanked them for the directions, and joked with them and said, 'Make sure you behave yourselves.' One of them replied, 'Yo bro- we are not criminals,' which made Johnny smile. When Johnny told Sophia about this, she said to him did you say to them, 'You might not be, but I am!' 'No', Johnny smiled and replied. I used to be, but now I am a published author. The look Sophia gave him was Priceless!

The journey from Pimlico to Hyde Park was just a few stops. Johnny had got to Hyde Park in plenty of time to enjoy the occasion. There were a lot of support acts before Billy Joel, including

Darryl Hall from Hall and Oates. The park was packed and was a sellout – everyone seemed to be in really good spirits. When Billy Joel came on and performed, he was everything Johnny thought he might be and more. Johnny realised he was such a talented piano writer, songwriter and singer. He lit up the crowd with hit after hit after hit, and Johnny was so pleased that he had bought the ticket. He realised Billy Joel was now in his seventies, and those opportunities to see people live were going to become fewer and fewer. He got home later that evening and thought how lucky he was. He had to do the same thing tomorrow for Bruce Springsteen. On Saturday, Johnny took the train to avoid car parking, congestion charges, and possible traffic delays. He arrived at Hyde Park, not knowing what to expect. Bruce Springsteen came on around 7 pm, and Johnny was blown away from start to finish. Johnny thought he would come on, sing the track about back in the USA and go off the stage. He hadn't heard many of his songs over the years. After listening and watching him perform with a band, he understood exactly why they called him the Boss! He was also in his seventies and was running around the stage like a forty-year-old, very fit man! It was clear he just loved playing the guitar and singing. He shared that he had started as a child and had just been invited to participate in a band when he was around 15. The band had lasted two or three years, which was a long time for a teenager, and that was where it all started. He had since been playing all over the world and acquired his reputation. He came across to Johnny as a nice, genuine family guy who just loved music. It was such a treat to see him play live, and Johnny enjoyed recording him on his phone while he was singing various tracks. The whole evening seemed to fly by as the next thing Johnny was on the train home, thinking about how lucky he was to have been to two concerts over the last couple of days. Both artists were not disappointing in any way. Johnny had 100% admiration for Billy Joel and his talent, which was different from Bruce

Springsteen's. He had been a big fan of Billy Joel all his life, but even he had to admit, Bruce Springsteen was just at the top of his game and probably, in Johnny's humble opinion, was just the better entertainer, which had surprised him!

Johnny was back in regular meetings, enjoying his recovery and enjoying his life. He bumped into a guy called Tim, who seemed to be quite shy to Johnny. Johnny tried to chat with him and at least guide him in the right direction – they seemed to have a connection – and exchanged numbers. After bumping into each other at meetings, Johnny had listened to Tim share in the meetings and had been for coffee before and after meetings with him on several occasions. Tim then asked Johnny if he would consider sponsoring him and guide him through the 12 steps. Johnny said he would if Tim was prepared to do the work. Tim had come out of rehab for about the sixth time! Johnny found Tim fascinating and liked talking to him. Tim was the only cocaine addict that Johnny had ever met who moved to Columbia so he could get the cocaine cheaper and feed his addiction. Tim had never really managed to make anything of his life, it had appeared. However, he had always thought that he had massive footsteps to follow because his father had been amazingly successful in the legal industry.

Tim had tried to follow in his steps but somehow never managed to live up to his father's expectations. He was an only child, and every time his life hit the rocks, he needed financial assistance or someone to pay for rehab. His mother and father would always pick up the bill for him. He was probably his own worst enemy, as he had been letting himself down rather than letting his father down. He was a nice guy who had travelled around the world during the Covid pandemic and met a woman from Singapore, with whom he got on well and eventually married. He took her around the world. She wasn't an addict, but Tim was travelling to different countries that were the best places to feed his drug addiction. He had spent years in Eastern

Asian countries before ending up in Columbia. He then had to sort out a visa for his new wife. His biggest problem was that he didn't have employment in England and could not support her according to the legal requirements for letting a foreign spouse settle in the UK. His mother and father had managed to resolve the issue for him by depositing a substantial amount of money in his bank, which he could then show he had the financial resources to support himself and his wife. He had the natural right to be a British citizen.

Even after his parents had put the money into his bank account, he started spending the money on drugs. Johnny would sometimes meet Tim and his wife for a coffee before the meeting. Johnny could never understand her name. Her English was poor, and Johnny used to call her Miss Ting Tong, but only in his head. Tim had started with a really good attitude in recovery, doing what was suggested. Very quickly, he had a small period of sobriety, and he was going to the gym seven days a week. After a while, he stopped phoning Johnny, and one evening, he called Johnny late at night and said to him he was on drink and drugs. Johnny asked him, 'What do you want me to do about it? Take care, and I wish you well.'

Within a few weeks, Johnny would see him again in a meeting, and he had shared with Johnny that he had become homeless and penniless again very quickly because his wife had kicked him out and taken his bank cards off him. Johnny was surprised at how everything had gone wrong for him so quickly yet again. He explained to Johnny that he had ended up begging on the streets in Canterbury for drug money. He did come back to the rooms for a short period and then disappeared again.

Johnny had noticed Tom Jones was playing at Dreamland on Thursday, the 27th of July. Johnny had grown up listening to Tom Jones. His father had been a massive fan. In those days, George had an 8 track in his car and lorry, so often Tom Jones would be the entertainment as they went on various trips together. Johnny had taken to Tom Jones, who went on to be one of the most successful musical artists and entertainers. Over the years, his womanising also got an awful lot of attention in the press. He managed to grab a ticket and thoroughly enjoyed listening to him share things about his life and career as well as listening to him live. He certainly lived up to his billing. That voice had probably earned Tom Jones more money than Johnny could imagine. In Johnny's opinion, he was a true professional and still had it all. Johnny had a great evening and even had some good childhood experiences and memories of Dreamland amusement park when he visited and used all the rides on hot summer days. What a beautiful way to spend a Thursday evening, Johnny reflected on the short journey home.

The book signing evening was approaching quickly, and Johnny was so excited at the prospect of signing books and taking photos with everyone, which he could use for publicity. Emma had called in all of her chips with journalists she knew, and three contacts had agreed to attend the book signing, listen to Johnny, and interview him for a written piece for the local newspapers.

The event went off with a bang. Johnny couldn't have been more pleased because all the seats were taken, the journalists attended, and people seemed to enjoy having their books signed and pictures taken with him. The journalists said they found the story interesting and would publish it in next week's paper. Johnny was pleased and excited about the possibility of reading about the event in the local papers. It would make a refreshing change for Johnny to be in the local papers in a more positive light.

When the article came out, Johnny was delighted with what had been said. They had reported on the event and written about the novel with their interpretation and understanding of what the book might mean to different people. Johnny thought all publicity was good publicity if you're trying to sell a novel and make a film.

Johnny had now started to write the sequel and was beginning to wonder how Bubba would be the lead character in the story. He realised that his relationship with Bubba was never going to be the main event in the book, or so he thought. He decided in regards to the first novel, that he had been fortunate with reviews, sales and the recent book signing event. He had no other ideas to promote the novel besides word of mouth and sales in general. He understood that in part an author would be able to live on their reputation, and he knew he didn't have one yet or a massive public relations team to do the work for him. He was grateful to Emma and a few of his colleagues for the help they had given him, but he didn't have the public relations team to generate the publicity he craved. He decided he had done his best and would continue to do this and see how that rolled out. Little did he know what was about to happen next.

Bubba and Johnny had met up a few times. They had been to see Ricky Gervais in his new show Armageddon at the London Palladium one evening. They seemed to be getting on well – maybe she wasn't going to be the love of his life that he thought she was, maybe they would end up as just friends. He enjoyed her company, but maybe the energy and chemistry he had with Jemima were just not there. He was beginning to realise that it was more of a physical attraction than a meaningful relationship, so his attitude towards Bubba had slightly cooled. He did ask her out again, and she hadn't gotten back to him. He took that as the answer and the fact she hadn't confirmed, he just decided to just move on and get on with his life. Within a few weeks, she was sending him very sexual graphic pictures and texts, suggesting she would be the best lover he had ever had, fulfilling all his fantasies and games in the bedroom. It was a tempting offer for Johnny. She had also started asking him about the details in the first book. In general, she was curious about certain facts that she thought may well be true. Johnny didn't discuss individual facts in the novel with anyone. He couldn't see the point of that.

After a week or so, Johnny and Bubba decided she would go over and stay at his place for the weekend, and they would get to know each other a lot better, particularly in the bedroom. She made it clear to him she would fulfil all his sexual desires and turned up with a small suitcase filled with lingerie, leather outfits, as well as handcuffs and, of course, a compulsory blindfold for the weekend that they intended to spend together. She was not an angel or a virgin, he thought. Rather than going out, they ordered takeaways through an app and had all their meals delivered. Bubba was drinking the red wine she had brought with her, and she knew Johnny didn't drink anymore. Johnny didn't mind that she was drinking; she had always been honest that she liked a drink, and the fact that Johnny didn't drink, he knew full well that was his choice and certainly didn't hold drinking against anyone else. The weekend was astonishing. They even filmed some of the events and games. They spent half the weekend in bed, playing out all of their fantasies and endlessly making love. Although Johnny had a wonderful time, on reflection the next week, it had just been great sex. Bubba had realised that Johnny's attitude towards her was cooling now, and he did tell her that she was in his next book and that she was the leading lady, but the spark had somehow gone, which she was very aware of. Johnny never knew how manipulative and deceitful she could be. She had taped some of their time together without his knowledge. Johnny got carried away that weekend and started telling her things he would regret later. That weekend, she had also gone through his phone when he was sleeping and looked at messages that Nunes had been sending Johnny. She had continuously been in touch with him wanting her part in the film, and he had no real interest in her as she was far too young, but Bubba had seen her as a threat to being the lead role in the first film, and maybe becoming the leading lady in the next novel and film. Bubba was furious as she thought Nunes was going to steal everything she felt entitled to, and she was going to put a stop to it. Shortly afterwards, she started asking Johnny about Nunes and why she was continuously messaging him about being in the film. He had promised her that part, and she let Johnny know she expected him to honour that agreement. The relationship with Bubba sounded more like a business arrangement rather than a romantic interest, and she was beginning to show a very cold, hard, and ruthless side to her character.

One night, while they were chatting on the phone, she said to Johnny, 'If you double cross me with Nunes, I will make sure you regret it for the rest of your life.' Johnny told her to calm down and that Nunes was just a young, aspiring model he had met at a function several months earlier and wanted to get into the film business. He said it had practically been a joke getting her number as he had no interest or desire for her. He did think and discuss in the long text messages they had exchanged that, of course, when the film was made, he would say to the powers that be that he knew a young Brazilian model who was an aspiring actress, and if they wanted to use her, he would welcome that, but that would be a matter for them. He wasn't going to push her onto anyone. Deep down, Johnny thought that she was only trying to get work and a break in life, and Johnny admired people who wanted to pursue a chosen career and try their best to keep knocking on doors in the hope one would open. He did know that she was young and very attractive, and there were probably several parts in the book she could play, so his attitude towards her had changed from when he first met her. He was now warming to the idea that if he could help her, he would.

Johnny then questioned Bubba and asked how she knew about Nunes. She then told Johnny that when his phone was on the side, he left messages showing on WhatsApp with the conversations left open. Johnny knew that wasn't true – he didn't leave his phone in that position, and he realised she had gone through the messages on his phone without him knowing. He was beginning to wonder how it had all come to this. He thought bumping into Bubba was going to be a positive experience, and maybe they would get on well, and that would grow in time. Of course, he would have been happy for her to be in the film and the sequel. He didn't like the idea of being dictated to, threatened, and told what to do by someone he now thought was quite cold and calculated. Perhaps he should've seen it coming, but Johnny felt that Zac and Bubba would never have lasted long without his drug importation business.

Johnny was enjoying life on the whole – apart from the change of heart towards Bubba, he couldn't have asked for more, in all honesty. He was very grateful for all that he had in life daily. He was meeting and talking to some very interesting characters from all walks of life. The dream of the film and the second novel were ongoing. He knew his publicity drive appeared to be almost exhausted, but he had no idea what Bubba was capable of or how events would turn out in the future.

Bubba was now making accusations to Johnny that he was seeing Nunes and involved in some sort of relationship with her. Other than the fact that they had met, there was a slight possibility that she might be able to do some film work in the future, there was no other relationship whatsoever. She had misunderstood certain texts or put her interpretation on the text messages which she had read. Johnny would often receive sarcastic messages from her like 'Are you out with her tonight?'

The relationship between Bubba and Johnny had deteriorated very quickly based on her insecurities and jealousy. Johnny and Bubba were still on talking terms, just about. Johnny had let Bubba know he was going back to Turkey soon for his last appointment and final fit at the dentist, and he would be out of the country for ten days. He was just letting her know. She then said that it sounded great and that she would go with him. Johnny didn't want her in Turkey with him for ten days, especially how things had been going. He told her he didn't think it would be a good idea for him to go with him. She then accused him of going with someone else, probably Nunes, but in any event, she believed he was going with another woman. In reality, the trip was planned for Johnny on his own - of course, he could've booked another ticket and upgraded the room, but the last thing he wanted at the moment was to be in a foreign country with a woman he wasn't getting on with. He thought he would enjoy himself on his own and have more time to reflect on his life and where he might be going in the future. Bubba couldn't understand why he didn't want to take her, and it ended in another row.

Johnny had now received his new consultation date with Doctor Harjeet at the William Harvey Hospital in Ashford. He was looking forward to meeting the doctor again. There would be very little to discuss because of the initial meeting, and Johnny would at least be able to get placed on the waiting list for his operation.

Johnny had been out with Sophia for dinner, and his relationship with her was on such a level that he could talk openly and honestly about other women in his life because she had David in her life. In reality, Johnny and Sophia had a great friendship and respect for each other, but it was never going to go past that again. It was always interesting for Johnny to listen to Sophia's opinions about life and women in general. Of course, Sophia never knew the women and could not speak for them, but it gave Johnny further insight into the relationships. Her advice regarding Bubba was that, as always, you should do what you want to; after all, the relationship was between them. She said that it appeared to be very unhealthy and toxic from what

Johnny was saying. Johnny always liked her opinions, and she would remind him that he was only sharing his side of the story. If she had spoken and listened to Bubba, then maybe her view of the whole situation would be different. She did laugh at the idea of her wanting to be referred to as Lady Bubba; she said, 'There was a clue there for you if you had spotted it.'

CHAPTER 6
TURKEY TEETH

JOHNNY HAD RECENTLY BEEN INVITED to a golf event in Sheerness. It was a fund-raising event for children with cancer. It was in memory of his old friend Lee, who died of COVID-19 in the pandemic. The last text Johnny ever sent him when he was in hospital was, 'Only the good die young – don't worry, you will be out soon'. Next thing, he was unconscious in intensive care and never made it. He was such a lovely, kind guy, and it seemed somehow a lovely thing to do in his memory now that all the COVID restrictions had passed. Johnny remembered attending the funeral when there were all the restrictions on around funerals. Johnny knew Lee's wife, Jan, and his mother, Janice. The funeral had been a moving event for many reasons, but the one stand-out reason Johnny remembered the service was that Steve, his best mate, spoke, he said 'he had never spoken to as many people in his life after Lee died who told him he was my best friend'. What an amazing tribute from so many people. He was a loveable rogue, and Johnny had many amazing memories of him in his heart to be grateful for. Lee was always laughing and had a very kind side to him, which Johnny admired. There was to be a golf tournament all day to raise money, and in the evening, in the clubhouse, food, entertainment, a raffle, and an auction to raise money.

Johnny had thought about participating in the golf tournament but knew he could not even guarantee that he could play a round of golf or walk around a golf course for a day. He decided not to participate in the golf event and just attended in the evening. His wife, Jan, organised the event with help from his mother, sister and close friends. There were so many raffle prizes, and there had been a lot of wonderfully generous donations of a whole range of events and gifts to be auctioned to raise money.

Johnny had arrived and was enjoying the food and drink and meeting up with many people he had not met for years. Many people also recognised Johnny, and there was a great atmosphere that evening. Ironically, Jan had now stopped drinking alcohol and was drinking soft drinks like Johhny. Johnny grabbed a load of raffle tickets. Then he started looking at the list of things that were going to be auctioned. He wanted to buy or at least bid on some things to add or contribute to the proceedings. A lot of the items were holidays and trips, which Johnny was not going to be able to use. There were also a lot of golf memorabilia, rounds of golf and golfing equipment, which Johnny couldn't seriously use. Then he spotted an MOT and a full service on any make of car. So that was something Johnny could seriously bid on and get the benefit from. Johnny knew the couple Steve and Shelley, who owned the garage that had donated the gift. He had a quick chat with Steve before the bidding to check for any restrictions. Steve said no. Johnny laughed and said, 'Don't worry, I am easy to deal with.' Shelley laughed at Johnny and said I miss hearing that laugh. Johnny decided he would buy that, and that way, he had with his raffle tickets at least added something to the occasion. Johnny and a guy got involved in a small bidding war for it, but he just kept bidding, winning the day on this occasion.

Later that evening, he went to the gents, and as he walked in, there was a guy he knew from many moons ago, Adam, who was in the toilet selling or at least giving a couple of guys what looked like half a kilo of cocaine. Johnny started laughing. The two guys didn't know Johnny and started panicking; Adam told them to calm down, and the fact that he and Johhny knew each other. He then joked with Johnny about having the cocaine himself. Johnny laughed at the whole performance, went into the cubicle, spent his penny, so to speak and left smiling. Johnny was so glad he could just ignore all that madness today. Later on, after saying goodnight to everyone, he left just before the end and gave Jan a copy of his novel to read before leaving. It had been a great evening; more importantly, Johnny had enjoyed the whole occasion drinking Diet Coke. On the drive home, he was able to conjure up so many memories of Lee and him playing cards together, drinking, socialising and creating havoc on occasions, no doubt, but it had never been spiteful. It had been playful and just got out of hand. They had done business together, shared beds and hotel rooms, ran out of some amazing restaurants without paying, and had a lot of fun and laughs over about a 10-year period that they knew each other. Lee had never really conformed. He lived his life on his terms and had at least lived a full life. People like Lee are a once-in-a-lifetime experience. They are very hard to find, a bit like diamonds in the street. Johnny later found out the evening had been a great success and raised about £14,000 for Children with Cancer. Lee would no doubt have approved of that if, as Johnny hoped, he had been looking down on the event that evening.

Johnny had recently been approached by Kate, who was a really good friend of Jemima's, and she had asked him if he would like to sponsor her. Johnny was surprised to hear from her as she had been the reason that Jemima and Johnny had fallen out. He didn't like the fact that Jemima had chosen to help her rather than go out with Johnny. He had no idea that Kate had been drinking again and didn't have a sponsor. He hadn't spoken to her in a long time but had met her before as a result of knowing Jemima. Johnny thought this could be interesting, and he agreed to meet her and run through the idea of sponsorship. He did make it clear that, in all honesty, she had an awful lot of sponsors, and in truth, what he was going to suggest to her would be very similar, if not the same, as the others.

Kate and Johnny had agreed to meet to discuss sponsorship a few days later. Johnny said he would go to her place, and they could talk it through. The previous evening, Kate had tickets for UB40 and asked Johnny if he wanted to go, but Johnny had already made plans for that evening. He was going to the Marlowe Theatre to see a production of Agatha Christie's 'And Then There Was None'. The following day, Johnny went to Kate's, and she poured her heart out about how her life had collapsed in recent times, and she was drinking again. She had problems with an ex-partner of hers when she went to see Mickey Flannigan earlier in the year. How ironic, Johnny thought – Jemima and Johnny never got to see Micky Flannigan together because of Kate's problems with her ex that evening they were meant to go to the show. Kate's life was in bits in reality. It was true she was drinking again, but it was worse; she was facing eviction and now had to come to terms with the idea of attending the same meetings that her ex went to. Both of them were in early recovery again, if indeed she was in recovery at all. Johnny said he would sponsor her but made it crystal clear that she needed to commit to the work in recovery and put it first every day; otherwise, she had no chance of recovery whatsoever. She had been at it all of her life from a very young age. She had been in and out of the rooms for a few years and never seemed to fully grasp the fact that her life probably depended on her recovery. The more she opened up about her past, the more Johnny realised how difficult a life she had, albeit with some of the choices she had made in active addiction, mainly with her choices in partners.

They decided to start working together, and Johnny accompanied her to meetings to encourage her to share – not because it was anyone else's business – but because he wanted her to try and get honest with herself and not have a fear of the rooms and that would hopefully help her with her recovery. Very quickly, Johnny realised that Kate and Jemima had fallen out, which surprised Johnny as they had been very close before. Johnny had some time on his hands and decided to try and help Kate as best as he could – if she was prepared to try and help herself. After a while, she picked up again, and they went through the same conversation. She had a relative staying with her who could rent a room from her, which may have helped her financially. Johnny liked the guy; he just seemed like an honest, clean-living lad who cared about his auntie. Johnny thought he was a positive influence in her life. He and Johnny would often talk openly about her addiction issues in front of her. It was clear to Johnny that he wanted to see his auntie get well, too. This situation continued for a while, and Johnny made it clear that she should not date a guy who attends the same meetings as her. She couldn't go through a repeat of getting involved with someone in the same meetings she attended in case it didn't work out and the repercussions would be too much for her to face.

He told her that if she wanted to date someone, she needed to find someone to go out with to the cinema, bowling, and do something other than using drugs or drinking with. It became apparent within a short time that she had a new interest in her life. Johnny had met him one day. He was either drunk or drunk and high. Johnny couldn't work it out, and he didn't seem like a particularly nice guy to Johnny. Johnny wondered why she was in any way attracted to or wanted to be involved with him, not that he knew that they were involved or maybe about to be involved. It would later transpire that she and the new guy, Matt, had known each other long before Johnny appeared on the scene. He was just totally off his head, saying the most inappropriate things at the wrong time. Johnny noted that he had no tact or diplomacy skills whatsoever!

Johnny was at Kate's one day, and her nephew had made it clear that Matt had been staying at Kate's and that she was never sober. Johnny said, 'You can either ring him and explain you don't want anything to do with him again, or we will call it a day.' He said, 'There appears to be something wrong with you; the chance of a quick fling with him could kill you, and you don't seem to understand or comprehend that.' She told Johnny she would let Matt know that it was over.

The following week, it had been decided by the court, in her absence, that she was to be evicted from her home. There was a guy at the council who had tried to be helpful to her and discuss the idea of clearing up her arrears and paying the rent monthly. She just ignored him constantly, as well as the letters. When she received another letter from the council, she sent the guy at the council a text and told him she couldn't cope and was going to kill herself. Thank God the bloke at the council contacted the police, who went to her place, kicked the door in as she wasn't answering, and defused the situation as best they could. They told her she needed to seek professional help and encouraged her to do so. Johnny went over to Kate's, and a friend of hers, who was also in recovery named Lisa, was trying to help her as well. They ended up having a huge argument because Lisa was far more sympathetic to Kate's plight, whereas Johnny was trying to tell her to get a grip, stop using, and begin to rebuild her life. Lisa had no boundaries in her recovery whatsoever. He explained to her, in no uncertain terms, that if she weren't a willing participant in her recovery, then everyone would just be wasting their time and, more importantly, that she was wasting her life away. Johnny wasn't trying to scare her; he was just trying to explain to a broken woman that although her life was in bits, ultimately, it was her responsibility to start to rebuild from the bottom. Maybe if she remembered the pain and hardship she was going through, it wouldn't be a bad lesson to learn.

Johnny, Kate and Lisa all decided to go to a meeting that evening, and on the way to the meeting, Kate received a call from the guy at the council. He was trying to offer her some support to help her in her hour of need. It was agreed that Johnny would attend the council the following day, and Kate would attend an appointment at which the eviction, or the possibility of keeping the house, could be discussed. They went to a meeting that evening, and Johnny was laughing at Kate as they turned up. On the way to the meeting, she had asked Johnny if her ex went to that meeting, and Johnny said, 'No, he hardly ever goes, but on this occasion, he was there'

The next day, Johnny attended the council with Kate, and the council bent over backwards to help her. Three representatives, all with different roles, are at the meeting with Johnny and Kate in a private room. There was a brief mention of the previous events where she had sent the text about how she had intended to end her life and couldn't cope; then they moved onto the idea of her being able to suspend the eviction and keep her home. They were trying to support her, although she had not helped herself at all. Her arrears had continued to increase as a result of an unusual situation she found herself in where she was not working but not claiming benefits. She had been working previously before drinking again, so had stopped claiming benefits, then found herself in a position where she couldn't work again, but the claim for benefits had not been processed properly – mainly due in truth to her actions and lack of co-operation with the benefits department about the information they were asking for. It was just a complete mess. One of the men at the council named Steve told her he specialised in helping people and had direct contacts at the benefits office who could assist going forward. Kate was then advised that if she went to the Citizens Advice Bureau, they would help make an application to the court to suspend the eviction due to her circumstances. So, Steve spoke to a woman at the Citizens Advice Bureau in Ashford and arranged for Kate to attend after leaving the council officers to start the process of appealing the eviction.

Johnny and Kate then went to the Citizens Advice Bureau, sat down with two ladies in a private office and filled out the forms together, which was the basis of the appeal for the eviction. They had been really helpful. Johnny dropped Kate home and told her he was off to Turkey in two days to get his teeth done. She thought it would be a good idea if she went to Turkey with him for the holiday; he laughed and said, 'You're not coming anywhere with me; you need to start getting back on track and doing what we've discussed.'

Three days later, Johnny was up and packed and on his way to Stansted Airport for his final dentist appointment in Turkey. It was a ten-day trip. This time, he had booked to stay in the Hotel Ilayda, which was just down the seafront from the hotel Johnny had stayed in on his previous trip. Johnny had his regular taxi driver now, who would pick him up at the airport and take him to the hotel in Kusadasi on Sunday evening.

The flight had been a good one and landed on time. As Johnny left the plane and was heading towards passport control, he nipped into the loo and thought he would whizz straight through passport control and be in Aydin's taxi on his way to Kusadasi in no time at all. When Johnny got to the two queues for passport control, there did not seem to be much staff at the booths, and he thought both queues seemed extremely long. Maybe another plane had just landed, which may explain all the people. Johnny chose the right-hand side queue, and it seemed to be moving very slowly indeed. Then he noticed a woman in a blue jumpsuit ahead of him in the queue. At first sight, she seemed to be the perfect-looking woman for a magazine shoot. Johhny was about twenty feet away from her. She was on the phone texting continuously, and Johnny realised she probably looked how she did as a result of surgery and enhancements. The closer Johnny got as the queues were going side to side, he realised she was almost plastic. Her breasts were large and very firm. She appeared to have had Botox, fillers and injections, no doubt, all over her face and body. Then Johnny thought it may well be a man who had had a sex change and surgery. The closer he got on occasions, the more he was confused about whether the person had originally been a man or woman. There did appear to Johnny to be more signs that it was a man who had had the work done. He thought that the posture and walking somehow seemed to lean towards a male. Then, the face close up looked like a man with lots of plastic surgery. It was certainly a conundrum for Johnny. Of course, it was not his business, obviously, but he was intrigued, to say the least, and it did help pass the time away while he moved along the queue slowly. Johnny thought he might ask the question at one stage and then thought better of it. He thought leaving it as a mystery on balance would be better. Then he passed through passport control and customs and was very quickly at the terminal exit looking for Aydin. He didn't know if he would recognise Aydin because it had been a while. They had been messaging on WhatsApp, but Aydin's profile picture was not a picture of him; it was his taxi card. Johnny thought he would be helpful and let Aydin know he was bald. That might help Aydin when they would be looking for each other. Aydin had messaged him back, 'I know'. Johnny smiled to himself and thought, of course, you do – Johnny's profile picture was a picture of him. Still, very quickly, Aydin spotted him and smiled at Johnny from a distance. Johnny instantly recognised him again. They were soon in the taxi leaving the airport car park.

When Johnny arrived at the hotel, Aydin explained that Turkey was celebrating 100 years as a republic on that day. The streets were filled with people partying, roads were blocked off, and there was a large music event to celebrate the occasion opposite the hotel Johnny was staying in. Johnny quickly put his bag in his room and went out to what he would describe as a concert for the evening. It was a really enjoyable evening. Everyone seemed to be in high spirits, and the music kept playing, but of course, Johnny couldn't understand a word they were saying or singing, although Johnny was enjoying listening to the music. It was a nice surprise.

Ironically enough, Johnny realised that the restaurant at the front of the hotel he was staying in this time was the restaurant that he had been walking to when he stayed in the other hotel the last time; he stayed in Kusadasi for just a few days. His dentist appointment on Monday morning was at 11 am. He was up relatively early, and it was a beautiful morning compared to the weather he had left behind in England the previous day. He knew that the dentist was approximately a 10-to-15-minute walk from his hotel and decided to stroll along the beachfront, grab some water, and relax before attending his appointment. He realised that he had a 10-day break, so he also wanted to make that time a holiday. Monday morning at the dentist, it turned out that one area of Johnny's gums, the previous bone graft, was now not deep enough for one implant to be inserted and completed. The dentist suggested he could have another bone graft and try again. Johnny decided against that and accepted that he would end up with a completely new set of teeth minus one implant.

Johnny's next appointment at the dentist was going to be in three days for his first final fitting, as they called it. The weather was pleasant in Kusadasi, and Johnny spent a lot of time sitting and walking along the beach opposite the hotel, eating and occasionally talking to the odd stranger here and there. He knew from his previous trips that there was an AA meeting in Kusadasi at the Saltbox restaurant on Tuesday and Friday evenings. Tuesday evening, Johnny thought it was something to look forward to. The meeting had been set up and run by a couple of Irish guys who had settled in Turkey. Johnny went to the meeting, and as is traditional or seems to be the way in meetings, if a new person is just visiting and has some sobriety, they often get asked to do the chair. It was a small meeting upstairs from the restaurant. Johnny had 13.5 years of continuous sobriety, and amazingly, he was the baby in the meeting of five people. Two of the people had nearly 40 years of sobriety, and the other two both had 20+ years of sobriety. Great meeting, Johnny thought. It was two Irishmen, one Irish lady, one Swedish man and Johnny. As is always the case when meeting new fellows, it astonished Johnny what people would share or share back. Johnny enjoyed the evening and let the secretary, Ken, know he would be at the next few meetings as he was in town for ten days. After the meeting, they all went to the restaurant, drinking coffee and chatting about life in general. Johnny had always been fascinated with Irish people – he loved their accents and attitude towards life and always seemed to enjoy their company. Later that evening, he returned to his hotel and retired for the night.

The next day, it turned out that Lisa, Kate, and Jemima had different opinions about certain events. The next thing was that Johnny was somehow involved. Johnny had received a message from Jemima's sponsor on social media to address some of the concerns and allegations being made about certain individuals. Johnny didn't know Lisa particularly well, who was now a good friend of Kate's in recovery, but he did know Jemima and Kate well enough to know an awful lot about the allegations and events. Jemima's sponsor, Susan, was trying to suggest to Johnny that it would be helpful if Johnny and Susan had a chat about the situation, as she knew Johnny was sponsoring Kate.

Johnny did know Susan was Jemima's sponsor and agreed in principle to at least discuss the situation with Susan. He explained to her he was in Turkey, but she already knew that from looking at his social media. They exchanged a few messages about Johnny in Turkey and pleasantries. Johnny said he would give her a call the next day. After that, Johnny messaged Jemima and asked for her permission to have the conversation with Susan because he felt that it would all come down to gossip without Jemima's permission. He messaged Jemima explaining the situation, and he thought she might be well aware of what was happening but wanted her permission. A couple of hours later, Johnny realised, as is often the way, that there were an awful lot of things Johnny knew about Jemima and Kate that Susan didn't know. He also realised Susan probably knew an awful lot of things about Jemima that he didn't. He then realised that the whole thing had become like a can of worms, and once it got opened up, none of these worms would be able to be put back in the can. He said as much in a message to Susan. She messaged him back a couple of hours later, agreeing with Johnny's take on the situation, and she explained that in reality, she or Johnny were not their parents or guardian angels; they were just trying to sponsor, and maybe it would be a good idea if the conversation never took place. Johnny was happy with the outcome and thought, on balance, it was in everyone's best interest. The only thing that had changed was now that Johnny and Jemima had started talking again after several months. Next thing, messages were flying back and forth for a few hours. Johnny suggested that when he got back to England, it might be helpful if Kate, Lisa, Jemima and Johnny sat down in a McDonald's with a cup of coffee to resolve the outstanding issues.

Later on, once Johnny had connected to the Wi-Fi, Kate told Johnny they had all spoken. He realised he had a missed call from Jemima. Later that evening, he rang Jemima back, and they had a wonderful conversation for about two and a half hours and discussed all the problems and issues that had gone on the day they were meant to go to Mickey Flannigan's show together. Johnny had realised that the situation's interpretation and communication had been very different on both sides. It had just been one big misunderstanding. In reality, Johnny regretted not phoning her on that occasion and talking to her rather than sending her an unhelpful message, which had effectively put a lot of space, with no communication and emptiness between them.

At least all the other issues, which Johnny wasn't interested in, had been resolved. How strange, Johnny thought. As a result of trying to help Kate, Johnny helped himself in the situation with Jemima and learnt a lot about himself and Jemima, too. They agreed to catch up when he got back from Turkey. Johnny was now in a great mood in Turkey. He was certainly glad that Bubba wasn't with him, and he had not taken up Kate's offer to join him on the trip. The next day, he had his second final fitting at the dentist – it was an afternoon appointment. Johnny attended, which lasted a few hours, and all seemed to go well.

In Kusadasi, the beach was the main attraction. There were other things to do. Johnny did go to a spa for a full body massage and went to a couple of Irish pubs to eat in for a laugh and a change of scenery. He relaxed in a good space and tried to enjoy the rest of his break. He was now looking forward to his next meeting on Friday. His second final fitting was due to take place on Monday, and if there were no complications, that would be the end of the treatment.

Friday morning came, and he decided to go for a walk along the beach, get some water, and enjoy the sunshine and atmosphere. He nipped into the city just along from the beach-front and treated himself to a haircut and massage before popping into a meeting that evening. There were some new faces at the meeting that evening, and he enjoyed it. The Irish lads were in good form, and Johnny loved listening to their stories. It wasn't exactly what they said, it was the way they said it, with their sense of humour.

The first time Johnny attended the meeting, he had grabbed a cab but had now been walking to and from the meeting as he realised it was up a few back streets and only about one mile from his hotel. He was walking back to the hotel after his meeting when he saw a group of guys chasing another guy out of a store and beating him! How strange, he thought. Was he a shoplifter, or was it something more sinister? They certainly did give him a beating in the street. He seemed to take it on the chin, get up and run off, and Johnny thought, well, in England, they would have been arrested for what they did to the guy. It appeared to Johnny that he wasn't complaining too much. Maybe it was more sinister, or perhaps it was how they dealt with shoplifters at that store; how could you tell?

That weekend, Johnny spent time on the beachfront, relaxing and chatting with locals, passing the time away. He was watching a local fisherman casting out to see, and as he cast out, he seemed particularly happy that he had caught something instantly. Johnny continued to watch this fisherman, thinking to himself, 'Wow, that was amazing to watch a man cast out and catch a fish so quickly.' Johnny was certainly very impressed. When the guy reeled his line in, Johnny realised he hadn't caught anything at all – maybe he was just practising, he thought, after laughing at his previous thought.

Monday afternoon came around quickly. Johnny attended the dentist, and the second final fitting went well. Johnny now had his new set of teeth and was over the moon.

Hopefully, he would return on a plane from Izmir to Stansted in a couple of days to return to his life in England as an author. He arranged for Aydin, his local taxi driver, to pick him up at the hotel on Wednesday at 6 am so he would arrive at the airport in good time for the flight.

On the flight home, Johnny sat next to a young lady, a student from London, Zoe. Her card was declined when she tried to pay for a coffee, and Johnny paid for her rather than her having to hand it back as she appeared to be carrying no cash. She had not asked him or expected him to, he just thought it seemed like the right thing to do. She was very grateful. It was probably really helpful for the flight home as it now meant they had struck up a conversation. Johnny told Zoe that he had just fitted a new set of teeth and was very pleased with the results. Zoe was a young woman, Johnny guessed about 29 years of age. She told Johnny that she lived with her fella in London and was studying at university and that her boyfriend was a software developer. They then started to talk about the cost-of-living crisis, as it was named in England, and the recent period of particularly high inflation, which had affected so many British people since the pandemic. Johnny explained to Zoe that he went to the dentist in Turkey because of the immense savings compared to having the same treatment from an English dentist. She said she understood as she had been to Turkey and had got new teeth, breast implants, and a Brazilian bum lift. It had cost her a fortune. Johnny was speechless and thought to himself, why on earth would a woman in her twenties want that work done? Her teeth were not a result of an accident; it was all about the look. They continued their conversation for most of the flight home, which Johhny enjoyed. Johnny thought that it was always interesting to just strike up a conversation with a stranger in a situation like that. It certainly made the flight home a more pleasant experience, as Johnny never considered reading or watching a film on flights. He always preferred a real conversation with a real person.

Johnny whizzed straight through passport control and customs before exiting into the car park where his car was parked. Then straight back home to Canterbury with the tunes on. It had been a successful trip overall. He always loved being back in England whenever he travelled. He always reflected that there is certainly something very special about being on English soil. Maybe it was just familiarity and safety as he perceived it. He had his bathroom and bed in his own home to look forward to that evening.

CHAPTER 7
FILM DEAL

WHILE JOHNNY HAD BEEN in Turkey for his trip to the dentist, he had picked up some colour and now had a tan and a new set of teeth. Johnny felt that was nice as he would no doubt look better on the front cover of magazines and in newspapers when he signed his first film deal shortly, or was that just wishful thinking on his part? Time will tell!

Johnny agreed to meet up with Jemima and sort out their misunderstandings and differences. It was a really interesting evening. There had been a lot of misunderstandings, and Johnny realised her perspective of certain situations and her reality, which was different. It was lovely to meet Pistachio again, and Johnny felt that it had been a healthy conversation and experience and enlightening in many ways.

They both agreed that they were very good friends. They got on well and enjoyed each other's company. Jemima explained that she had a few issues that she wanted to work on herself, and they agreed to catch up soon. Johnny would take that, especially with the circumstances.

Kate wasn't and didn't have the desire to continue doing the work that Johnny had suggested. He decided that it would be far better for Kate to do her own thing and have her own experience. About a week or two later, she got back in touch with Johnny and explained to him that the new guy on the scene called, Matt, had fucked her over. Johnny said he felt sorry for her and didn't lecture her. He didn't ask what that meant because that term could be taken in so many ways; in reality, it wasn't any of Johnny's business, and he didn't want to make it his business.

He didn't enquire on what that meant and hoped that Kate would learn from the experience. She shared with Johnny that her father had told her she would be far better off on her own for a while. Johnny agreed but didn't say anything as he thought, 'Kate is going to do what Kate wants to do in any case.' Johnny did take a certain amount of satisfaction from the fact that he had least played a part in helping her keep a roof over her head as the eviction process had been suspended.

She was working with the council and benefits office to resolve the issue of arrears and at least pay her rent on time going forward. Of course, it was far better for her and her little dog that she had a roof over her head. He hoped she would find a new sponsor and do the work she needed to soon. Johnny felt content with himself at the moment, certainly on the up and very comfortable about his part in at least trying to help her. He decided on balance; he was going to prioritise the new novel, the new audiobook, and a film deal for the first novel.

At this time in his life, he felt the option for a film deal was to wait a few months more to see if he managed to get a reply from any of the film production companies, directors, and producers he had approached already. He would then see if Nalani still had any contacts and friendships in the film business that he could pursue. Then he realised that the only way to guarantee the film was made would be to do it himself if all else failed. That was a big ask! How would that work?

He then researched the real cost of making a film for the big screen. Of course, there isn't a set answer to that question, but without big-name stars and dramatic action stunts really necessary for the production, the best estimate he could come up with that was realistic would be in the region of between £2m and £4m. He also then realised that a few people that the characters were based on in the book had read the novel and joked with him that they would love to be in the film.

Johnny thought, if necessary, this could be a bonus, as if you employ well-known actors and actresses, you would have to give them the script, allow them to learn the part and the character of the person they were going to play in the film. The people that Johnny knew could just turn up and be themselves. He knew many people in recovery and some not, who had expressed interest in being in the film when it was made, and of course, it would mean Bubba could play a role in that process as well.

Johnny didn't have the technical know-how to make a film. So, his dream would be as follows… if no offers came forward in the future, then he would have serious conversations with film production companies about the costs of the production once he had ascertained a very close and realistic budget, the novel could be used to make the film, or maybe it would be more professional to do an adaption of the book to a screenplay, which could be used to make the film. Suddenly, actors and actresses like Nunes and Winston were very appealing because they were aspiring, very keen and would be cost-effective. Johnny would certainly be able to approach many people and sell them the idea that the film would be the making of them and, of course, in reality, it is true for so many film stars as everyone has to start somewhere.

Once Johnny had worked out the real cost in terms of money, the big issue was going to be a backer for the film. Johnny figured he needed someone prepared to invest, say in the region of £3m. On that basis, Johnny needed to find someone incredibly wealthy, someone with a wealth of £3m; the likelihood of them investing that in a film would be highly unlikely. In contrast, if someone had, say, a personal fortune of £50m, Johnny felt that if he could get a sit down with that person face-to-face, he could sell them the idea that if they funded the production, the only other costs involved would be his fees for writing the novel and his fee for organising the production of the film. Johnny liked the idea that if he could find an up-and-coming director and producer, he could become an executive producer and at least be able to insert some of his originality and authenticity into the film. If someone else made the film, they would employ a director and producer and rely on their interpretation of the novel. Johnny felt that although he didn't have the necessary talents to direct and produce a film, his creative ideas and recollections of people and events may prove helpful.

Then Emma piped up about her current squeeze; he was a filmmaker. He had made several films which were used for educational purposes. Although that was a world apart from making a film for the big screen, he certainly had the creativity, understanding, and expertise to put a film together. That was food for thought. Maybe in the future, Johnny may like to get in touch with him and at least talk with him about films he had made, and if he could offer any assistance, or maybe like to get involved. Emma then explained to Johnny about Pat, whom she had been seeing off and on for about a year now. Emma was relatively early in recovery, and the romance had first blossomed when they met at work. Emma had not been in recovery then, and the romance had hit the rocks before being rekindled. Now Emma was in recovery. Listening to Emma talk about Pat and her gave Johnny much comfort and a great perspective on his private life. Emma had reached a point in her relationship where she enjoyed and liked being a modern independent woman but wanted to know if she and Pat were going to become an item or not. After discussing the whole relationship and how she felt with Johnny, she decided to ask Pat if they were exclusive. She could adjust her sail accordingly depending on how he saw them and the situation. Johnny suggested that if she made the conversation light-hearted rather than putting a gun to his head, metaphorically speaking, he was far more likely to be honest with her, which is all she wanted. If she had made it a, are we exclusive, or I am out conversation, he may have lied if he was not serious about her or just playing for time while enjoying the sexual side of the relationship. Johnny and Emma agreed that if he didn't think it was a great idea for any reason, he was just buying time without committing. Emma preferred that approach on balance. Next time they met up to do something together, she would bring this question up at the appropriate time, and if he did not confirm that was what he wanted for any reason whatsoever, afterwards, she would just tell him nicely that she was done and out, then wish him well in the future. The fact that they needed that conversation was probably the answer. Johnny knew it was between them and wished her well.

It was all going to come down to getting an offer or doing it himself. At least he felt that he was on the right path. He also now liked the idea that when the second novel was published, he may well like to do the audiobook for that himself. On balance, now he had a little more understanding about publishing a book and an audiobook, and he felt that it might be an enjoyable experience for him to do the audiobook himself. Of course, Christian Neale would always be an option as the narrator for the second novel.

Finishing the second novel, getting the audiobook sorted, and seeing if any offers materialised over the coming months would be his chosen plan to follow. Of course, now that Johnny had his other options on the table, he wasn't too bothered about a firm offer from a film production company. He thought, on balance, it may be far more fun to put the thing together himself.

Finding an investor, or maybe investors, would be tricky. It may be a big ask to ask people to fund a film on the back of a novel, but Johnny did feel that the eye-watering returns that would be possible if the film was a success in England or worldwide may prove too tempting for someone to turn down. For an investment of approximately £3m, the sales and returns could be in the tens or hundreds of millions of pounds.

After checking his bank balance, Johnny decided in the meantime, he would keep buying lottery tickets and networking if and when opportunities came up. Of course, the idea of crowdfunding a film with this budget was an option, but it would be far easier to deal with fewer people – one or just a few investors. Johnny decided to leave the idea of crowdfunding on the back burner for the moment

One morning, Johnny left his house as he had to pop to Boots to collect a prescription at Oaten Hill chemist. As he arrived and tried to find somewhere to park, he noticed that his regular parking spot on Cossington Road had been taken. There were three parking spaces at the bottom of the road on the right-hand side, and normally one would be available. It seemed to him, on balance, that a lot of people who went to the chemist used those spaces just to stop in for five or ten minutes. When Johnny arrived, there was a British Telecom van at the front of the three spaces, an old Peugeot behind the BT van, and a Jaguar in the third spot. The van driver appeared to be going as he was manoeuvring in and out and maybe getting enough of an angle to get out of the parking space he was in. Suddenly, he got out and was gone, which left the first parking space available. Johnny realised he could get in the space quite easily. He took a couple of turns as he pulled up, reversing his Aston Martin into the front space. He didn't want to block the woman in the Peugeot in her space, although he knew he would only be 5-10 minutes.

After parking up, he opened the door, and there was this

immaculately dressed and very well-groomed lady peering down at him. She said, 'Hi, my name is Melanie. I just wanted to say I love your Aston Martin.' Johnny took one look at her and nearly gave her the keys but on balance decided against the idea. He got out of the car, and they started chatting. She was very friendly, and Johnny was confused about whether she was just politely passing the time of day or maybe had an ulterior motive. It was a really interesting conversation. Johnny explained to Melanie that he had always loved Aston Martin cars ever since watching James Bond as a child. She very quickly brought up that she worked for an estate agency in Canterbury and was viewing the property at the end of the road. A very pleasant conversation occurred, and then Melanie said that she 'only drove a little old Peugeot now'. Johnny said that 'seems like a nice little car gesturing towards her Peugeot'. She pulls a face looking at Johnny as if to say are we talking about the same car?! It was a very old, slightly beaten-up model, but Johnny felt she could make her judgement about her car; he would rather choose his words more carefully to try and see the positive in what was in front of him. She then said that previously, when she was married, her husband had a Range Rover, and she used to use that. Johnny smiled to himself and thought he wasn't going to tell her he had one of those at home as well – that might sound a bit flashy! Johnny also found it interesting that she was sharing that she was divorced but decided with his personal life, as it was, he had no real interest in Melanie, apart from the fact she was very attractive and knew how to make the most of her appearance.

They were laughing and joking about life walking down the street together, and as they got down the end of the road, Johnny wished her well with the viewing, nipped across the road and into the chemist. As Johnny was crossing the road towards the chemist, he started smiling to himself, he remembered a comment Jemima had made to him about his Aston Martin. It was probably the best comment he had heard and made him laugh. One day, she said, 'It's a lovely ride, like its owner.' Johnny would never find out if Melanie had an agenda or not. Johnny had to admit he had never owned or driven a car before, like his Aston Martin, from the perspective that people would often approach him just to talk about the car or give him looks when he was waiting in traffic. After Johnny had bought his Aston Martin, he saw what he thought was probably the best advert ever for an Aston Martin. It certainly put a smile on his face; he burst out laughing when he saw it, and he certainly could relate. It was a picture of a stunningly beautiful and sexy woman standing in a kitchen in a man's white shirt in a seductive pose. It was a tasteful photograph. It was very suggestive but not too revealing. The picture would automatically grab any man's attention; it was not too revealing but left very little to the imagination; it would certainly conjure up all sorts of images and thoughts in his mind. Then there was an Aston Martin logo, and the words read, 'Pre-owned Aston Martin – you know you will not be the first, but does it matter?'.

Johnny was at the car wash the following day, and his phone rang. It was Joe. Johnny knew an awful lot of Joe's from the rooms and was confused as to which one it was calling him. Once Johnny figured out which Joe it was, they started talking about recovery and sponsorship. Joe was honest with Johnny that he had relapsed again and had been drinking for a few days. He was trying to suggest to Johnny that the relationship with his previous sponsor somehow had not helped the situation. Johnny disagreed and told him, 'You do not need to drink just because you can't get hold of your sponsor – you're not meant to rely on your sponsor. You're meant to grow up, be accountable and take responsibility for your actions. Whenever my mood is low or high, I always find that a meeting is a great leveller. It puts me back in reality and takes me out of my head.' Joe was a nice young guy whom Johnny had met a few years earlier. They had always got on well, although they had never really been close. Joe asked Johnny if he would sponsor him, and of course, Johnny was grateful that he had been asked. Hopefully, Joe may well be up for the work. Johnny said to Joe, 'Rather than saying yes, I think it would be in both of our best interests if we sat down, had a coffee, and discussed what the relationship would be based on and the work involved.' Johnny realised that many people would say they would do anything and were up for everything without understanding what that meant. In Johnny's experience and view, it was far easier to lay out all that was required and would be required and leave the person to go away and think about it for a couple of days, to go away and think about it before they decided to commit or not. All this rushing about business in meetings when people would ask Johnny to sponsor them would agree, and they wouldn't even speak after that; it was now going to be just a memory for Johnny. In Johnny's view, for him to want to sponsor someone in the future, he wanted to see a certain level of commitment to meetings and the principles of recovery before they would do any step work together. There had been way too many occasions in the past where people would say one thing and do another. Johnny did know for certain that all people's words are cheap unless they are backed up with actions. That is true in any area of his life, but particularly in recovery. Johnny and Joe agreed to meet for coffee before a meeting the following Saturday. They could meet at McDonald's Canterbury at 6 pm and discuss the idea of sponsorship. When Saturday came around, there was no message from Joe. Johnny called Joe to confirm they were still on, and he got no reply. That was the end of that.

A week later, Johnny bumped into Joe in another meeting, and Joe said to Johnny, 'Maybe rather than you sponsoring me, I could ring and check in now and again.' Johnny said to him, 'Maybe you use the rooms just to have a break from the drink occasionally rather than being serious about your recovery.' Joe seemed to take offence at that, then Johnny said that in his experience, recovery was a lifetime commitment, albeit one day at a time. Johnny didn't mind the idea of Joe phoning him occasionally, as getting a phone call from someone in the rooms was always nice. Johnny realised that there are many people in recovery, and from all walks of life, who want the results without doing the work.

Johnny and Bubba's relationship had cooled a lot in recent times. They used to keep in touch on social media and with messages occasionally. Johnny would often joke with her about being the leading lady in the second novel. He told her, 'Not to worry, and everything was going to be alright.' She would then say, 'We don't seem that close anymore.'

Johnny had been fortunate enough to get two tickets to see Arsenal play in the Champions League the following Tuesday. Johnny always loved watching Arsenal play. Of course, it was always a treat for him to go and watch a live match. He had spent all his life following them and had many warm and wonderful memories of attending football matches with members of his family, friends and people he had met in the rooms. He even took Sophia to a couple of cup finals when they had first met. He asked Bubba if she was free for the evening, and she was. They agreed they would drive rather than catch the train, and she decided she would book a day off work. They would leave Canterbury in the early afternoon to arrive in plenty of time to watch the match.

Johnny still knew the places he could park around that area, and he was within walking distance of the stadium. Bubba confessed she had never been to a football match before. When they got to the stadium, they spent about an hour in the Arsenal football club shop, and Johnny got Bubba an Arsenal top with her name printed on the back, with the number 11.

She chose the number 11 because she thought her legs were her most attractive feature. It was a cold winter night, and the

Bovril they got at the cafeteria would no doubt keep them warm for the game. Mikel Arteta had been the manager at Arsenal for some time now. Arsenal had certainly experienced a resurgence in form in recent times. They would be on top of the league one week and third or fourth the next week. They seemed to have a few really good performances and then lose their way occasionally. Consistency was not there week in and week out like it would need to be if they were to be serious challengers in either the Premier League or the Champions League. Deep down, Johnny felt that although, in theory, they could challenge for honours in both competitions, it was a bit of a stretch of the imagination to think that they would win the Premier League or the Champions League this season. Stan Kroenke was investing in the club again now, and the funds available for purchases in recent times had been far more than they had been in the previous years. Now that a lot of debt had been paid down for the purchase of the new stadium, he was prepared to invest in the future of the club. Of course, he never really appeared at the games, but it seemed to Johnny he was not a great football fan but a very astute businessman. He had his son Josh Kroenke in London overseeing the club. There was at this time a great time of football people running the club as it should be. It was a wonderful evening, and Arsenal played exceptionally well and won the match. The atmosphere in the crowd had been breathtaking that evening. At one stage, a large part of the crowd had been standing up, dancing and singing in sheer delight at the performance of the team that evening.

As they exited the stadium, almost by chance, Johnny and Bubba bumped into David Dein, the former co-owner and Vice-Chairman of Arsenal Football Club. It felt a surreal moment for Johnny as he remembered bumping into David Dein and having photos taken with him many years before when Johnny had gone to a match with Lenny. Johnny had first met Lenny in HMP Standford Hill when he started going back to prisons to do AA meetings in the prison service. Lenny was a Gooner through and through – he had come from North London. He was mixed-race, and he had shared with Johnny how when he went to school, black lads had it in for him as well as the white lads. He had been in and out of prison for most of his life for various crimes, a lot of which centred around drink and drugs. He decided he had enough of that way of living and was trying to get clean and sober, enjoy sober living and change his life entirely.

Johnny and Lenny had exchanged numbers so that when Lenny left prison, they would keep in touch occasionally. Lenny had on occasion come to Canterbury to meet Johnny, do a meeting together, and catch up. Lenny was living on the outskirts of London and had managed to adjust back into society, remain clean and sober, and was trying to become a better person, as he saw it. At the time, Johnny had tickets for a match, so they met up at the stadium, and as they were walking along, Lenny suddenly shouted, 'Look, it's David Dein.' On that occasion, David Dein was with a small group of people, and they had enjoyed a very jovial conversation about the football club and what it meant to be an Arsenal fan. On that night, they had taken photos together as a memory of the meeting. Lenny had also shared with Johnny that he knew all about David Dein. David Dein had made an awful lot of money in the sugar business many years earlier, was a lifelong Arsenal fan, and had started investing in the club decades before. At the time he started investing in the club, his mother said to him, 'Don't you go up that football club wasting all your money there.' Many years later, he would sell his shares in the football club for £75m to Red and White Holdings, the investment vehicle of Russian Oligarch Alisher Usmanov.

At that time, the vast majority of Arsenal Football Club was owned by Red and White Holdings and Stan Kroenke. Lenny had asked David Dein point blank when he would be returning to the club in a formal capacity. It was clear that he was very much in the Usmanov camp. David Dein joked that he was in 'the reserves at the moment, hoping to get back into the first team shortly.' That was a reference that he hoped or knew Usmanov wanted to buy the whole club from Stan Koenke in the future. It would later transpire that Alisher Usmanov's investment company Red and White Holdings would, on two occasions, make Stan Kroenke substantial and serious offers for his shares in Arsenal Football Club. Stan Kroenke made it clear his shares were not for sale, and shortly after that time, he bought Alisher Usmanov's shares from him, which meant he now owned the whole club outright. Johnny joked with David Dein that he had met him many years ago and it was lovely to bump into him again, not that he probably remembered him, but they both agreed it was nice to see the team playing well again and wished each other a pleasant evening.

On the journey home, Bubba suggested to Johnny it may be nice if they were able to get away somewhere together for a break in the sun, just the two of them. It was a tempting offer, and Johnny couldn't deny that. He said he would let her know what his plans were, and he would get back to her over the next few days about making some arrangements. They drove back to Canterbury, and Bubba let Johnny know she wanted to stay at his place for the evening. Johnny was naturally delighted at that prospect. Just before arriving back at Johnny's, they managed to grab a takeaway on the way home since they had not eaten at all. Johnny managed to grab a couple of bottles of Chateauneuf-du-pap which was Bubba's favourite red wine. They sat down and enjoyed the pizza, and Bubba had a few glasses of red wine. They started chatting about Johnny's plans and their future together. Shortly after, Johnny was tired and said he wanted to call it a night and go to bed. She said, 'I will come and join you soon' as she said she wanted to finish watching a film on Netflix, and she would join him a bit later and wake him up. Johnny agreed and headed off to bed. When his head hit the pillow, he was out like a light!

In reality, Bubba didn't want to watch a film on Netflix. She spent the time going through all his emails, messages, and WhatsApp conversations with various people, although Johnny was unaware of this behaviour. She had become neurotic and obsessed about fame, and she thought everything was about her; she needed constant reassurance that she would be the absolute centre of attention, regardless of how events would play out in the future. Johnny was unaware, but now she had gone through lots of private messages on his phone and misinterpreted half of them. Sophia and Johnny would often share messages, chat about life, and meet up for dinner from time to time. Johnny realised he never had a life story with one woman as some couples would have. He had more of a collection of love stories. Johhny always admired couples with a life story together, but it had not been how his life had panned out. Although being good friends with Sophia and they could enjoy each other's company occasionally would be the closest he had to a life story. She knew him better than anyone alive in reality. They had now been friends longer than they had lived together. Often, when she travelled, Johnny would feed and look after her cats. Johnny would often sit on her sofa when she was away while feeding her two cats talking to them telling them all his secrets and laughing with them. They were both very affectionate, and Johnny liked seeing them happy. The messages from Nunes were nothing out of the ordinary, it was more of a discussion about acting and work going forward. Bubba saw her as a major threat because she was a young, beautiful model with acting skills and was maybe relying on Johnny for her big break in the film business. There was a nice single mother Johnny met in the rooms recently called Michelle. They had exchanged a few messages. They were simply agreeing to meet for coffee and discuss recovery. Johnny quite liked her; she had suggested it would be nice to meet up for a coffee and a chat about recovery. Then, the messages from Jemima were self-explanatory and had been the nail in the coffin. She had read many messages that went back over a long period, which were private, intermate and very revealing. Messages from Nalani and Emma had just added to Bubba's suspicions and theories. Bubba wasn't at all happy Emma was helping Johnny write the new novel. Johnny had made many other contacts in the film business with what amounted to very harmless business messages and conversations. Bubba had been acting like a private investigator and now had almost a complete dossier on him. She was coming up with an awful lot of speculative theories. Her final assessment is that Johnny was just a total womaniser and was using his novel, the sequel, and his ambitious film plans to promise young, beautiful women fame and fortune in the film business to seduce them in the bedroom.

Johnny had been to a few luncheons and events lately and asked to sign copies of his novel by men and women who would often take a snap or a selfie. Johnny had to admit he liked the mini book signings and the pictures, which he would share on social media for publicity. Bubba had been looking at some of the harmless pictures and drawing the wrong conclusions about the pictures as well. Perhaps she fancied herself as Miss Marple. She had certainly gone out of her way to delve into Johnny's affairs.

After a few hours, she joined Johnny in bed and simply slept beside him. In the morning, she said she tried to wake him because she felt 'amorous' but couldn't wake him. The following morning, they had breakfast together. Johnny agreed that he would look into the idea of a holiday, and she went to work. On the way home, Bubba thought to herself Johnny had just been using her and misleading her. He was nothing more than a man on a mission to become rich and famous. Then she realised how she would make him famous, but at the same time become more famous herself. 'Hell, hath no fury like a woman scorned', so the saying goes.

Johnny was unaware of what Bubba was planning and scheming behind his back. If he had known what was going on, he certainly would never have worried about publicity because of how events were about to unfold.

CHAPTER 8
A WELL-DESERVED BREAK

JOHNNY HAD MANAGED to get a ticket to meet the footballing legend Paul Gascoigne at an event at the Mercure Maidstone Great Danes Hotel in Hollingbourne. Johnny knew the hotel well, as he had learnt to swim there as a child. It was on a Sunday afternoon/ evening. When Johnny arrived by chance, he bumped into a guy called Ryan, whom he had sponsored in the room's a few years ago. Ryan seemed to take to recovery like a duck takes to water. He was still clean and sober several years later and seemed to be getting on well in life. They met in the bar, grabbed a couple of soft drinks, found a table and started catching up. Ryan was a single lad and was on a few dating apps looking for romance. He started showing Johnny his Tinder profile and some of the girls he was talking to on there. Johnny recognised a couple of women he knew from the rooms, which made him smile; then he saw Bubba's profile. Wow, that was an eye-opener. It was the first dating app he had looked at for years, and Bubba just happened to be on there. more importantly, he had been fortunate enough to see her profile courtesy of Ryan that afternoon. Johnny never said anything to Ryan – no need to, but he just noted the fact.

Shortly after catching up and putting the world right, so to speak, with Ryan, the photos with Paul Gascoigne started for about an hour and a half, followed by an auction of signed memorabilia. Then, the host of the afternoon showed some videos of Paul Gascoigne and talked a little about him before introducing him to the audience. As you would expect, he got a wonderful round of applause and a warm welcome. Johnny thought because he was an England international who was, to say the least, a little crazy, fans from all teams loved him. He spoke honestly and openly in an interview about his family, football, his career and life; he spoke about his alcoholism and shenanigans. He shared that he was currently about eight months away from his last alcoholic drink. Some of the stories were hilarious. He said he was and came across as a non-material person. He had earned about £30 million in his career, and as a result of the life he led and the journey he went on, he thought he had about £80,000 left. It was the main reason he was doing the events. Johnny got tempted to bid on a few bits of memorabilia. Still, there were so many either England or Paul Gascoigne fans there that the prices of all pictures and other stuff started quite reasonably but within minutes had reached thousands of pounds and really Johnny didn't want them or something that badly. He settled for his photo with Paul Gascoigne mounted in a picture frame with several other pictures. It was a lot of fun and was another memorable experience for Johnny. On the way out, Johnny managed to wish Ryan well before driving home.

Christmas only seemed just around the corner now. Johnny had so many wonderful memories of Christmas in his heart. His first big memory of Christmas was one Christmas Eve when he was about seven years old. He remembered being very excited about Father Christmas coming to visit and seeing what presents he may leave him. He had left out a carrot for the reindeer and a mince pie for Father Christmas as welcoming gifts. He was asleep when he was disturbed; he woke up and saw his dad in his room. He was shocked that his dad was in his room. He remembered saying that you better leave dad, as Father Christmas will be here soon. His dad, George, agreed and said he was just checking in on him. Johnny did prove to be right on that occasion when he got up in the morning, Father Christmas had left his Christmas presents very close to where his dad had been standing a few hours earlier. He also remembered talking to his brother Alex on the phone one Christmas day while he was in prison, and Alex asked him, 'What the lunch was like?'. Johnny replied, 'It is probably made from the food that a cheap Supermarket can't sell.' that was the best description of the Christmas fayre that day he could conjure up at that moment. In Johnny's childhood, he had also been a big fan of snow at Christmas. That always seemed to add magic to the occasion, in his opinion.

Johnny had put his decorations and tree up relatively early this year and wanted to make the most of this year's Christmas period. He felt like he wanted to take 'a well-deserved break'. After pondering the situation for a while, he thought it would be nice to have time to reflect, slow down, spend some quality time on his own, peruse the situation and recharge his batteries. A break or holiday without Bubba became his first choice, all things considered. He would let her know he was just going on his own. She accused him of going with someone else. He said, 'I am not going with anyone else at all; I am simply going on my own'. She became abusive and put the phone down. He wasn't going to phone her back or chase her. He decided to chase his dream, not any women; he was always happier chasing his dreams because he enjoyed that always, whereas, with the young ladies, it seemed very up and down, to say the least. He had an idea the private life would just work out when it was ready to one day; whether that was sooner or later, he never knew how could he. All his life, he had always attracted complicated women, and he was complicated as well, so just having a break was his best decision: attract rather than chase and let nature take its course.

Then, a friend of Johnny's from India, Ravinder Boparai, asked Johnny if he would like to join Ravinder and go to India for his brother's wedding for 20 days. It was quite an unexpected offer, totally out of the blue. The timing of the offer was perfect for Johnny to have a well-deserved break. Johhny considered the offer very seriously for several days. He had never been to India, and it could be an amazing experience, but it may just be like hard work. He knew Ravinder but not that well. They had started speaking during COVID-19 about business ideas on social media. He seemed a likeable chap who had lots of business ideas and dreams. He was a young Indian man about 30 years of age. He was always polite. He seemed to have a desire to live in England. Johnny had encouraged Ravinder to look around India at certain products or ideas whereby they could import products from India to England and clean up. Ravinder came up with counterfeit goods or copies of expensive labels in the fashion industry. Johnny was not interested in importing counterfeit goods that Johnny didn't even consider to be that cheap in reality.

Then Ravinder explained about legal immigration and helping people enter with visas from India. Johnny knew nothing about that process at all. It all sounded great: find companies to offer and sponsor Indian citizens to come and work in England. Find accommodation for them in England before they arrive, help them with their visa application, then charge a fee for the assistance and help in the help entering legally, having a home and a job waiting for them when they arrive. It sounded to Johnny very similar to sending people across the channel in boats, only on a larger scale and in a legal manner. Ravinder explained to Johnny some so many people wanted to come to England and work. Many of them were non-skilled men and women who could and would be good at agriculture and caring work. They could improve their English while they live in England and make a new life for themselves. Johnny knew he could find unlimited decent accommodation in and around Canterbury. That would not be a problem at all. There are also a lot of farms on the outskirts of Canterbury that employ hundreds of migrants, mainly picking fruit or working in pack houses. There are also a lot of care firms and care homes all over the Kent area that seemed to be always crying out for staff it seemed. Neither job would pay a great salary or wage, but it would be a starting point for them.

The next thing was that Ravinder turned up in England. He had just got his visa sorted out and recently arrived in England. He was living with a relation of his in Wolverhampton. Johnny and Ravinder agreed to meet. Ravinder travelled to Canterbury on the train to stay with Johnny and put things together about accommodation and employment for future clients and to meet and enter into a business relationship. Johnny was very excited about meeting Ravinder and getting things sorted out. He arrived at Canterbury East on a Thursday evening, and Johnny picked him up after a meeting and took him out for an Indian at the Kashmir in Palace Street. He seemed a decent guy, and his English was not great, but as Johnny spoke slower, they seemed to communicate reasonably well. The owner of the restaurant knew all about Ravinder from his head scarf and where he came from. They were very quickly talking about all the different regions in India. Ravinder only stayed at Johnny's for a few days. They spent a little time sightseeing, and then they visited some farms in the Chartham area. Johnny went to the second farm with Ravinder, and the manager was very helpful indeed. He explained that they would love to be able to offer Indian citizens jobs working at the pack houses. He then explained that there was a great need for unskilled labour in the agriculture industry. He then explained to Johnny they could only employ certain types of foreign nationals, and he listed the countries to which the English Government would issue visas. India was not on the list. The government would not issue visas to Indian citizens who were unskilled. They would consider citizens with certain skills and qualifications. The whole scheme had been a nonstarter, really, but no harm done. It had not taken too long to find out the truth, and there had been no real loss.

Johnny and Ravinder had stayed in touch and chatted occasionally, mainly about some business ideas. While Ravinder had been in Canterbury, he would FaceTime his family in India and put Johnny on the phone to speak to them. They seemed like a nice Indian family to Johnny, always smiling and happy, but they spoke hardly any English at all. On balance, Johhny concluded it was a nice thought and offer. Still, the idea of travelling to India to stay with an Indian family who lived in a small village and spoke hardly any English might just be a bit too much and may not be a break at all! He also has some prior commitments for the travel period. Johnny sent him a lovely reply thanking him for his offer, declining the invitation, and sending all his best wishes to his brother for his big occasion.

Johnny decided he wanted to go to the Maldives for a break on his own. After returning from Kusadasi earlier in the year, Johnny realised his passport would expire in 2024. He knew that to visit some countries, you need a current passport that has at least six months left before expiring. He and Jemima discussed the possibility of travelling to Valencia together in 2024, and of course, in any event, having a new 10-year passport only had advantages and no disadvantages as he saw it. He knew he would get decent weather; apparently, it was meant to be paradise on Earth. That was a big statement. Johnny wondered whether it would live up to that billing or not, but if he went, he would find out for himself. Johhny started looking at deals and options for after Christmas online.

Shortly after that, a new couple moved in next door to Johnny. The place had been up for rent for a few weeks, and then suddenly, they appeared one day. Johnny thought they seemed to be a really happy young couple, obviously young and in love. They were very friendly and couldn't wait to introduce themselves. They were Peachy and Stavros and sounded like a couple of strippers to Johnny. Nothing could be further from the truth. Peachy was a midwife who was pregnant with their first child and was very quick to point out that with a big grin on her face. She was now on maternity leave. Stavros was a landscape gardener, and they met as a result of Peachy living in her place and needing help in the garden. Stavros was her gardener; the rest is history, as they say. It was unclear whether they had tied the knot or were just living in sin, so to speak. Stavros was a little reserved and friendly enough, but Peachy was over-friendly, keen to know who their neighbour was and all about him. When Johnny told her he was an author and had just published his first book, she seemed thrilled for him. 'Sounds like a great adventure', she said with a beautiful smile all across her face. What is the name of your book? What is it about? The next thing they do is sit in Johnny's lounge drinking coffee, and Johnny tells them the title and all about the book. She says, 'I would dearly love to get a copy; where can I buy it?'. Johnny pulls out a copy and says, 'I would like to give you a copy, sign it for you and in return, maybe you would be kind enough to review it when you finish reading it. She shouts, 'How exciting, I have never met an author before, thank you'. Johnny then offers Stavros a copy as well. He replies, 'I don't read very much, but thank you'. Johnny then says you can listen to it on Audible if you want to. Stavros says, 'Great, I prefer that idea; I can listen when I am working'. They all had a coffee together before Peachy and Stavros went on their way. Well, at least they had some life in them, Johnny thought. The previous couple who lived there were very quiet and hardly ever said a word all the time they lived there. On occasions, Smiles were exchanged – that was it.

Johnny researched the best deals and locations, and after a while, he managed to get a great deal at the Four Seasons Resort Maldives at Kuda Huraa. The reviews were amazing, the images certainly made the resort and location look and seem like paradise. He would take a punt on that one and book for seven nights full board with flights from Heathrow included. It was still expensive with the deal he got, but the book sales were still very strong, and he knew shrouds don't have pockets.

One day, Johnny walks into Canterbury and sees Agatha walking into Waitrose. He had not seen Agatha since his mum's funeral. Agatha was a very educated, well-to-do lady who had married a very successful businessman. They had been married about sixty years when he became ill, and she had cared for him until he passed away. She always had a smile on her face when Johnny met her previously. She was also a keen gardener, and Johnny knew his mum and Agatha had met many years ago on a computer course in Canterbury, they had got on well, both had a passion for gardening and rather than going out for coffee together they used to go round each other's homes for a day and do their gardens together, enjoy coffee in the garden and relax. They did it for years. Johnny joked with her and asked her how she was. She seemed thrilled they had bumped into each other and insisted they should grab coffee and cake together in Waitrose. Johnny liked the idea, told Agatha to grab a table and got the coffee and cakes. She had always been a good conversationalist and company. She loved to talk about everything. She had several children and was always keen to share how well they did with their families, homes and jobs. Agatha always seemed a realist to Johnny, a no-nonsense, straight-talking lady. After a while, they had finished their coffee and cake; she told Johnny that she and her late husband had been going to a ukulele club in Deal for years before he passed away. As she put it, she continued to go and had a new admirer there. He had asked her out a couple of times. She was now 89 years old, and she said her new admirer, who was called Dennis, was in her nineties. So, Johnny says, 'That sounds nice. Do you like him?' Agatha replies, 'Well, I told him I don't do tricks, and I am not going to be his nurse'. Johnny is in tears laughing at how eloquently Agatha had put her cards on the table with Dennis. She then replies, 'he has stopped asking me now'. That seemed like an appropriate moment to give her a big hug and wish her well. Her passing comment to Johnny was, 'You know where I live if any afternoon you want a coffee and a chat'. What a lovely lady and offer Johnny smiled and left the coffee shop.

The film project didn't need much work doing on it just at the moment as it had not been long enough to assess whether an offer may come forward or not realistically. Still, Johnny was always looking at film events, and there seemed to be a new idea being promoted. Whether it was new or not, he was not certain, but as well as crowdfunding for films, Johnny was now aware that there were investment platforms now available to invest in feature films. That would certainly warrant Johnny's attention and closer inspection. That may prove to be just what the doctor ordered, so to speak. It probably was exactly what Johnny was looking for if he didn't receive an offer in the post from Guy Richie, with Jason Statham being suggested as the lead man. After all, Johnny liked his book a lot and believed it could be made into a feature film for the big screen. He also believed that the right directing and production would make a great film and be commercially successful. He also believed that when he got the chance to pitch to investors if that were the direction things were going to go in, his passion, humour, and desire would come across in his presentation, as well as his desire to play a role in being part of the production. He also was not worried about any of his fees in advance. He was more than happy not to receive a penny in advance and work tirelessly on the project to see it through to completion, letting investors recoup their investment first before he saw a penny. Johnny did know and would often say to himself; 'the money has already been printed and is in the vortex to make the film'.

Peachy was always just popping around for a coffee and a chat when Stavros was at work, mainly talking about her baby and Johnny's book. She would often comment that she thought maybe Johnny had lived a very colourful and amazing life as a result of speaking to him and reading the book. Johnny thought she seemed very inquisitive and quite good company. Johnny thought she was a little lonely at home while Stavros was working.

Sophia asked Johnny what his plans were for Christmas, and he realised he didn't have any plans for Christmas day; maybe he would cook himself or find somewhere to book. She said she had booked a table at a local restaurant for Christmas day, and he was more than welcome to join her if he wanted, and they could catch up. What a lovely offer, he thought. They agreed, and he thanked her. That had now sorted Christmas day out, and he had his holiday in paradise to look forward to after Christmas. Johnny mentioned to Peachy he was going away after Christmas on holiday for nine days in total. The next thing she says is fab darling – good for you! While you are away, I will check in and look after your home for you. Johhny was speechless – no need for that, but it's a very kind offer. She replies you would be doing me a great favour if you let me just keep an eye on your place while you are away, give it a clean, pick up your mail for you to put on the side and just see everything is in order. It's better to be safe than sorry; it would give me something to do. I can manage a little light cleaning and hoovering; it would keep me occupied. Johnny says OK, but please let me pay you. She says how about when we are away in the future if you are free, you could feed our cat; that would be very helpful she smiles. Yes, it is a simple trade of one neighbour doing another neighbour a good deed and the other repaying it in the future. They smiled and shook hands; it was a deal.

Johnny is off to a meeting in Canterbury at the Baptist Church on Thursday evening. His old friend Shaun Gill had been in touch on the off-chance, Johnny might be free for a bite to eat and a quick catch-up before Christmas, either in the afternoon or in the evening. Johnny said late lunch or early dinner suited him best. Shaun was going to spend the day in Canterbury doing his Christmas shopping. They agreed to a late lunch at four o'clock. They agreed on Cote restaurant in Canterbury. Johnny liked it in there. The food and service always seemed good to him. He would regularly go in for lunch or dinner on his own or with others and, over the years, got to know some of the staff well. One young lad was a waiter in the restaurant, and Johnny would regularly end up chatting to him. Johnny thought he was in good shape, a nice youngish lad with something about him. Once, Johnny asked him if he was married or had a girlfriend. Johnny never forgot his reply; he said no, I prefer to be happy. Johnny thought he was joking, but he was serious. Johnny thought you had just not met her yet, that's all. Johnny and Shaun met each other at the entrance more by luck than judgment and greeted each other before going in. The food was good, as always. Shaun could be a little over the top sometimes, especially if he were hyper, but, on this occasion, Johnny thought he seemed really in a good space and on his best behaviour. He had two sons he was very proud of; the eldest one had married earlier in the year to his childhood sweetheart and had his own building business that, if Shaun was to be believed, was bigger than Barratt Homes. Johnny understood that, in reality, he was doing alright. He would always get carried away when he talked about his sons, but he clearly loved them, and that always showed when he shared about them. It was an enjoyable catch-up, and they got to speak about some recent events in the area. Shaun was a character for sure and could talk for England. He knew so many stories about travellers and people he had come into contact with over the years. Johnny and Shaun were from the same generation and could bounce off each other just chatting about their younger days and how much the world had changed. It had been a nice catch-up just before Christmas, that was for sure. Shaun had given Johnny a Christmas card. Johnny remembered he always did every year, and he had not even thought about exchanging Christmas cards. He felt a little embarrassed and asked Shaun to write his address and postcode on the back of the card. He would send Shaun and his family a card in the post the following day. They wished each other well, and Shaun insisted on picking up the bill. It had been a good catch-up and enjoyable meal, that was for sure.

Johnny starts walking up to the meeting, and outside the old Wilko store, which has now closed down, he sees a guy on a blanket whom he has seen a few times before. When Johnny walked past him, he never asked for anything, he had a cup in front of him. Johnny realised he was a genuine homeless man. He slept rough on the streets; people don't do that for fun Johnny knew that much. Johnny leans down to him and says I want to buy your dinner for you this evening gesturing towards Burger King and the KFC, which are next to each other. He was so grateful. Johnny nips into Burger King to get him a Max meal and lots of extras, almost a banquet for two. He goes back outside and gives it to the guy, whose face lights up instantly. Johnny wished him well, walked up the street and realised again that they were worthwhile actions in life. After doing that good deed for the day, he felt lit up inside, walking up the street and feeling like a king for a day. It was always the same. It was by being of service and giving that he found real happiness. When he got into the meeting shortly after, he saw a rather distinctive young lady he knew from his former life. She used to work as a hooker. She looked at him, but it never seemed to register with her who he was or the fact that their paths had crossed before.

That was quite a common experience over the years; Johnny would bump into hookers who had previously worked for him who were in recovery or getting into recovery. He couldn't remember her name, but he knew it was her. She had not changed; that must have been about 16 years since their paths had crossed. Johnny never mentioned the work or job title when he met some of his previous staff. There was one who would say to him,' You're a criminal' rather loudly. Johnny smiled and said, 'I used to be, but I am not today and have not been for several years.' Johnny was way too polite to share back to her, 'and you're a hooker.' She was new in the rooms and needed help, not judgment or judging. That is the problem with judging others, Johnny realised. It is easy to judge others, but it is probably better to mind your own business, go home and work on being the best version of yourself. The real flex is working on yourself, not others.

A few sleeps later, and it's Christmas day just like that! There was a meeting Johnny could go to from 1 to 2 o'clock, and he agreed to meet Sophia in the restaurant, which was a ten-minute drive from the meeting at 2 o'clock. He thought he could do the meeting and leave 10 minutes early, and that would work well. It was a cracking meeting with a lot of laughter and fun. It was a person reading the day's reflection from the Daily Reflections and sharing back on it before opening up the meeting for general sharing. They had put on a small buffet with lots of nibbles, cakes, mince pies and Christmas treats. It had been well attended and a very uplifting meeting certainly for Johnny. Johnny had noticed recently that there seemed to be many younger people in Canterbury attending meetings, both male and female. Some were University students, and a lot of them seemed to flock together. It was a great thing to witness; Johnny admired young people, recognising they had a problem, acknowledging their issues, looking at themselves and their souls and getting into recovery so young. In reality, Johnny admired anyone in recovery, but Johnny thought it always seemed a bit more special to find the rooms at such a tender age. Lunch in the restaurant at Bridge did not disappoint at all, and Sophia was in good form. Maybe she had a couple to drink before he arrived! Her partner David was spending time with his children, and his ex-wife was going to be there, so that was how it was, Johnny guessed. He never enquired any further; it was none of his business, and he knew that much. It was a nice lunch with good conversation and laughs. Halfway through the lunch, Johnny reminded Sophia about something she had agreed to do. Within a couple of minutes, she replied I have not done that, then she said she changed her mind; I think there is a misunderstanding; what was it we agreed on? Johnny replayed in his mind what she had just said and thought, wow, what can you say to that? He would have asked her what she was playing at in the old days. He simply sat there speechless and reflected on how it lasted as long as it did, then smiled and said, "Let me know when you know what you are doing, and that will be fine. They always had many memories they could talk about, some good and a few maybe not so good, but mostly they would catch up on where they were currently. She was sharing her honest opinions about how David was carrying on at the moment. He was going through quite a bit with health and family issues. Johnny said it sounds a little like it is a bit of a problem for you now. She looks at Johnny and says, 'Yes, but nothing like the bollocks I put up with from you'. At that point, Johnny smiles to himself, looks at the waiter and asks for another Diet Coke. The moment passes. It had been a thoroughly enjoyable Christmas lunch with great conversation, as it always was with her. She had recently been on a ten-day break to the Canary Islands with a friend. They both talked about the difficulties of travelling with a friend and how that works when trying to allow for different tastes, desires and expectations of two people from the same event and experience. Sophia had to shoot off to Heathrow later on as she was picking up a friend who was flying from China to stay with her. Johnny knew the woman, Susu. Sophia and Susu had been friends for about 25 years, Johnny thought. Sophia insisted on paying, which was a nice touch, Johnny thought. Probably cost her an arm and a leg because it was Christmas day. Maybe there would be something special on the TV that evening. Oliver Twist was Johnny's all-time favourite. There was something magical about that film for him, Johnny realised later in life. He enjoyed it as a child and loved it more now, a bit like Chitty Chitty Bang Bang.

He gets home and gets lucky. He finds Olver Twist on the BBC I player. That will do nicely, he smiles. It's not the original film but a five-part series with a host of great stars, including Tom Hardy, Timothy Spall, Sarah Lancashire and Edward Fox. It's not like the film with Ron Moody and Oliver Reed, but it is a perfect end to a rather enjoyable Christmas day. Watching Oliver and Timothy Spall reminded Johnny about when he did some extra film work in 2015. He did it for only two days as an experience. On one day, he was an extra in the movie Denial, which starred Timothy Spall. It turned out it was about a character who was a historian and trying to rewrite history effectively. The character was trying to argue that the holocaust never took place. Johnny remembered his small part in the film in which he was part of an audience that Timothy Spall's character addressed with a speech. Interesting flashback and memory before bedtime.

CHAPTER 9
FROM HEAVEN TO HELL

Just like that, Christmas was over! It was now the time between Christmas and the New Year. The Boxing Day sales were in full swing; holiday adverts started appearing on TV. Johnny thought that they might start advertising easter eggs in a day or two. Johnny had no plans for this period; he would do some light walking as and when he could; of course, he had to factor in his hernia daily and get to some meetings. He certainly didn't need anything in the sales he knew about. Johnny spent a couple of days reflecting on what an amazing year he had just had. There had been some very special experiences with some lovely ladies. The most important thing was that it was another calendar year that he had spent free from alcohol and all other mind-altering substances. He now had a complete set of new teeth as a result of a couple of short stays in Kusadasi; the novel was completed and published, the audiobook was now published, and he had a lot of fun around most aspects of his life. He thought on reflection that his life was now really about getting up each morning and going out to play just like Habib, a jolly bartender whom he had not even met yet, but he would articulate in a way that Johnny could relate to. He had certainly met a host of colourful characters over the last 12 months, and most of them knew something he didn't, which he could learn from when he listened to them. He had also learnt an awful lot about himself and life, which would be great lessons he could take forward and build in the future with the beginning of and starting to learn a little about the film business, the various options that are available to all exploring that route. He never envisaged that he would be writing a sequel which he would be able to publish in the future. He had bought his dream car, the Aston Martin, and put his own James Bond number plate on the car as he saw it. The new Range Rover with a private plate was lots of fun to drive about in. He knew the material things and toys would never fill his soul, but owning and driving an Aston Martin was a bucket list job in his world. He had also been fortunate enough to see many entertainers and visited the theatre on several occasions. Billy Joel, Tom Jones, and Bruce Springsteen had all been worth the time and money. He thought it would, on balance, go down as a vintage year. New Year's Eve was just around the corner now, and then Johnny was soon going to be off to heaven for a seven-night stay at the Four Seasons Resort Maldives at Kuda Huraa. It certainly looked like heaven, but Johnny knew that, in reality, the best place in the world to be is in someone's heart and prayers, and he believed that heaven, in reality, is just a state of mind.

The last few days of 2023 flew by, and within a flash, 2024 had arrived. Johnny decided he wasn't going to take too much on holiday with him and would pack light. He only needed to wear shorts, a T-shirt, trainers and some nice clothes to wear in the evening. Apart from wrapping up warm to go to the airport and come home at the end of the holiday, everything else he needed would be to live in a warm beach environment for seven days and seven nights. He felt fortunate that he had managed to get direct flights from Heathrow to Malé International Airport.

He would give the key to Peachy, who would look after his place while he was away.

On the morning of his flight, he set off early to Heathrow Airport and had already booked and paid for parking, which left him plenty of time to get there and allowed for the fact that he needed to arrive two hours before the flight. Once he had checked in, he strolled through the duty-free area and food hall, then decided to have a light breakfast before the flight. The flight took off on time, and on this occasion, Johnny decided because the flight would be over 10 hours, he wanted to be more prepared and decided to take a decent book with him for the duration of the flight, or maybe he would watch films on his phone. He was undecided. It was a British Airways flight, and Johnny always felt that British Airways was one of the better flight companies to travel with. The staff, food and service on BA flights always seemed to have something a little more to his liking and taste than some of the other low-budget airlines that he flew on in the past. He knew that when he arrived at Malé International Airport, he would get his speed boat transfer, which he had been told would last about 25 minutes, to get to the resort. Johnny was excited and excited at the prospect of getting a speed boat to the resort. He had never had this type of experience before. It sounded very much like the type of place James Bond would have had to travel to in one of his adventures. Johnny loved the idea of arriving at an international airport in the Indian Ocean, grabbing a speedboat to transfer to a luxury resort where he would stay for one week. The primary purpose, he thought, was to relax, enjoy the vacation, unwind, and reflect upon his life, where he was at the moment, and, in particular, where he was going in the future. Of course, he always knew that he depended on his higher power to open up the right doors for him at the right time, whether that be in his personal life, work life, or, in particular, recovery.

The speedboat pilot was a young, well-groomed guy who

was immaculately dressed and introduced himself as Aden, whose English was very good. He seemed very happy to be of service, helping with the luggage and welcoming Johnny to the Maldives. Johnny thought he would make a great representative for the Maldives Tourist Board if he weren't the speedboat pilot. There was one other couple and Johnny on the trip. They were a middle-aged couple from Scotland named Trudy and Kieran who said they were celebrating their 20th wedding anniversary and decided to treat themselves to a week in the Maldives. They told Johnny they had stayed at the Four Seasons Resort a few years ago and were super impressed by the experience. Johnny was in for a treat, according to Trudy and Kieran.

Kieran had grown up near Loch Ness as a child and moved down to London as a teenager, started working as a trainee solicitor and had qualified and landed a great job at BP. He worked in their legal department, dealing with in-house contracts that covered all of the legalities regarding drilling and oil production. They had two teenage children whom they had left at home, and although they both loved their kids from the bottom of their hearts, they were looking forward to getting away from them for a week. Trudy worked as a freelance photographer and would often be found at fashion events, snapping away with her camera and selling her photos to the tabloids in London.

It was a pleasant journey, and Aden offered them complimentary drinks and sandwiches for the short trip. Next thing, they were arriving at the resort. They were greeted at the Four Seasons arrival dock by two members of staff who took their luggage directly to the lobby for them, and they asked the three guests to follow them. The receptionist who greeted Johnny with a beautiful smile was named Faiza. She welcomed Johnny to the Four Seasons Resort and told him he had been expected. He was asked if his flight and transfer were to his liking. He smiled and said to Faiza, 'I think I've been very fortunate; it was a smooth flight, and I thought Aden was a great Captain and host on the speedboat', which made her smile. Johnny was asked to sign his registration form, which had already been completed for him, and she asked if she could take a copy of his passport if it weren't too much trouble. After completing the registration process, Johnny was asked to follow the porter, who would take his suitcase on a luggage rack to his Deluxe Beach Pavilion with a private pool.

It was a short stroll from the reception, and within around 5 or 6 minutes, the front door of the beach pavilion was open. Johnny's suitcase was put by the side of his bed. The porter suggested that if he needed anything whatsoever, he had to contact the hotel concierge, who would be more than happy to provide him with all the information he required about activities, dining, and any other questions he may have. It was explained to Johnny that nothing was too much trouble, and he said, 'All we want for you is for you to enjoy your stay with us as much as possible.'

Johnny was hungry again and decided he needed to grab a bite to eat. He was blown away by the number of dining options available to him. Johnny decided to head off to the Handu Grill for steak and seafood. It was only a short walk from his Beach Pavilion. It was a very small and beautifully designed restaurant that specialised in steaks. The staff were really friendly, and the menu offered a great selection, Johnny already realised that the food was going to be to die for. He was looking at some of the other guests in the restaurant, and what they were eating looked exquisite. After a delightful dinner, Johnny took a stroll back to his Beach Pavilion, looked at the pool in the moonlight, and thought to himself, 'What a way to live'.

He got in bed, and surprisingly, for Johnny, who usually struggled to get to sleep, he did relax and fell asleep very quickly. The following morning, he took a stroll to the Poolside Bar and decided to spend a few hours there to consider his options and what activities he might like to try. A friendly member of staff explained to Johnny that light snacks and refreshments were available to him all day at the Poolside Bar, seven days a week.

At lunchtime, Johnny spoke to the concierge, a very funny man who took his time to explain to Johnny all of the activities and amenities available as a guest at the resort. He decided he would relax for the rest of the afternoon, and the following day, he booked to go on a dolphin cruise and a turtle and shark safari. That sounded amazing to Johnny, he had certainly not done that before.

The following morning, the chartered yacht picked up the passengers and sailed into the Indian Ocean. The views were breathtaking, the water was crystal clear. Johnny had never seen seawater like it in his life. It was nothing like Margate at home. The yacht was luxurious, with only a few passengers on board. Johnny didn't realise that he would see dolphins who would be swimming very close to the yacht. Everything seemed to be at a leisurely and sedate pace. The whole point of the experience was to relax and enjoy the occasion. Johnny was very happy to take pictures and videos of the sea life that was almost within touching distance right next to him. The trip lasted about two hours, and Johnny thought he had done well to start with that activity if he was going to take in some of the local scenery, culture and views. Of course, he knew he could sit by the pool all day at his Beach Pavilion or one of the larger resort pools, but he wanted to make the most of his time and keep himself busy – he would use the idea of sitting at the pool for a fallback plan when he didn't have much to do, where he could sit and reflect in private.

For the following afternoon, Johnny booked kayaking for his next adventure. He had tried it before in England, quite local to where he lives, as a Kayak experience went from Fordwich to Grove Ferry, along a river. He remembered seeing some wildlife on the banks of the river, but there were no views of what was in the water. He thought the main difference would be that in the kayak experience, he was about to go on, he would be able to view the marine life in the crystal-clear waters.

That evening, he decided he would go for Italian at the Reef Club, and of course, he knew in advance that all of the dining experiences were going to be to his liking. The staff were so friendly in any case, and nothing was too much trouble. All the restaurants were happy to change the dishes on the menu and would cook anything you wanted as long as they had it in the kitchen. The menus were more of a general guide than a fixed dining plan. That night he retired to his Beach Pavilion and decided he would relax by the pool and soak up the atmosphere.

The next morning, Johnny was back at the Poolside Bar, and Johnny had become friendly with the local friendly bartender Habib. Johnny offered to buy him a drink, and Habib smiled back and said, 'Thank you for your kind offer, but we do not have a till at this bar as the food and drinks available are free. However, I do appreciate your gesture.' Johnny then started talking to Habib about how long he had been working at the Four Seasons and what type of firm they were to work for. Habib responded and said he liked working for the hotel, that they treated their staff very well, and that it was a friendly environment to work in. He had always looked forward to going to work and didn't think of it as going to work; he thought of it more as play because everyone was so friendly and he enjoyed it. He couldn't remember the last time there were any problems at work. Habib was married and had one young daughter Lilah. Habib always carried photos of his wife and daughter in his wallet and very quickly showed Johnny the pictures. Johnny found Habib to be a really interesting company, and he talked about some of the celebrities who had stayed at the resort before. Johnny had not heard of some celebrities but realised they were more American than English. Habib asked Johnny if he knew

Mickey Flannigan, the comedian from England. Johnny told him he was a big fan! Habib said that he and his family had stayed at the resort several times, and Habib knew very little about him, but a lot of the guests told Habib that he was a very popular, funny comedian and well paid for his entertainment services. Johnny had to agree that he thought Mickey Flannigan was very funny and entertaining. He had seen him live once and many times on TV and loved his sense of humour, direct approach and attitude towards comedy.

The kayaking experience was great; he was given his kayak, and he could return it when he was finished, and he was free to go wherever he wanted within the boundaries laid out on the map to explore the local area and sea life. It was a leisurely kayak in the Indian Ocean. It was so peaceful there were hardly any other guests in the area doing water activities, although there were certainly lots of activities available, including snorkelling, jet-ski hire, catamaran sailing and windsurfing. He felt the water sports available in his location were probably among the finest in the world. He thoroughly enjoyed the experience and afternoon, and when he returned, it had relaxed him.

When he got back, he decided that evening he would spend it at the Serenity Pool, drinking mocktails while reviewing his draft manuscript. That would be an enjoyable way to spend his evening.

Johnny found that, in reality, a lot of people in the resort wanted to spend time on their own in peace. He felt that hardly anyone was drinking much alcohol; it wasn't that type of holiday, and people weren't there getting intoxicated. When you stayed at a place like this, he realised, you didn't need anything else to add to the occasion. The resort and location were simply spectacular.

The staff and guests were very friendly, but it wasn't the type of place where Johnny thought he would make friends or get involved in long conversations and share life experiences with other guests. The fact that the range of accommodation at the resort was suites, the bungalows and villas were individually located with their pools, and people were seeking solitude, not lively conversation and activity; it certainly wasn't like Butlins, that was for sure!

The next few days, Johnny felt very comfortable and relaxed at the Serenity Pool, enjoying the occasional mocktail. He was now engrossed in his draft manuscript of the 'The Butler Really Did It.' He was checking for spelling, grammar, and the accuracy of the text. He enjoyed reading the manuscript and making the necessary corrections that he felt would take it closer to being published in the fullness of time.

He had decided while staying at the resort that he would try all the different restaurants and dining experiences available. Over the next few days, he sampled the cuisine of Baraabaru, a fine Indian restaurant, and a spectacular Asian place, Café Hurra. He spent time in the Sunset Lounge, and he experienced the in-suite dining in his suite and staff from the restaurant and cooked him the most sumptuous three-course meal. Between the courses, the chef would share information about each dish being prepared for him. They also shared a little about their own lives.

Before his time at the resort finished, he wanted to do a little bit of yoga and snorkelling, and he would at least feel that he had made the most and the best of his time at the resort. He enjoyed the snorkelling experience. He hadn't practised yoga in the past, he loved to meditate and relax by trying to concentrate on his breathing. Before he did his yoga practice, he booked a private masseuse for a private massage, which he thought would relax his muscles before he started yoga.

Johnny had not considered his overall opinion of the resort; the only thing he could say for certain was that there was nothing to complain of whatsoever, and everything was done to the highest standard possible, as you would expect from a Four

Seasons, five-star resort. The overall experience was outstanding. The time had simply flown by.

The following morning, after his spa and some more yoga, he would check out of his room to enjoy a coffee in the lobby while waiting for who he was now calling Captain Aden to pick him up and escort him to the speed boat for the return trip to Malé International Airport.

Captain Aden remembered Johnny and asked him how his stay was. Johnny decided he would grab a couple of photos with the staff before he left with Faiza, the delightful receptionist with the beautiful smile he would ask Captain Aden to take the picture, and then Faiza would take the photo with Captain Aden. On reflection, he regretted not getting a picture with the jolly bartender Habib or the in-dining chefs from the experience. However, he did have several photos with people he had met.

They set off for the airport; on the journey, Johnny thought what beautiful views, beautiful memories and a priceless experience. Very quickly, they were arriving; they exited the speedboat. Johny and Captain Aden shared a hug, and Johnny tipped him and wished him well. Johnny arrived in good time for his flight. When he arrived at the airport, he had a little bit of time to wait before the flight home would start boarding. He heard his flight called over the tannoy, so he headed through security and passport control before waiting to board the plane. On the British Airways flight home, he sat next to a delightful lady called Rosa. Very quickly, she shared with Johnny that she was an author and that she specialised in crime and romance novels. She had been writing successfully for the last ten years and had her own publishing business. It had started as a hobby. Before writing professionally, she was a teacher, which she thoroughly enjoyed, but she had left the education system in the UK because, over the years, she had seen the pay conditions in the education system deteriorate remarkably for teachers in general. A friend of hers had started teaching foreign language students

English as the pay and conditions working for a private language school far exceeded anything that the UK education system would offer a teacher in today's world. She had enjoyed teaching students from all over the world – she found it particularly interesting to talk to students from all countries and backgrounds about the different cultures they had come from to live and learn in England. Of course, the most common reason people chose to learn English was not to stay and work in England; it meant at home; they could advance their employment opportunities with major corporations because English is the most spoken language in the business world. A good command of the English language is highly sought after in many different countries. A lot of her students had really interesting stories to tell her about where they came from, and when she started writing novels, she often would pick destinations they had lived in to create the experiences from some of the conversations they had shared.

Rosa was her real name, but she wrote under a pen name. She preferred that and liked the idea that she could use her pen name to be an author and create the most elaborate crime and romantic novels possible, but she understood that was just a job that she enjoyed. She thought she was very down to earth in her private life. The biggest pleasure in her life was her two grandchildren. She was amazing company for the flight home. Johnny shared with her that he had recently become an author, was enjoying it, and wanted to have films made about his books. She hadn't thought of that idea before, she thought it sounded like a good plan, but she thought it would not be easy to achieve, but she said to Johnny 'after listening to you talk for a few hours, about where you would like to take the experience, I think it would be great if you manage to achieve your plans and dreams. I hope you manage to get the film made soon; I will certainly look forward to that.' Johnny thought that she meant it. Neither Johnny nor Rosa had any copies of their books available to exchange with each other, which may have been a nice touch, but there you go. It was certainly nice for her to encourage Johnny with his dreams and plans. After a couple of what were only reasonable meals, compared to what Johnny had been accustomed to, they were coming in to land at Heathrow Airport. As the plane landed, Johnny reflected on how pleased he was with the holiday overall, and it was certainly a bucket list experience which he could tick off.

Shortly after passing through passport control and customs Johnny picked his car up from the secure parking area and glided back to Canterbury. He had not kept in touch with Peachy while he was away. He was sure that if anything had cropped up, she would let him know, or maybe on balance, he thought he would be better off not knowing while he was away. He may well be better off finding out when he got home. On the drive home, he wondered if he needed to get some milk. He didn't message Peachy after getting home, he would see if there was any milk in the fridge or not. Sainsbury's was less than five minutes away if need be.

After arriving home, Johnny knocks on Peachy's door. She comes to the door smiling and says, " I wondered what time you would be home. She invites him in for a coffee, chat, and to give him his key back. Stavros is asleep on the sofa, and Johnny takes an armchair. Peachy says Johnny looks good with his tan and asks him how the holiday was. Johnny jokes that Stavros is probably knocked out with all the excitement about becoming a father for the first time. They sit chatting, and Johnny tries to share his recent holiday experience with her, showing her some snaps as well. She said there have been no problems at your place. I had a little clean-up for you as well, just to keep myself a little occupied. Johnny then asks how long it is before the baby is due. Less than six weeks, she replies, smiling and placing her hand on her stomach. Johnny then makes his excuses and says I am going to unpack now; no doubt we will catch up soon. As he is about to leave, Peachy says I finished your novel 'The Butler Did It'. She jokes with Johnny, 'he certainly did do it, what an amazing story'. I will review it for you in the coming days. She says Stavros has also listened to it, and he thoroughly enjoyed listening to it and will review it as well. How nice, Johnny thought as he reached his front door. He opens his front door, pops his suitcase in his bedroom and realises he needs to nip to Sainsbury's to get a couple of bits.

Wow, he thinks! She certainly has cleaned up and, at the same time, moved a lot of stuff around. It was certainly very tidy; a lot of things have been moved about, he noted. Later on, he unpacked and caught up with his mail before grabbing an early night. The flight has taken its toll on him, he has now realised.

Johnny is woken by a firm and consistent knocking on his door a few days later. Johnny rarely had visitors at home, certainly not unannounced or unexpected ones. It may well be the Amazon delivery driver or Hermes man going to ask him if he could leave parcels for one of his neighbours. Johnny didn't mind taking in parcels for neighbours from time to time, but he didn't want to be woken up while still sleeping for the experience. Johnny just turned over and tried to go back to sleep without looking at the time. The delivery driver wouldn't stop, just kept knocking. Johnny slowly climbs out of bed and walks to the front door, opens the front door and is greeted by two armed police officers who ask him to put his hands above his head, step outside and keep looking at the officer who is doing all the talking.

Johnny had only had one previous personal experience with armed police officers, and in a flash, he recalled it at that moment. It had been about 20 years earlier outside the Royal Bank of Scotland in Canterbury. Sophia had a lot of his money at the time on deposit in her Royal Bank of Scotland account. It was a Friday, and Johnny's brother, his wife, and three children had been coming down to Canterbury for the day. They had all agreed to pick up Mum and spend the afternoon at Howletts Zoo. Johnny and Sophia had agreed to meet at the bank. She would withdraw the cash, and Johnny could then meet up with his family. When Johnny arrived, she wanted to talk to him about something personal between them. He said I don't have time. I am in a hurry. They were standing in the car park at the side of the bank at the rear of Slatters Hotel. The conversation became heated. As it went on, it became louder and louder. Johnny became frustrated with Sophia. He just kept saying, get the cash, I am in a hurry, we can chat soon. She was saying that without having the conversation, she would not withdraw the cash from the bank. It became blackmail as Johnny saw it. The conversation could start with two sentences and go on for an hour or so easily Johnny knew that. The conversation probably reached an abusive level to an on-looker. They knew each other, and neither was prepared to back down or compromise. The absolute worst-case scenario would be Johnny telling her a thing or two about herself and storming off. However, that was not how it appeared to the members of the public passing by. A member of the public had rung the police and told them a man and a woman were arguing in the car park behind Slatters Hotel. He is going to kill her. That triggered an armed response unit to drive straight to the scene to investigate. Two police cars turned up very abruptly outside the bank. Johnny noticed them turn up. Then, when he saw they were armed, he thought something heavy must be going on around here; best keep out of that. There was a rather short police officer who had bulletproof clothing on, carrying a Glock pistol in a side holster, walking towards Johnny. Following him were armed officers carrying what looked like Heckler & Koch MP5 submachine guns. Johnny didn't think anything of it at all. He then says something to grab Johnny's attention and distract him from the conversation with Sophia. Johnny turned and faced him, and clearly, he could see

Johnny had nothing in his hands at all. As Johnny looked at him and he got closer to Johnny, he then just kicked Johnny's left leg, which brought Johnny crashing down on the concrete in the car park. Johnny was then put in handcuffs and arrested. He protested his innocence and the fact that there must have been a mistake, but to no avail. He was led away and taken to the local police station. All Johnny wanted to do was get to the zoo and meet his family. He was checked in at the police station. Sophia was being interviewed about the whole incident. She had a statement taken. Johnny was interviewed about the incident under caution and explained it was a conversation between two people, nothing more. As for the phone call by a well-intentioned local passerby, what was that all about?! Johnny could not remember the exact text of the conversation and what was said. He said what's it got to do with anyone else? The conversation was between Johnny and Sophia. It was a simple negotiation, which should have been simple, but it got out of hand as neither of them would back down. After Sophia was interviewed, Johnny was released without charge, but the process took about four and a half hours, which ruined Johnny's plans for the day to spend the afternoon at the zoo with his family. He told his brother half a truth that he had a problem with his car and was arrested, but it was all a mistake, and it took several hours to clear the matter up.

Then back in the present moment Johnny is handcuffed outside the front door and led back into his home, sitting on his bed at the same time as having the recollection of the previous experience running through his mind. Then a woman wearing a police combat jacket introduces herself as Detective Superintendent Hunt from the Major Investigations Team. What did she call herself? Johnny thinks. Is this some kind of dream, perhaps he needs to wake up. Then she says, 'Are you Johnny Butler?' he replies, 'Yes, I am'. She then pulled out what appeared to be a warrant, not that he could see or read without his glasses. She then says, 'Your home is about to be searched, and we will be removing all phone and computer devices as well as any documents and all other property that is discovered from the search that will assist us with our enquiries. She then tells Johnny; you are being arrested on suspicion of conspiracy to murder in 1999. Johnny couldn't hear the rest; his mind had just gone blank, and he could see her lips moving but could not hear what she was saying. Johnny is dressed in his tracksuit bottoms, has an officer put his trainers on for him, and grabs a jumper; Johnny then reminds the officer about his medication, which is in a seven-day pill box on top of a chest of drawers in his bedroom, which another officer picks up. He is then led out to an unmarked police car, where he sits in the rear of the car flanked by a police officer on either side and driven to Canterbury Police Station. The local police station was expecting them, and Johnny was booked in by the custody sergeant. He had all his rights read to him, he was then told why he had been arrested and was asked if he understood what was going on. He replied, 'Yes, I understand.' The custody sergeant explained in great detail what was going on and what would happen in terms of Johnny being interviewed about the alleged crime. He is informed that the search of his home will continue, and his cars will be searched as well. He is then asked if he would like a solicitor. Johnny replies 'I will reserve my position until I have had time to consider my position'. The sergeant asks him, 'What would he like to eat and drink? from a limited choice, he reels off. Johnny chooses the all-day breakfast and a coffee. He is then told he will be held in the cells until his interview is ready to be started. His handcuffs are taken off. The Sergeant then instructs another officer to put Johnny in cell 2. As Johnny is led off, he advises Johnny to let him know about a solicitor if he wants one.

Johnny is now lying on a hard mattress in a cell at Canterbury Police Station, waiting to be interviewed about a conspiracy to murder allegation. He was about to find out about a certain allegation as a result of new information, new evidence and witness statements which had instigated the reopening of an unsolved murder in 1999, or a cold case as is the more appropriately used term. After about an hour of thinking about his predicament and nibbling away at his all-day breakfast, he decides he at least needs to speak to a solicitor to try and understand what it's all about, which will allow him to gather his thoughts. He rings the buzzer, and a few minutes later, the food port on the cell door opens, and he is asked, 'Did you want something?' Johnny replies, 'Please let the Sergeant know I would like to speak to a solicitor'. The response is 'will do', and the food port shuts. About fifteen minutes later, the food port opens again, and Johnny is offered a cordless phone and told John Grafton-Williams from Grafton-Williams and Associates is on the phone. A loud booming voice introduces himself and asks, 'Am I speaking to Mr Butler?'. Johnny replies, 'Yes'. Good, he says. Mr Grafton-Williams says, 'This is a very serious allegation being alleged against you, Mr Butler. There is no need for you to do or say anything at all. I will be at the Police Station within the hour, and we can have a chat then. Johnny thanks him. The line then goes dead. Johnny then pushes the buzzer again; the food port opens again, and Johnny hands the phone back to the officer. About an hour later, the cell door opens, and Johnny is told his solicitor has arrived. He is led to the custody area, sits on a bench, and is advised that he can meet his solicitor and talk to him in private once there is a free interview room. Then Johnny looks up and sees Peachy and Stavros at the counter talking to the custody sergeant. How on earth have they been caught up in this mess, Johnny thinks to himself! Then Peachy turns round, and Johnny notices she is suddenly not pregnant at all. It was only about 24 hours ago she was a young expectant mother. Now the pregnancy appears to have ended, or maybe a miscarriage, Johnny thinks. She then turns around and is smiling; how on earth can she be smiling in the circumstances? Then, the sergeant referred to Peachy and Stavros as Detective Sergeant Mills and Detective Constable Meadows. It suddenly registered with Johnny they were serving police officers and operating undercover as a young couple expecting their first child. His cover was a landscape gardener, and she was a midwife. Then Johnny started putting it together in his mind. He had taken his new neighbours at face value. She was over-friendly from the off and Johnny had opened up to her about his life and was honest with her. She had opened up to Johnny about her cover story and set about gathering any possible evidence against him, he thought. Then he started laughing to himself. He had trusted her with his door key while he went away. He had unknowingly given a serving police officer his front door key, permission, and blessing to come and go as she pleased while he was away. Then he tried to work out what the ramifications of that meant to him.

Then, in walks a man Johnny thought was the local ring-leader from the circus. He had a face like a robber's dog. He was wearing what appeared to be a large top hat, a Victorian waist-coat and a vintage tailcoat, black trousers and what appeared to be highly polished Oxford shoes. He didn't have a whip in his right hand, but he had a cane, which he kept tapping and playing with, and in his left hand, he was carrying a leather briefcase which looked like it had seen better days. He looks at Johnny and says John Grafton-Williams at your service, Mr Butler. We are just organising a room; once that is done, we can get to the bottom of everything privately. A few minutes later, the custody sergeant tells Mr Grafton-Williams which room is free. It is obvious to Johnny that know each other on a professional level. It is obvious from the conversation and body language this is not the first time they have met. Johnny and his solicitor are directed to an interview room. They sit down. Mr Grafton-Williams runs through the introductions and formalities. Then he hands Johnny his business card. He then explained that he had had dealings with the Major Investigations Team and knew Detective Superintendent Hunt from a previous case. He has spoken to her about the allegations, and she has advised him in brief terms that as a result of new evidence, an unsolved murder case was reopened. He had then come under suspicion as being primarily responsible with another or others for a murder in 1999. It was about the murder of Mikey at the cab office. He then told Johnny the investigation centred around the possibility that he had hired a contract killer to kill Mikey on his behalf. As a result of new evidence, all the old case papers had been taken out of storage and examined thoroughly. Then, permission had been granted to tap Johnny's landline and mobile phone. Then, an undercover team of police officers had been inserted into the property next to his with the sole purpose of trying to extract information from him about his background and, in particular, the alleged crime. They had inserted listening devices in your home and cars without your knowledge to assist with the gathering of evidence and building a case against you when, totally out of the blue, a woman called Lucy Bale contacted the Kent County Constabulary and explained she had proof that you had ordered the hit on Mikey in 1999. You had admitted the crime to her. She could prove that. She had a tape recording of you admitting it to her. You had confessed the crime to her. She also made it very clear that she was prepared to give a statement about what she knew and give evidence in court against you. Then he smiles at Johnny and says apparently, you may know Lucy Bale as Bubba or Lady Bubba and smiles.

Johnny sits and listens and thinks this can't be happening. He looks at Mr Grafton-Williams and says, but apart from what you have just said, is there anything serious to worry about?! Mr Grafton-Williams raises his eyebrows and looks straight at Johnny.

After a brief pause between the two men, Mr Grafton-Williams says, 'Does any of this make sense to you now, Mr

Butler?'. Johnny considers his response and says, 'Well, thank you for the summary and explanation of why I am here today, Mr Grafton-Williams; I do understand the information you have relayed to me and am aware of what is being suggested'. I do know a woman called Lucy Bale, aka Bubba. I have certainly met my new neighbours recently. I had become aware just a few minutes before I met you that my neighbours were, in fact, police officers. I am aware of the unsolved murder you are referring to, and after listening to you about other information, I have heard what you have said. I understand the process which has taken place, which has led us both to this room and to the conversation we are currently having. Perhaps you don't mind if I sit here for a short time and process all that information before we continue any further. Johnny then drinks his glass of water and peruses the situation; I wonder exactly what Mr Grafton-Williams is going to suggest is the best course of action in the circumstances, and then he considers if he is the man for the job. At that moment, it suddenly hit home to Johnny that he had gone 'from Heaven to Hell in the last week.'

CHAPTER 10
POLICE INTERVIEW AND CONSPIRACY CHARGE

AFTER A FEW MINUTES HAD ELAPSED, Johnny considered his options in the circumstances. Rather than ask Mr Grafton-Williams for advice based on his previous experiences and how those events turned out as well, together with his knowledge of the current situation, Johnny smiled at Mr Grafton-Williams and simply said, 'Well, I am certainly grateful for you attending and representing me today – I will need to reserve my position about any future legal representation by you or your firm depending on how events play out in the future, in the circumstances and taking everything into account I am more than happy to answer any questions the police have to put to me in an interview under caution.' Mr Grafton-Williams replied, 'Have you considered the possibility that a no-comment interview may be a better way to proceed?

Johnny explained to Mr Grafton-Williams that although that made sense on some level and that he did understand based on letting them prove the case, he had a previous experience where the judge looked at the jury and said, of course, he could have answered these questions at the time. His previous solicitor on that occasion had said he would explain that it was on legal advice that the interview had been 'no comment', but that didn't happen as, in Johnny's experience, solicitors and barristers do not get to challenge the judges' words when they sum up or address the jury.

Mr Grafton-Williams looked at Johnny and said he understood. 'I will let them know, he said. 'We are ready for any questions, and you will be answering the questions to the best of your ability, even allowing for the time that has elapsed since the event. There may well be parts you cannot remember because of the length of time involved.' Of course, that made sense to Johnny. Mr Grafton-Williams left the room about five minutes later. He returned and said, 'They're going to put you back in the cell, and your interview will start within the next half an hour or so.' Johnny was put back in cell number two and sat on the mattress, deep in thought. After a brief period, Johnny's cell door opened, and he was led into a room where Mr Grafton-Williams was already sitting down. After about 5 minutes, two police officers entered the room and sat down opposite Johnny and his solicitor. They explained they were going to start the interview, which would be taped. They gave Johnny the formal caution explaining his rights. Before they entered the room, Mr Grafton-Williams and Johnny decided that he would answer the questions and if any of the police officers broke the rules or went too far, in his opinion, Mr Grafton-Williams may intervene to protect Johnny and his rights, but apart from that, Mr Grafton-Williams would not comment.

The two officers identified themselves as Detective Superintendent Hunt and Detective Sergeant Ryan. The tapes were turned on, the formalities were dispensed with, and the questions began. The initial questions go directly back to the events of 1999, the statement he gave to the police at the time and the crime itself. The questioning went on for about an hour and a half. Johnny answered all of the questions to the best of his ability, and then they suggested it would be a good time to take a break before continuing. Everyone agreed that a break would be a good idea in the circumstances. After about twenty minutes, they resumed the interview. The tape was turned back on again, and everyone confirmed that they were present in the room and happy to continue. The questions start to change, and they come more into the past year, the circumstances surrounding the novel, their actions, and, in particular, what Bubba said. Johnny answered all of the questions to the best of his ability, but there were occasions where some of the questioning was very repetitive. At that point, Mr Grafton-Williams would occasionally interject and explain that his client had already answered the question, and they couldn't keep asking the same question. Apart from that, the interview did seem to flow in a manner in which questions were asked and the answers were given.

Johnny addressed all of the issues as best as he could. They then explained about the undercover operation and undercover officers. They also talked about the search that was continuing at his home, and they made it clear that his computer and phone records were all going to be checked. They also explained that because of the severity of the allegation, they were speaking to the Crown Prosecution Service staff about the best way to proceed. They let Johnny and Mr Grafton-Williams know that they would be applying to Canterbury Magistrates' Court for an extension of Johnny's period of detention for up to 96 hours in total. After around another hour and a half of questioning, they suggested it would be a good time to take another break, and in fact, they would end the questioning there and continue the questioning the following day. The interview was suspended for the day, and the officers left the room, leaving Johnny and Mr Grafton-Williams alone. It was explained to Johnny that when Mr Grafton-Williams would leave, Johnny would be returned to his cell.

Johnny was grateful that he had reminded the officer earlier that morning to pick up his pill box with his medication so he would have that for his four-day period in detention at the police station. After the police officer left the room, Mr Grafton-Williams said to Johnny that, in reality, because of the seriousness, they would prefer to finish the questioning and charge him within the next few days. That way, they could apply to have him remanded in custody, and that application would be granted. He would not get bail for that offence. He said that now because Johnny had been happy to co-operate and answer all of their questions, they would probably try to weigh on balance whether they have a successful chance of getting a conviction if they charge him. There would be a barrister at the Crown Prosecution Service running through the evidence and letting the police know what needs to be tidied up and what issues and evidence needed to be dealt with in terms of the interviews; based on the answers, Johnny would give it may be necessary for a further period of investigation to take place to determine what is true and what is not. Johnny understood what he had said. They parted company, and Mr Grafton-Williams said he would be back tomorrow before continuing the interview. He said he didn't know what time that would be but that they would let him know in advance so he could be there.

The following day, after breakfast and a wash, Johnny was advised that his solicitor, Mr Grafton-Williams, would be at the station around 11 am, and the interview would continue. Shortly after 11 am, they were back in the interview room with the tape running again, answering more questions. Someone had been looking at documents seized from Johnny's home the previous day. They then decided they would take another break and reconvene after lunch.

Mr Grafton-Williams and Johnny discussed the process, which was continuing. Mr Grafton-Williams explained to Johnny that they needed to put all of their questions to him and would then be seeking instruction from the Crown Prosecution

Service. He said, 'If they feel they are not in the position to charge you currently, they will release you on bail pending the outcome of their further investigations.'

After lunch, the same two officers conducting the interview explained to Johnny that they only had a few more questions for him, which would conclude the interview. After the interview, they would consult on the next step in the case based on the evidence, their statements, and Johnny's interview. The final part of the interview didn't take too long. After 45 minutes, Detective Sergeant Ryan looked at Detective Superintendent Hunt and said, 'I think we are done,' and was looking for reassurance and confirmation. Detective Superintendent Hunt agreed, and the interview process was concluded. Johnny was then advised by the officers that he would be informed in due course on what would happen, and until then, he would be held in the cell and was free to talk to his solicitor at any time. The officers leave the room, and Mr Grafton-Williams says to Johnny, 'It's a waiting game now, and they may be out investigating as we speak. There is a large team of officers involved in the investigation. It is impossible to know exactly what they are doing or checking, but they will speak to me directly before they speak to you about their intentions over the next couple of days.'

They said their goodbyes to each other, and Mr Grafton-Williams said he would be in touch once he knows what's going on. Johnny returned to his cell feeling slightly better than he did originally as he had answered the questions to the best of his ability and felt that, on balance, it was an awful lot of hot air over nothing, but would they see it like that or not?

The following day passes with no explanation or answers from the police or Mr Grafton-Williams. Johnny is now aware that the fourth day in custody would be his last day, or he must be charged. Johnny slept quite well that night, especially allowing for what was possible the next day. He realises that it is far from an ideal situation to be in, but the whole matter is out of his hands. He decides it must all be in the plan and would hand it all over to his higher power as he always does. The next day a police officer informed Johnny that Mr Grafton-Williams would be coming to the police station later that afternoon to see Johnny. Johnny didn't know what to make of that as he realised that Mr Grafton-Williams would need to be present in the event of a charge or a release on bail for a period of further investigation to take place.

Later that afternoon, Johnny and Mr Grafton-Williams are reunited again. Mr Grafton-Williams informed Johnny that, from his understanding, Johnny would be charged later that day! Johnny was shocked in reality but accepted what had been told. Later that afternoon, in the presence of Mr Grafton-Williams, Johnny is charged with conspiracy to murder and informed that he would be taken to the local magistrates' court first thing the next morning.

Due to Johnny's period in detention, Johnny was unaware of outside events. He was taken to the local magistrates in the morning, where he knew the case would be referred to the Crown Court and he would be remanded in custody until his next appearance at Crown Court. Johnny was unaware that the local press had been informed of the charge in the case, and the police had held a press conference and informed them that a 56-year-old man, whom they did not name, had been charged with conspiracy to murder. That news had spread like wildfire overnight. Johnny was unaware, and the next day, Canterbury Magistrates' Court was filled with newspaper and media journalists to cover the events in court.

Mr Grafton-Williams came to the cells to explain the procedures for the day to Johnny, and all he needed to do was confirm his name and date of birth. Mr Grafton-Williams would be personally representing him, and he said, 'As you might expect, there is an awful lot of media attention in this case already. This may become a factor in the case, although you should know that the media are legally responsible for only reporting the facts and what is said in court. They are not allowed to report any information that may prejudice the case, and they will be reminded of that today, but it is always the case.'

Johnny appears in the dock, the charge is read out, and everyone agrees and knows that the matter will be referred to the Canterbury Crown Court. Johnny's next appearance will be at Canterbury Crown Court in 14 days. He would be remanded in custody until that day. The court was chocka block with people with notepads who Johnny assumed were reporters. His appearance in court was brief and lasted less than 20 minutes. He was sent back down to the cells, and Mr Grafton-Wiliams explained he would be in touch. About two hours later, Johnny was put on prison transport and sent to the local remand prison on the Isle of Sheppey. After taking stock of the events, Johnny realised the matter would almost certainly end up at trial, and effectively, his life would depend on the trial's outcome.

The following day, the national newspapers covered the story on the front pages, and as a result, public curiosity about the case and the novel began to grow. The case was being discussed on news channels on the TV as well as radio. The book sales rocketed due to the charge and appearance in court. Within a few days, the publisher was struggling to keep up with demand and print the book quickly enough. In the first week after the charge, the novel became the fastest-selling book ever in the whole of the UK. Johnny was nicely tucked up in his cell and unaware of what was happening outside in the real world.

He had decided he would try to make the most of his dark situation and wanted to become very proactive in any recovery meetings that were available in the prison. He could use his time in a very productive way, and he would reap the rewards for trying to help others in prison who may have addiction issues with alcohol or substances.

As the press became aware of the book sale numbers, the

book sale story started to gain more media attention than the criminal charge story.

Johnny is back in the dock at Canterbury Crown Court two weeks later. Mr Grafton-Williams had visited Johnny in the remand prison and said he knew an excellent woman he would highly recommend to represent him in the Crown Court. Her name was Elizabeth Butler KC. Mr Grafton-Williams then said, 'I thought it may be appropriate in the circumstances to have Mrs Elizabeth Butler KC representing Mr Johnny Butler!' Johnny quite liked that idea. Clearly, he knew nothing about the lady but thought it was meant to be. Elizabeth Butler would be at the Canterbury Crown Court that morning to represent Johnny and start his defence. Johnny Butler entered a not-guilty plea. After that day, she would visit Johnny to run through the evidence with an associate from Grafton-Williams & Associates at the prison as soon as she could. The biggest issue that morning seemed to be the most suitable location for the trial to take place, bearing in mind some of the witnesses who lived near Canterbury. The crime took place in Canterbury and how that may play out for the prosecution and defence. Mr Grafton-Williams, who was also at court that morning, explained to Johnny that Mrs Butler thought that a trial in London, or out of the local area, would certainly be to Johnny's advantage. Ironically the Crown Prosecution wanted to try the case outside of the area. On this matter, the prosecution and defence were in agreement, and the judge then ordered that the case be referred to the Old Bailey, where a trial would take place at a future date to be decided.

Johnny was then remanded in custody for 28 days to appear at the Old Bailey. After the hearing had finished, Mrs Butler came down to the cells with Mr Grafton-Williams to talk to Johnny and go through the process to explain that after his appearance at the Old Bailey, he would be remanded at a London prison until a trial date had been set, and the matter could be dealt with. She thought, on balance, that always favoured the defendant to have a trial heard outside of their local area. She explained she would visit Johnny in the next couple of weeks with the papers and discuss the case. She wanted time to read through the papers and understand the evidence against him before talking to him. Johnny was then sent back to the Isle of Sheppey before being transferred to HMP Wandsworth a couple of weeks later.

As a result of the media coverage of the trial, it has now become a point of discussion all over the world. News agencies were sending reporters to the UK to report on the trial as the media attention and speculation from the general public had grown, and the trial had become a worldwide phenomenon. This now meant that book sales had exploded internationally as well as in the UK.

Mr Grafton-Williams had told Johnny that the trial had attracted unprecedented media attention, and Johnny had been informed of the fact, but it hadn't sunk in, and he didn't quite know what that meant in terms of reality.

Mrs Butler visited Johnny one Wednesday afternoon at HMP Wandsworth with an associate from Grafton-Williams & Associates. The man introduced himself as Robert Jones and explained he would be taking notes and had brought the papers. He gave Johnny a copy of all the papers, and the firm had also sent Mrs Butler all of the papers for her to examine and read. Mr Jones is an unusual individual – he is a very tall man, slightly rough and ready round the edges, unkempt, and his trousers too short, Johnny thought. He looks more like someone you might find from an amateur dramatics event rather than a legal clerk. Johnny felt his taste in clothes and appearance left a lot to be desired, but Johnny did know what he looked like and dressed like was irrelevant. All that mattered was how his brain worked, his experience, and his attitude towards the case. After a three-way conversation, which lasted about an hour and a half, Mrs

Butler tells Johnny she will do her very best for him. She would see him at the Old Bailey in a couple of weeks, and they could go from there. Elizabeth Butler was growing on Johnny Butler quickly. He thought she had a natural ability to think like a gangster and talk like a lawyer. Johnny was now totally convinced that he had the right person representing him. Saturday 17th February soon comes around. It meant Johnny would spend his 14th Sobriety Birthday on remand in HMP Wandsworth, waiting for his conspiracy to a murder trial. He certainly had not seen that coming.

Johnny's next appearance is in Court 1 at the Old Bailey in front of Judge Turpin two weeks later. Judge Turpin speaks in a gentle, soft manner and does not raise his voice at all, it appears to Johnny. Johnny got the feeling that the barristers who appeared in front of Judge Turpin understood that he didn't need to raise his voice to improve his argument, and the last thing you would want to do in Judge Turpin's presence was raise your voice. The biggest issues to be discussed that morning, now that the location and venue had been agreed, were a date for the trial and the intense media speculation. What followed was a three-way conversation with Elizabeth Butler KC, Judge Turpin and Charles Smythe KC, the prosecutor, about a realistic time frame to bring the matter to trial, and the judge welcomed any comments that the prosecution and defence may have about the media in such a case. After a very thorough and deliberate conversation about the media and the coverage of the case, everyone agreed that Judge Turpin clearly understood the situation and allowing for that fact, everyone agreed with the rulings he made, which were, in effect, that he would continue to remind the press of their legal responsibility of reporting the case. Under no circumstances should there be any reporting that would prejudice the case, and anyone behaving in such a reckless manner would be held accountable before the court. Regarding the trial date, the prosecutor asked for a brief adjournment so that he may be able to take instructions from the Crown regarding witness availability and possible dates. After the adjournment, Mr Smythe ran through dates with the judge's clerk, and they concluded the trial would start on Monday, 20th May. Mrs Butler confirms her availability. A few matters of disclosure are then discussed, and the prosecution is ordered to disclose any other information they intend to rely on to the defence within the next 28 days. Judge Turpin then asks Johnny to stand and explains that he will be remanded in custody until Monday, 20th May, when he will be brought back, and his trial will commence.

Johnny is then remanded and sent back to HMP Wandsworth Prison to wait for his trial date. Mrs Butler had informed Johnny she would like to meet him again for a conference before his next appearance and the start of the trial. She needed to understand the differences in what he was saying, what the witnesses were saying and what the Crown Prosecution intended to rely on. She felt that, in all honesty, the matter was going to come down to who the jury would believe on a few crucial points; it was as simple as that. She had time to examine all of the papers, and a lot of the evidence and the unused material in the case suggested that they were generally of little relevance to determine innocence or guilt. She felt that, on balance, the case was highly speculative until they had the witness statement from Lucy Bale. Without the statement from Lucy Bale, there would not be any case to answer, but the stark reality was that if Lucy Bale was to be believed, then he may well be convicted and in reality, that may mean serving the rest of his life in prison. That was the case at its lowest point, she felt. She was very keen to know about Lucy's background, their relationship, any details he could offer, and any other evidence he felt could support his statement about Lucy Bale. She said for the avoidance of doubt, 'we need to demonstrate to the jury what type of a character she is, has been, what her motives may be, and how all this came to pass.'

Johnny now had a few months to wait for his trial. In Wandsworth Prison, there were an awful lot of addicts and alcoholics who were actively using, even though they were in the prison system. Drug use in the prison was rife, and alcohol was not very widely available, but there were a lot of inmates drinking hooch, which was the nearest equivalent. Johnny now, as a result of looking at his own life and behaviour, had far more empathy and compassion for addicts because he knew from his own experience that once addicts are in active addiction, they are in a never-ending cycle of destruction. As a result of their being in active addiction, their behaviour and morals will change dramatically and breaking the law to feed their addictions becomes a way of life. He could see that in his own life, and he had met many people in the rooms and in recovery who had been to prison and or had been in trouble with the law regularly.

There were two 12-step recovery meetings in Wandsworth Prison every week. Johnny felt it would be the most productive way he could spend his time there, by at least trying to help fellow addicts and share the message of recovery about using a 12-step program. Johnny was fully aware by now that he was responsible for carrying the message of recovery. He certainly was not responsible for carrying alcoholics or addicts. He had by now at least managed to understand what healthy boundaries looked like in a relationship between two addicts or alcoholics, where one sponsors the other. When Johnny was fortunate enough to be able to sponsor, he always made it clear at the first sit down and chat that he was merely the guide and, as he would put it, 'he would shine the torch, and the person he was sponsoring would need to do the digging.' He had come to realise over the years that some people were so broken in the rooms in their early days that they thought the art of recovery was getting a sponsor, and that was the solution. When of course, in reality, that is just the beginning of a positive process which can be undertaken by an addict, who wants to go through the 12-step programme, find and have a relationship with a higher power of his or her understanding, look at their soul, and behaviour, after understanding what an addict or alcoholic is. They need to fully concede that they are one and have the desire to change.

In many ways, recovery is such an unusual journey because you can meet a Chief Executive Officer of a public company or a homeless man sleeping outside a supermarket, and they are both suffering from the same disease, albeit their lifestyles appear to be very different.

Johnny always enjoyed the prison meetings more than the meetings in the outside world because you could often meet some intriguing characters and career criminals with amazing stories, which included all the highs and the lows. In everyday life, of course, you would meet people who had lived extreme lives, crossed all the boundaries, and were effectively rebels on some levels. Their behaviour would still seem to conform to the laws of the land. One of the saddest things Johnny felt in prison was the people he would meet who were not very bright or well-educated and who did not understand the words that they were using. They would often use the words totally out of context, which would mean, in some instances, they would probably be better off learning to read and write first. Johnny always tried to share a positive message in the meetings with the lads, and he very quickly became part of the furniture in the meetings. He got to know a lot of the inmates from the meetings. They had alcoholics and addicts coming in from outside to take the meetings, and there was certainly a very good foundation for anyone who was trying to get clean and a great understanding of what recovery could be like before release from the prison system.

Johnny took a particular liking to a guy called Frank, who attended all of the meetings. Frank had a great sense of humour and could tell a great story. They often shared some of their experiences over coffee before and after the meetings. Frank had been a career criminal all of his life; he grew up in the east end of London the hard way and had a difficult upbringing. He left school early and went on to become an armed robber. In his twenties, he had been caught as part of a gang robbing a Securicor van. They had robbed a few vans before that occasion and been successful. On this occasion, a police chase had developed after the robbery. They did get the cash, but their getaway had failed because several police cars had surrounded them and come at them from all angles. They were convicted of that one-armed robbery.

When he had spent time in prison after that conviction, he had met an awful lot of people who were serving a lot less time than he was for the importation of cannabis and making far more money than he could dream of. It didn't make sense, he thought, so his career path had changed from armed robbery to the importation of cannabis. He had been successful for a while and had done it with other criminals who had been part of a network, but because he was only a small player, it had taken him time to build up his funds in that business the real money was to be earned from being an investor in the importation, rather than being just associated with it and having a role in the process, as well as selling it in England and collecting the money. It had taken him a few years before he had managed to accumulate any decent funds.

Frank had married a wonderful girl named Charlotte and had two lovely children, living on the outskirts of London. She had never asked him what he did for a living, but she knew he didn't have a regular nine-to-five job and was probably operating outside of the law. He had a reputation in the criminal underworld as being a guy no one would want to cross, and he had progressed from the importation of cannabis to the importation of cocaine later in life. He had then become hooked on cocaine which was the root cause of all his problems, Johnny believed.

As a result of a loss of shipments coming into England, he had lost all of his money, but a large cartel of drug dealers from London who were very well known employed him to collect their drug money and debts for them. He always carried a gun and had the reputation that he would use it if necessary – he was a very feared individual. He had managed to avoid prison for most of his life but had been caught delivering five kilos of cocaine in Bromley. He had been unaware at the time, but he had been under observation by the National Crime Agency as a result of a wider investigation into the drug dealers and criminals that he was working for. He had not realised that he had been under surveillance for several months. He had no choice but to plead guilty and received a 10-year prison sentence. His wife, Charlotte, had told him on many occasions, 'I don't mind what you do, but I don't want to be married to a man who is going to be in and out of prison all of his life.' After the conviction, she had simply told him that she wanted to move on with her own life. Of course, it was in the children's best interests that they would always know who their father was, but she was going to instigate divorce proceedings as she couldn't cope with visiting him in prison for the next five years. She told him that she still loved him, but enough was enough.

There was another guy in the meetings called Ben, with whom Johnny had become friends. He was certainly not a career criminal – he had a problem with alcohol. One night, he had drunk too much at an office party, and on the drive home, he was driving down the motorway, and he missed the exit that he wanted to turn off to take him home. He was over the legal limit and wasn't thinking properly as a result of the intoxication, rather than drive to the next exit, turn around and come back, he reversed back up the motorway so he could then exit at the correct junction. Unfortunately for him and the oncoming vehicle, which was being driven by a mother of two, he caused a fatal road traffic accident. The emergency services were called, and the lady was pronounced dead at the scene of the accident. Ben had to be cut out of his car by the fire service. He was breathalysed at the scene, and the police informed the hospital that they wanted a blood sample taken. He had been arrested and charged with manslaughter as a result of being over the legal limit for alcohol in his blood while driving a motor vehicle for which he was charged as well. He was a Senior Manager working for a large telecoms provider who had a successful career, a wife and family, and a nice home. On that evening, everything changed in one moment. He pleaded guilty to the charge of manslaughter and received a 4-and-a-half-year custodial sentence. He had, by his admission, driven a motor vehicle under the influence on too many occasions in his life. He didn't realise, until he found recovery, that he was, in fact, an alcoholic.

Johnny started attending and using the gym again. He was back using the cross-trainer, but more gently than he had in the past. He was just trying to get some daily exercise rather than become obsessed with it. It didn't take too long before the obsession of the cross-trainer and how it made him feel, got hold of him again, and he wanted to start going daily and spend more and more time using it.

Johnny did feel fortunate that, from time to time, he would receive visitors. Sophia popped in a couple of times to let him know that she was more than happy to try to help him and look after his home while he was awaiting trial. He had a key hidden in the garden to his place, which he had told her about the first time she visited. She now had regular access and could lock up and come and go as she pleased. She would open his mail for him, and he had also told her his login details for his publishing account. He asked her to log in and check the bookshelf for sales reports, as he was also curious to keep up with how the book was doing. He would sit there in disbelief when she came back to tell him the number of books sold and the royalties being paid into his bank account while he was in prison. It was simply astonishing. The book had sold several million copies since he was first charged. The royalties and sums of money that were being paid into his bank account were eyewatering. He now realised, ironically, that he could afford to fund the production of his film, and he no longer needed an investor or backers if he did not receive an offer from a film company.

Sophia and Johnny didn't discuss the case at all as there never seemed to be the time, and perhaps it was better that they didn't discuss it. Once he was remanded in custody, Johnny decided that he wouldn't talk about the case, as he was aware of true stories where prisoners would become witnesses against other prisoners being held on remand. They would give statements to the Crown Prosecution Service alleging other inmates had confessed crimes to them. The stark reality of this was that in some instances, it may well have been true, but it was also true that some inmates were willing to embroider and make up stories and confessions to try and negotiate a more lenient sentence and conditions for themselves.

Simon, a guy whom Johnny knew from the rooms in Canterbury, had written to Johnny and suggested he would be more than happy to visit. Of course, in prison, a visit from someone you know, a good laugh, and a joke in the visiting area with access to the canteen are big treats for any prisoner. When Simon visited Johnny on a Saturday afternoon, Simon explained the story was on the daily news and being described as the most fascinating case and trial with plot twists and turns that you couldn't make up. It became apparent that it related to the criminal underworld, which, if the allegation was proven against Johnny Butler, ended with a gangland execution hit of a major criminal.

Grafton-Williams & Associates would often send letters informing Johnny of any new material, new witness statements, or other legal matters concerning his upcoming trial.

It suddenly dawned on Johnny that Bubba had made the novel a success beyond his wildest dreams because of her behaviour. Deep down, he knew that she wanted to be famous for being responsible for seeing him sent to prison. She was now clearly seeking fame and attention by being a witness for the Crown Prosecution Service. Johnny thought that if he were convicted, she would be expecting to be on the front of every magazine and daily newspaper in the world as the woman responsible for putting him behind bars. She would probably milk it for all it was worth, with interviews selling her story and perhaps starring in a film or documentary about her own life. The whole thing had exploded and was out of control. The only certain thing was that someone, or maybe some people, would become very famous as a result of this trial, even if it was only for a short period. Stories in the media, like anything in life, have an expiration date.

The trial date was fast approaching. It was only ten days away, and Johnny would be fighting for his life as he saw it. He was happy with Grafton-Williams and Associates. He liked Elizabeth Butler too. She always considered every aspect and possibility of all situations. She weighed up situations very well, Johnny thought. He felt she was a very good judge of character on the whole. She was articulate as well as having an assertive style, she always carried herself well. Her clothes were always immaculate, and she made a big effort with her appearance. She had a presence; whenever she was in a room, whether a visiting room in a prison or a Crown Court, you could not help but notice the energy and vibrations coming off her. What Johnny liked about her was that he had never heard her talk about herself or how good she was at the job; it was so apparent to Johnny that she was at the very top of her game and took her profession very seriously. The part he admired was that he believed she had a steely determination to win at any cost. Johnny once joked with her in one of the meetings about an advert he saw on social media for a lawyer, which read, 'Just because you did it doesn't mean you're guilty.' She replied, 'Mr Butler, we're not here to play games today. I want to win your case, and I would appreciate it if you would give me all the relevant information for me to do that for you. I'm not here to judge your innocence or guilt; you told me you are not guilty of the charge you are facing, and based on your claim, I don't question your innocence or guilt; I take instructions and pursue them to the best of my ability within the law.'

Sunday, 19th May, Johnny tried to go to sleep early as he knew that in the morning, he would be taken to the Old Bailey in prison transport, and the trial was due to begin in front of Judge Turpin in Court 1, he presumed. He had a great feeling about the experience; in particular, he had total faith in Elizabeth Butler, KC. In Johnny's mind, the whole occasion was turning into a world title fight between Charles Smythe KC and Elizabeth Butler KC. If this were a boxing match, it would probably be on a par with George Foreman vs Muhammad Ali. Would the Judge stop the trial?! Would there be a knockout punch that the prosecution or defence could not recover from?! Would the trial go the distance and get a verdict?! Would the verdict be unanimous or a majority verdict of at least ten people?! Johnny knew there was a total frenzy in the media about the trial already but could not understand it in reality while he was on remand awaiting trial. He watched the news on TV and read the tabloids and broadsheets occasionally but tried just to remain calm and work on the facts and his relationship with Mrs Elizabeth Butler KC.

CHAPTER 11
TRIAL AT THE OLD BAILEY

ON MONDAY, 20th May, Johnny is woken up by a bang on the cell door and a voice telling him to get ready for his prison transport. He is now awake. He does his daily prayers and thanks God for everything he has in his life as well as asking to be of service to others where he can and trusts God will use him as he needs him in all. Then, a simple 10-minute period of meditation will calm his mind down and give him that peace he craved. He then made a gratitude list of everything he has in his life to be grateful for. He had grabbed a shower the previous evening and was just going to have a wash at the sink and brush his teeth before getting dressed. The journey from HMP Wandsworth to the Old Bailey was only about seven miles. He knew they liked to leave early, allowing for traffic and getting all prisoners to their arrival place in good time. By arriving early, Johnny knew it would be helpful to spend some time having a short conference with Mrs Butler on how she expected things to start and, more importantly, what her strategy and plan were just for that day.

The drive to the Old Bailey is straightforward enough.

Johnny had wrongly assumed that the Crown Court was called the Old Bailey. In reality, it is the Central Criminal Court of England and Wales, commonly referred to as the Old Bailey after the street on which it stands. Live and learn every day, he thought! Though the Old Bailey has always been primarily concerned with London cases, it has come to play a wider role in the Criminal Justice System, where there are fears that trying a case in the local area would make it difficult to secure a prompt or fair trial.

He is due in Court 1 in front of Judge Turpin at 10 am. As the prison transport turns into the Old Bailey and is about to enter the Crown Court, Johnny sees a woman waving a plaque which says, 'Johnny B is Innocent.' It brings a smile to his face. He arrives nice and early, which is handy as it will give him a chance to have a mini-conference with Mrs Butler and the legal clerk from Grafton-Wiliams and Associates.

A charming and delightful lady from Grafton-Williams introduces herself as Mrs Jill Canon. She then explains to Johnny that last night while at home Mrs Butler fell down her stairs late in the evening, was taken to hospital and has broken a leg as a result of her tumble down the stairs. Her husband let her chambers know about her situation and the fact that she will now be off work due to the fall. They had let Grafton-Williams and Associates know first thing this morning. The chambers do not have a KC available today to send as a replacement this morning.

They are sending a Junior to explain to the trial judge that an adjournment will be required to allow the defence to take instructions and a replacement KC to be sought. Johnny thinks I didn't see this coming. It's such a shame for Mrs Butler and Johnny. He remembered all their conversations about the crux of the matter and what it would all come down to after she had read the case papers and unused documents and evidence. Johnny and her were at least on the same page about his defence. Before a trial starts no one knows how the evidence will come out, and for the most part, that is what matters, as well as how the prosecution and defence will use the evidence presented in court in their arguments to the jury, before the judge summarises the facts and evidence presented, just before instructing the jury on points of law before they retire.

Then it hit Johnny Mrs Butler was never really going to defend him. God had put her in his life to educate him about the important matters of his case. Mrs Butler was his teacher, not a person to represent him. She had certainly done her job well, that was for sure! Johnny would always be grateful to her for that. Johnny then asks Mrs Canon to instruct the barrister, who is on his way from the chambers, that as a result of Mrs Butler's fall, Johnny had decided he would represent himself. He will continue to use the services of Grafton-Williams, particularly Mrs Canon, for the duration of the trial to look after all the case papers and assist him from behind in the court.

He had been in so many Magistrates, County and Crown Courts over the years, he had plenty of experience with court procedure. He could certainly address people and the Judge, that was for sure. He could think like a gangster and talk with some sense, even if he could not talk like a lawyer. He understood the case better than anyone else and knew the truth. He knew how to cross-examine witnesses, present his case, and closing arguments. He had the right to be represented, but he had the right to represent himself. By representing himself, he would never doubt or regret that he could have done better himself. After all, it was his life on the line. The difference between a conviction and acquittal was hard to put into words, but life-changing was a bit of an understatement; he knew that.

Due to all the media hype about the case, Johnny knew or thought that the press from all over the world was going to be there to follow and report on the case. The only question on everyone's lips all over the world was, 'Did the Butler Do It?' No doubt, some would be allowed in the court, and there would be a lot of live reporting from reporters outside the courthouse. The trial was not going to be televised. Judge Turpin was never going to allow the trial in the court to become a media circus. There was zero chance of that. He could not control the reporters outside the Old Bailey, but they could only report facts and follow the case as it unfolded hour by hour and day by day. Johnny did not have a wig or the appropriate attire, but that was not going to be an issue. He was grateful he had a decent suit to attend court in. It had been sent into the prison by Sophia, who had grabbed it out of his wardrobe. Nice to be smart, but it was not a fashion contest, that was for sure.

10 am and Johnny is taken up to Court 1 for the start of the trial. Mrs Canon signals to Johnny that she has instructed the junior barrister, who is now in court, that Johnny intends to represent himself in the matter. The court is full to the brim, Johnny notices. There is no jury, just barristers waiting for Judge Turpin to enter. His clerk asks the prosecution and defence barristers if they are ready. Then, the clerk leaves the court to let the judge know who is still in his chambers and that everyone is ready when he is.

Judge Turpin enters Court 1. Everyone rises. The court is now in session. The judge addressed the barristers and asked about Mrs Butler KC. He had been made aware that Mrs Butler had had an unfortunate fall at home the evening before and would now not be representing the defendant, Johnny Butler. The prosecutor, Charles Smythe KC, told the judge that the defence had informed him about Mrs Butler's situation that morning. Judge Turpin turns to the defence barrister Mr Michaelson. Mr Michaelson informs the judge of the events the day before and the current situation. After careful consideration, he informed the judge that the defendant, Mr Butler, had decided to represent himself before the court in this matter. Those are my instructions.

Judge Turpin looks at Johnny, who is in the dock, and says, 'Does your client fully understand the consequences of what he is suggesting?' Judge Turpin then explains all his rights as the defendant; he then raises his concerns and addresses issues such as the consequences of representing himself in a matter like this. He confirms that this is a highly unusual situation. The defendant will need to be handcuffed to a court security officer for the duration of the trial. He will sit at the front, where a defence barrister would sit. Then he will be allowed to represent himself in the matter. Jury selection can then take place. Mr Michaelson's services are no longer required. The necessary arrangements will be made in the court. Then the court clerk will randomly select 12 out of the 15 potential jurors to sit on the jury.

The judge explained the probable length of the case to the jurors and asked if there was anyone who knew the defendant or had any reason why they could not serve on the jury. One lady explains she is due to have a hip operation in 8 days and does not want to miss it due to the length of time she has been on a waiting list. Judge Turpin says he understands and has some experience with the process. He is sympathetic to her plight and excuses her. An alternative juror will take her place. No other issues are brought before the court. The jury has been selected and the clerk swears them in. Judge Turpin informs them that the regular court hours will be 10 am – 1 pm and 2 pm – 4.30 pm. He then informs them in light of the time the case will start after lunch at 2 pm. He then rises and leaves the court. Johnny will be taken back to the cells during lunch and any breaks. He has the defence trial bundle in the courtroom and can refer to that anytime he is in the court.

There is a live feed in the court, but there are no cameras, and the general proceedings can be followed by anyone on the live feed, which just updates about the session, the trial details, and so on. As the court adjourns for lunch, the press and media are now reporting the case with another unbelievable plot twist. The news that Johnny Butler's barrister had broken her leg and Johnny Butler was now representing himself in the most media-covered trial of the modern era was sensational. Reporters were now asking, 'Is there anything the Butler has not done?' Then, many legal commentators and journalists were offering their views on why he would do that. How may this change affect the trial? Would the change affect the outcome? Some suggested he had lost the plot and was committing suicide almost; others questioned whether Johnny Butler was mad or a genius. Was it a shrewd move? What were all the disadvantages and advantages of his choice?! No one knew the answers in reality. Some thought it was a very astute move, and others thought he would be buried without legal understanding and training. The loss of the experience of legal representation would prove his downfall. What would the headlines be in the papers tomorrow, was anyone's guess.

Lunch is a simple microwave meal and a carton of fresh water with an apple to follow. Johnny thinks it is certainly not up to the Savoy Grill standard, but variety is the spice of life, and it hits the spot. Johnny is grateful to eat and knows that in some countries, some people and a few in England may not eat today. Johnny has learned the art of and the benefits of being grateful for what he does have today. Johnny is taken back to court at 1.50 pm. The prosecutor is already in the court. Johnny says to Mr Smythe that at the end of the day, he will be happy to give him the list of names of the various witnesses, that Johnny will be happy just to have their statements read out in court rather than attend because Johnny accepts that there are a lot of people including serving police officers who merely collected information and statements from witnesses and their statements merely explain that procedure. Mr. Smythe is grateful to Johnny for bringing that up.

At 2 pm, the court clerk looked at the prosecution and defence and said he would let Judge Turpin know everyone was in court. The court clerk returns. Shortly after, Judge Turpin enters. Mr Smythe informs Judge Turpin that by the end of the day, Johnny has informed him that he will let Mr Smythe know which witnesses will not be required to attend court but can merely have their statements read out. Judge Turpin acknowledges the cooperation between both parties. He then looks straight at Johnny and says I have noticed the atmosphere that currently exists and welcome that. The very last thing Johnny wanted to do was upset the judge. He would very happily disagree with the prosecutor if necessary. He was looking to take guidance from the judge in reality. Johnny knew the judge would always have the last word before the jury was sent out whether Johnny liked his decisions or not. This was not a place to get emotional when rulings and decisions went against Johnny. It was a court of law, not a game of Cluedo.

The judge asks his clerk to get the jury. The jury filed in. Johnny takes his first serious look at them, even if he is trying to do it in cursory glances. From now on, they will have to sit in the same seats for the duration of the trial. One or two characters stand out to Johnny mainly for their clothes, general appearance, and presentation. Johnny decides it best not to start people watching and thinking about who they are, what they do and their backgrounds in general. His mind could run into all sorts of possible scenarios which, on balance, he knew may not even be close to the truth, but it would not be helpful to him in any way. Just accept them for what they were. They were merely a collection of 12 men and women who were randomly selected from the electoral roll.

The Judge asks Johnny to stand. The clerk reads out the charge. Conspiracy to murder Mikey in 1999. Johnny is asked how he pleads to the charge. Johnny answers, 'Not Guilty.' Johnny is told he may be seated. Judge Turpin then explained to the jury that the prosecutor would give his opening statement in light of the plea. Charles Smythe stands with his notebook in front of him. He then makes an opening statement about the Crown Prosecution case against the defendant. He explains the murder in question happened some 25 years earlier. At the time of the murder, a full murder inquiry had been launched. The deceased and the defendant had known each other for several years. They had been introduced to each other as a direct result of them both being taxi drivers and operators in Canterbury. They had formed a company and became business partners for several years.

The business had been very successful on a financial level, but this was not the type of business where people would work hard, operate within the law, pay taxes and employ people who would do the same. This business was run by two selfish individuals who broke all the rules and laws and cheated the authorities out of the revenue that should have been paid to the government in taxes. The firm's name was Lynx Taxis, and they were regularly under investigation by local and government authorities. The police had several dealings with the firm and often investigated one or other of the owners for illegal activities. It was at this point Johnny was listening intently to Mr Smythe that he remembered that saying he would occasionally reflect on his earlier life. It simply said, ‘Everything I like is expensive, illegal or won't text me back.’ To a large extent, he could relate to that. Mr Smythe then explains the deceased’s criminal background. He explains a prison sentence that effectively destroyed the relationship between the two men.

He then explains that they parted company in business terms after the deceased was released from prison. He was certainly giving all the background information about events. Johnny didn’t mind at all about all the so-called history and background. He knew the only thing that was going to count was whether he was innocent or guilty of conspiracy to murder. Did he hire a contract killer or not? Johnny remembered a remark a trial judge had previously said in court, he casually remarked juries cannot remember opening statements. Johnny thought on balance, it was true, and it was a dark picture in some respects but carried no real weight in this matter.

Mr Smythe then explains the facts about the murder and how the defendant was questioned about the murder at the time. He was questioned and stated his relationship with the deceased. He was also asked about his whereabouts when the murder was committed. He then acknowledges that the police checked and verified his alibi at the time of the murder. The statement then states that after a full investigation, which went on for over a year with hundreds of witnesses and lines of enquiries, no charges had ever been made by the police about the case. The case had been left unsolved. The appropriate authorities had stored the case, as all unsolved murder cases are in the hope and possibility that new or additional information and evidence may come to light in the future.

He then said this was such a case, and due to new circumstances and evidence which directly linked the defendant to the case, he had been charged. He then said that the jury would hear directly from a witness that he had confessed to the crime, and for the avoidance of doubt, they had a tape recording of the conversation in which the defendant admitted it in his voice. He then said after hearing the defendant's confession in his voice and hearing from the woman he confessed to, they would be in the proper place to render a guilty verdict in this case. Mr Smythe then indicates to the judge that he has finished his opening statement and is ready to call his first witness in the case.

The judge thanked Mr Smythe, turned to the jury, and said, 'From time to time, there will be times in the trial when I need to deal with legal matters and address the prosecution and defence. It is perfectly normal that will take place in your absence, and you should not infer anything about the case at all from these breaks.' He then says, 'It will help the trial to proceed in a timelier manner and follow the correct process according to the law.' He then explains that they have now finished for the day, and in the morning, when they return, the prosecution will start calling their witnesses. He then directs them not to read about the case in the papers or on the internet. He reminds them not to discuss the case with anyone. He reminds them of their responsibility to decide the case merely on the evidence presented and heard in the court. The jury files out. After that, the Judge looked at Mr Smythe and said, 'I thought it might be helpful to you and Mr Butler to have some time today to agree on all the witness statements.

The judge retires. After this, Mr. Smythe pulls out a full list of witnesses in the case he intends to rely on. Johnny recalls Mrs Butler's advice and attitude towards witnesses. They had been through all the witness statements together in great detail. Johnny had read all the statements several times. Mrs Butler simply said, 'If we disagree with the contents of their statement and we don't accept their evidence in chief after reading their statement, then they must attend court. If there is nothing in their statement we disagree with, then we accept the witnesses' statement, and we accept it will be read out by the prosecution and entered as evidence. The list of witnesses was long. Johnny knew exactly which witnesses he had no bone of contention with. He had finished his list earlier that afternoon while Mr. Smythe was reading out his opening statement.

After going through the list together and double-checking, Mr Smythe and Johnny had probably managed to cut the length of the trial down by some considerable time. A prosecutor could read a statement far quicker than he could have a witness sworn in and then question them and extract the contents of their statement from them, that was for sure. Mr Smythe indicated to Johnny he would start with Detective Superintendent Hunt in the morning. Day one is over. Johnny is taken back down to the cells and will be taken back to HMP Wandsworth in prison transport.

Tuesday 21st May Johnny wakes in his cell the following morning with the banging on the door and is directed to get ready for prison transport to the Old Bailey by a prison officer. He only has to worry about himself, all his court papers are now in the court. He wakes up and does prayer followed by meditation. He then makes his gratitude list, which is so long. He is on trial for a crime that will determine the outcome of his future, but he can see so many positives in his situation. He concedes to himself that it is a unique position and thanks God for everything he has and all God has given him. He asks God to give him the strength to help the jury see the truth in the mountain of evidence and testimony which is about to follow. Although he understands the case, the evidence, the allegation and the charge, he is mindful that the jury does not have that luxury. It was only yesterday they were chosen at random. They may well have read about the case in the papers or on the internet. They may also have watched TV programs discussing it for weeks and months on end; maybe they knew about the allegation and some of the circumstances leading to the charge and the trial. They certainly were not aware of the evidence and facts in this matter.

The trip to the Old Bailey does not take too long, and after arriving, Johnny is put in the cells. At about 09.30 am, the cell door is opened, and Johnny is told that Mrs Canon has come down for a chat. They sit in a room together and chat about the court procedure. She lets Johnny know she has access to all the prosecution case papers on the benches, which he is sitting at the front of. She also has access to all the unused material. There are reams and reams of paper everywhere. Johnny explains to Mrs Canon that most of the papers will probably not be required, but of course, it will depend on how the evidence comes out and if there are any surprises or shocks. Johnny knew a barrister called Jools, whom he had met in the rooms and who had been defending and prosecuting cases all his life. He was nearer the end of his career than at the beginning. He thought he had five good years left in him. Johnny had previously asked him if barristers and judges had a retirement age. He said that recently, judges had a mandatory retirement age put in place, which he believed was seventy. It was seen as more politically correct in the world as it is today, whereas, in the past, there was no mandatory retirement age for judges. Barristers could continue for as long as they like, especially bearing in mind that they exist to get new instructions continuously. He suggested that the mid-seventies seemed to be the general rule in the industry as a deadline for hanging up their wig and gown!

Johnny had been informed that Detective Superintendent Hunt would be the first witness and shared that with Mrs Canon. She simply smiled, got up and said, 'Let battle commence.' Johnny smiled. About ten minutes later, Johnny was led back up to Court 1 at the Old Bailey.

The judge's clerk asked Mr Smythe and Johnny if they were ready. They both indicate they are, and the clerk leaves the court to inform the judge in his chambers that everyone is waiting. The clerk returned to the courtroom, shortly followed by Judge Turpin. At this point, everyone stood up to acknowledge his entrance. He then asked everyone to be seated. The Crown Prosecution have provided the judge, Johnny and the jury with multiple copies of files of the five folders of the jury bundle, which they can refer to from time to time if required, some witnesses will refer to them. The judge then indicates to his clerk to get the jury. A few minutes later, the jury filed in and were seated.

The judge explained to the jury that the prosecution would now call their first witness. He reminds them of their responsibilities and points out that the copies of the five folders of the jury bundle are available to them as a point of reference so they can follow the evidence when required to do so.

Detective Superintendent Hunt of the Major Investigations Team takes the stand and takes the oath. Charles Smythe slowly asks her to introduce herself, her rank, her previous experience in the police force, and, in particular, her role and responsibilities in this case.

Johnny listens patiently while looking at Detective Superintendent Hunt. Then it hits him, who she looks like. She is almost a doppelganger for Marie, a woman he met about nine years ago from Gravesend. She is the absolute spitting image. Johnny had always remembered Marie. They had met on a dating site, and Marie had told Johnny she was a single woman with no family, liked an occasional drink, and lived in Gravesend.

Then after chatting for a while, she declared that she worked in the fashion industry. She sold clothes and ladies' accessories, and she had her shop online and did particularly well at it. It had conjured up an image of a retail fashion empire like Prada in Johnny's mind. They had talked for a few days and decided it would be a good idea to meet up, have dinner and at least break the ice with a face-to-face meeting and see if there was any connection. Johnny picked an Italian restaurant on the high street in Gravesend, and they agreed to meet there one Saturday evening. Johnny had arrived earlier than the agreed meeting time and waited for Marie. It was a wonderful Italian restaurant. It had a great atmosphere, and Johnny had high expectations for the evening.

In walks Marie, who is very nicely dressed. They had recognised each other quite quickly, and the conversation and introductions flowed. They ordered some drinks, and after choosing what to eat, they started to exchange small talk about life, and then she referred to her children, at which point Johnny did a double take because she had been single with no children on her dating profile. He casually remarked, 'Oh, I didn't realise you had children.' To which she replied, 'Only two.' The conversation moved on, but Johnny did note that that had been misleading, to say the least.

Johnny wasn't drinking alcohol, but very quickly, she was drinking wine by the glass, and Johnny realised it would have been easier to buy it by the bottle. Then, when they started to talk about work, she explained to Johnny she was selling second-hand clothes on eBay, at which point Johnny realised Marie was not quite the package he thought she might be. The food was exquisite, it was an old-fashioned Italian place, and the cooking was great. At least that part of the evening was going well, and Johnny and Marie enjoyed the food. Then, after dinner, while contemplating whether to have dessert or not, Marie said to Johnny, 'You need to ask me certain questions.' Johnny was speechless. What she was proposing to Johnny was that she was going to tell Johnny what questions to ask her on the date. Now Johnny realised this wasn't a match made in heaven, but at the same time, it was an experience, and he thought they could go with the flow and see what happened.

Johnny had never been told what questions to ask someone before, and it was certainly new for him. After dinner, Johnny asked her if she fancied going to a bar or a club for the rest of the evening. They had ended up in a nightclub in Gravesend. Johnny was drinking J20s, and Marie was drinking whisky and coke. Whatever it was and whatever it wasn't, it wasn't for Johnny; he had decided that and, a bit later on, made his excuses before exiting gracefully.

Detective Superintendent Hunt explains to the jury that as a result of various information from multiple sources on the Crimestoppers hotline, the 1999 murder case had been reopened and tentatively looked at. Then, as a result of initial investigations, further inquiries were made about the publication of certain books and the possible implications of the information contained in those books. She had been asked to lead the inquiry and see what evidence she could turn up about the case and if that evidence would merit further examination. She had taken this role on and led a team of officers who had conducted many enquiries in the Canterbury area and, as a result of those enquiries, led to further investigations into the potential guilt of Johnny Butler.

She had been performing this role for some time and was discussing her findings with fellow officers before asking for permission to tap Johnny Butler's phone to do a thorough investigation into his current emails, landline, and financial records. She had been informed that an apartment next to him in his block was available to rent. She thought it would be a good idea to place undercover officers in the apartment so that they could befriend Johnny, gain his confidence, and get to know as much as they could about him and the possibility of any role he may have played in the crime. They also set up listening devices in the flat next door so that he was continuously being listened to while he was at home. While furthering their investigation, they received evidence from Lucy Bale, which was shocking and explosive. It was a voice recording of Johnny Butler admitting the crime in his own words, which she had recorded when she had been in his presence.

It was at that point that the decision was taken to arrest Johnny Butler and confront him with the allegation and, more to the point, his involvement in the conspiracy of the murder of Mikey in 1999. She then explained to the jury that she had personally interviewed him for several hours over a few days while he had been legally represented at Canterbury Police Station. It was after conducting the interviews that the decision had been made to charge him with the crime of conspiracy to murder.

After lunch, Charles Smythe then got Detective Superintendent Hunt to explain that although she was the leading officer in the case today, the murder case had originally been investigated very thoroughly in 1999 by a large team of police officers with unlimited resources. She and her current team reviewed the original case papers, which drew no firm conclusions about any suspects at the time. There were certainly not any suspects that could be charged and put on trial for any crimes relating to the murder. However, after reviewing the original case papers and in light of the new inquiries and evidence available today, that position had dramatically changed.

Later that afternoon, Charles Smythe indicated to the judge that he had no further questions for Detective Superintendent Hunt. Judge Turpin then asks Johnny if he has any questions for the witness. Johnny replies, 'I do indeed, your Honour,' and stands up while handcuffed to his court security officer. He then looks down at his A4 pad and has a straightforward list of questions to clarify some information and points that he thinks will be helpful for the judge and the jury at a later time.

Firstly, he refers to the day she arrested him in Canterbury and the police interviews that resulted from that arrest. He asks her, 'Were there any questions that he had not answered that she had put to him in the interview?' To which she replied, 'I cannot remember the full details of your interviews.' Johnny doesn't mind that answer; he can live with it. He then gets her to confirm that because of the nature of the crime, the police did have unlimited resources at the time of the murder and in recent times. He then asks her, 'Who was the person that he had hired to commit the crime on the day in question?' She acknowledges she doesn't know the name of or the whereabouts of the person that he allegedly used for the contract killing. He then asks her how much he paid an alleged hitman for the contract killing. She acknowledges she has seen no evidence about this question. He then asks her, 'Where in the police papers is the evidence that proves a payment was made to a hit person at the time of the murder?' She acknowledges there is no proof of payment by Johnny at the time of the murder to an alleged contract killer.

He then asks her if she is aware of any police officers who had personally witnessed any evidence with regards to the hiring of a contract killer or money being paid to one. The reality was the police were relying on people for evidence – they had no first-hand experience and had not witnessed any events which were relevant in this case. They debate the point a little, and after a short while, she concedes to Johnny that no police officers were direct witnesses to any of the events being alleged against Johnny. He had decided that was the only information that would be helpful for his defence, since in all honestly, he didn't have too many qualms with Detective Superintendent Hunt's evidence in the case.

Johnny then thanks Detective Superintendent Hunt for her time and indicates to Judge Turpin he has no further questions for the witness. Judge Turpin asked Mr Smythe if he had any further questions. He does not. He then turns to Detective Superintendent Hunt, thanks her for her time and her evidence, and lets her know she is free to leave. At that point, he looks at the clock on the wall, which indicates 4.10 pm and decides that will be a good place to finish for the day. He then addressed the court and sent the jury home for the day while informing them the case would be adjourned until the next day at 10 am. He leaves the court. Johnny smiles at Mrs Canon while he is being led down to the cells. The second day of court is over, and he awaits transport to take him back to HMP Wandsworth.

Johnny is now totally unaware of the situation in the media. The reporters are outside the court and on TV, reporting the day's proceedings and sharing their views of what happened in court that day. When Johnny returns to his cell, he has a bunch of mail left on his bed. All envelopes have been opened, which is par for the course with all prison mail. The prison always reserved the right to read and check mail, and in reality, Johnny understood they read very few letters, just a few random ones. They just searched for contraband and maybe read some letters acting on the information they had received about the improper behaviour of certain prisoners, as well as crediting cheques and postal orders to prisoners' accounts if the letters contained any. Prison resources certainly did not stretch to all correspondence being read in full.

He was not too disappointed at how the day had gone. It had been straightforward, and he didn't challenge the integrity or honesty of Detective Superintendent Hunt. Still, he had certainly brought out a few points that at least showed the judge and the jury how fragile the prosecutors' case was in his view. A couple of letters from friends, and then Johnny opened a letter, a firm film proposal from a major film production company. They want to make a film or a possible series based on the novel 'The Butler Did It by Sean Joseph.' They had definite ideas and plans, either for a film or a possible series, and invited Johnny to get in touch as soon as possible so they could thrash the details of the deal out. Sophia had forwarded the letter from his home address.

Johnny was ecstatic. He now had one of the world's leading film production companies wanting to make a film or series. It was his dream come true. Of course, it was such a bonus on top of the sales from the novel. He could now afford to make his film in the future if acquitted, but a major film production company would have the resources and access to film stars and talent that he could only dream of. Maybe they would like his input into the project, or maybe they would just run with their creative department. All of the details could be agreed in the future. Johnny lay on his bed and reflected that he had now written a best-selling novel all over the world, and he had a firm offer to make the film. Life certainly couldn't get any better for him, apart from one minor detail – the fact that if convicted, he would be spending the rest of his life behind bars. In the circumstances, the Crown would be able to ask Judge Turpin to sign and start a proceeds of crime order to be attached to his earnings from the novel and any future film deals. It really would be life behind bars for the rest of his days with no money, or the flip-side was that he would have unlimited funds for the rest of his life and could pursue and live a life beyond his wildest dreams.

Wednesday, 22nd May, the process is now becoming familiar to Johnny. He is up early, washes and has breakfast, spends his daily quiet time and makes his gratitude list before being taken to the Old Bailey. Shortly before 10 am, he is taken upstairs to Court 1. The clerk goes to let the judge know. Judge Turpin comes into court and asks for the jury to return and the day's proceedings to start. The prosecutor indicates there is a large number of police statements that have been agreed upon by both sides; therefore, Mr Smythe intends to read out the statements to the jury as if they were being spoken by the witnesses themselves. As Johnny Butler had no questions for the witnesses, their statements in their entirety would be accepted and entered into evidence. There were 17 in total. The judge then looked at the jury and explained to them that the prosecutor would now read out the names of witnesses and statements they had made in this case. He then explained to the jury that the contents of the statements were not disputed by the defence at all. It was, therefore, the jury's responsibility to listen to the statements as if they were being spoken by the person themselves, and they were entitled to rely on these statements in their deliberations at a later date.

Mr Smythe starts with the first five statements, which were from serving officers at the time of the murder. They were all called to the scene of the crime on the day in question and were responsible for sealing off the crime scene and starting the investigation. Then there were four statements from officers who were charged with gathering all of the forensic evidence at the crime scene. This included fingerprints, DNA samples, blood samples, and a full analysis of the area, including gathering evidence at the crime scene.

Their investigations had all been carried out wearing white

suits, masks, shoe coverings and gloves to preserve the evidence from the original crime scene. This process continued for several hours before their findings would be sent off to the laboratories for examination and identification. All their findings had been published in reports available in the jury bundle and not disputed by the defence. A crime scene log had been created and was in the jury bundle. The body was then taken away by the police for a full post-mortem examination to confirm the cause and nature of the death. The findings of the autopsy would later prove beyond any doubt that Mikey had been shot at close range. He had been shot three times in quick succession, one bullet in the head, one to his heart and one in his chest, which had been instantly fatal as a result of bleeding and blood haemorrhaging as well as organ failure.

The judge then thought it was an appropriate time to have lunch and sent the jury for a break. He explained to the jury that he knew the sandwiches that were provided by the canteen were not the best quality he had ever tasted, but he assured them that they were of a reasonable enough standard that they wouldn't be left hungry and would keep them well-nourished and watered in the time that you spend with us. The jury left the court, and the judge indicated that the case would resume at 2 pm. Johnny was led down to the cells for lunch.

After lunch, the prosecutor reads out the statement of two officers who interviewed Johnny Butler at home and at the police station at the time of the murder in 1999. As a result of the interview, they then contacted other people to confirm what they had been told by Johnny Butler. Their statements were all in the jury bundle and confirmed that what they had been told by Johnny Butler at the time did prove to be accurate. Then the prosecutor read out four statements from serving police officers who were attached to the original investigation at the time, who had spent several months on the investigation, looking into leads and enquiries all over the country.

After a short comfort break in the afternoon, the prosecutor read out two rather lengthy statements from police officers at the time of the murder, which explained in great detail how they had thoroughly reviewed all of the evidence available at the time. They had given their findings to the senior officers in the case. After reading those two statements, Mr Smythe indicated to the judge that his next witness was available and outside the court. The judge looks at the clock and over to the jury, saying, 'Thank you for your service today. We're going to finish and adjourn for the day. Further witnesses will be attending the court in the morning to give evidence.' The jury leaves the court after Judge Turpin indicates the court will start at 10 am, before leaving the court. Johnny is led back down to the cells after managing to say goodnight to Mrs Canon briefly and waits for his prison transport back to HMP Wandsworth once more.

After returning to prison, Johnny reflects on the day and concludes that he hopes that the jury will be able to detach from the serious graphic crime that has been committed and his innocence or guilt concerning the charge against him. He doesn't want the jury to get wrapped up in the idea that the callous murder must be solved by them or the idea that someone must pay for the terrible loss of life.

CHAPTER 12
THE VERDICT

THURSDAY, 23rd May, Johnny wakes up and follows his daily routine of preparing to travel to court before waiting in the cells downstairs to appear in court. There is a knock on the door at about 9.50 am and one of the custody officers lets Johnny know there will be a delay in the start time of the proceedings, as Judge Turpin has to hear other legal matters before his case starts again. The custody officer explained to Johnny, as always with these matters, that you simply never know how long these things take, and he would let him know when he would be ready for court.

What seems like hours later, Johnny's cell door is opened, and he is led up to Court 1. It turns out it is now 11.15 am, so the delay was, in total, 1 hour and 15 mins. The judge asks the clerk to get the jury, and he then explains to the jury that from time to time, and in particular at the beginning of the day, there may be other matters not connected to the case he would need to deal with, in terms of applications made and sentence hearings. When that is the case, there may well be a delay to the start, but these other matters have no bearing on this case whatsoever. After the jury is sat down, Charles Smythe calls Detective Sergeant Mills, who is the first of two undercover officers who lived in the apartment next to Johnny and had gotten to know him over some time, while at the same time, trying to gather evidence and uncover the facts about the case. Detective Sergeant Mills explains to the jury that she was placed undercover with a fellow officer. They had created the identity of a young couple living together who were expecting their first child. Her colleague, Detective Constable Meadows, had pretended to be her partner.

She then went on to explain to the jury the part she had played in meeting the defendant Johnny Butler, talking to him, getting to know him, and at one point, she had been looking after his home for him while he had been away on an exotic foreign holiday in the Maldives. She also explained how she and her colleague would listen in on recording devices that had been inserted into the defendant's apartment. She then went through the jury bundle, explaining her findings and the reports that she made regularly to her senior officers. She then explained that on the day that he was arrested, her cover had been blown as a direct result of him seeing her and her colleague at the police station. In interviews, he had been questioned about his relationship with his new neighbours. She explained to the jury that she had used the name Peachy and she had pretended to be pregnant during the undercover operation.

Mr Smythe indicated to the judge that he had no more questions for Detective Sergeant Mills. The judge then asked Mr Butler if he had any questions for Detective Sergeant Mills. He only has a few questions for her. He asks, 'As a result of the various conversations that have taken place between him and her, what had he ever said to her in direct conversation that was evidence of guilt in this matter?' She then answered that all of her findings were in her reports. He then says, 'Please, can you show us in your reports where there is any incriminating evidence about the charge?' She accepts that he said nothing to her in person.

The evidence she had gathered and findings were passed onto her senior officers, who made the judgements about the significance of what she had discovered and the conversations that had taken place. Johnny Butler then asks her, 'In the hundreds of hours of recordings, what part on the tapes or where in the tapes does it refer to any conversations that took place in person or on the phone, about playing any part in the alleged crime?' She reluctantly agrees, she doesn't know any. He then thanked her for her time and let the judge know he had no further questions. After consulting with Mr. Smythe about any further questions, the judge thanked Detective Sergeant Mills for her time and evidence before releasing her.

After lunch, Detective Constable Meadows is called to the stand and sworn in. He gives evidence of the role he played leading up to the arrest of Johnny Butler. He explains he played Peachy's partner, and he told Mr Butler his name was Stavros, and he was a landscape gardener. He then explains to the jury the role he played with her in befriending Mr Butler. He admits that he spent more time away from the apartment, pretending to be at work when, in fact, he was at the police station or meeting senior officers, relaying his findings to them. He would take instructions on how best to proceed. All his findings are referred to in the jury bundle, which complements and effectively confirms what Detective Sergeant Mills had told the court. At this point, Mr Smythe tenders the witness for cross-examination.

Johnny Butler goes through the same process with Detective Constable Meadows that he did with Detective Sergeant Mills and manages to extract from him the fact that there was no real evidence in his gathering of evidence of any crime being committed whatsoever from the records in the jury bundle or unused material. Detective Constable Meadows runs through the reports and findings and explains to the court that they were informed one evening that there had been a breakthrough in the case. As a result of the breakthrough, Johnny Butler's home would be raided in the morning, and he would be arrested before being taken away for questioning, at which point their cover would be blown, and their work would effectively end. They continued the act of friendly new neighbours until after the arrest when they returned to duty at the local Police station and prepared full statements to give to their senior officers in the case.

Johnny finishes his cross-examination, and Judge Turpin asks Mr Smythe if he has any further questions for Detective Constable Meadows. He indicates he has none and the judge thanks Detective Constable Meadows for his time and evidence before releasing him, then looks at Mr Smythe and indicates a 15-minute break before the next witness will be called. The jury filed out, followed by the judge.

After the break, the prosecutor, Mr Smythe, calls Detective Inspector Keates to the stand, who takes the bible in his right hand before reading out the statutory statement and swears to tell the truth, the whole truth and nothing but the truth, so help me God as all the previous witnesses had. Mr Smythe takes Detective Inspector Keates through his evidence, which is not contentious. He is merely a building block that Mr Smythe is putting in place to present his strongest case and further show the jury the complete sequence of events that led to the case being built against Johnny Butler.

Detective Inspector Keates was part of a team of officers headed by Detective Superintendent Hunt that was given the case to investigate earlier the previous year as a result of certain allegations being suggested about Johnny Butler and as a direct result of the book being published, 'The Butler Did It'. He and his team had read the book, particularly Chapter 12, 'Unsolved

Murder', and looked at certain evidence in a new light. The jurors were given a copy of the book as a reference point to follow the events and the Crown's case. Detective Inspector Keates then went on to explain that he and one of his colleagues had spoken to Lucy Bale in great detail when she contacted the police.

He had taken her statement and evidence she presented to the police, a voice recording of a conversation between Lucy Bale and Johnny Butler. Johnny realised Detective Inspector Keates was not vouching for Lucy Bale or the voice recording. He was just explaining how they came into existence. Johnny simply asked Detective Inspector Keates if he knew how the recording had been made and the circumstances in which the words had been spoken. He explained he knew what he had been told by Lucy Bale. It was a conversation that took place and she recorded it because she had concerns about Johnny Butler and his behaviour. Johnny then asked Detective Inspector Keates if he was aware that the voice recording in question had been made in a video rather than just a conversation. Detective Inspector Keates says he did not know of that. He merely confirmed that the recording had been sent away for analysis and the laboratory voice recognition evidence was in the jury bundle, that the two voices were an exact match of Lucy Bale and Johnny Butler. Johnny thanks Detective Inspector Keates for his time and indicates to Judge Turpin he has finished his cross-examination.

Mr. Smythe has no more or new questions for Detective Inspector Keates, and the judge thanked Detective Inspector Keates before releasing him from the court. It is now 4.25 pm, and Judge Turpin says the court will adjourn for the day. He released the jury and explained that the prosecutor would call the next witness to the stand at 10 am. He reminds them of their legal responsibilities not to discuss the case with anyone at night and/or research it online or read about the proceedings. He then rises for the day and leaves the court. At this point, Johnny is led back down to the cells again to wait for his transport back to HMP Wandsworth. He gets back to his cell at about 6.15 pm and has time for a shower and shave before being locked up for the evening. He has got some tasty nibbles in his cupboard for dinner later on. It will not be a banquet, but Tuna and noodles followed by fruit and coffee will keep him going.

After dinner, he reflects that up until now, there have been no real shocks or fireworks in the courtroom. The case is constantly on the news channels, and although the case has been sensationalised mainly because of the events and people involved in the case, which has gripped the nation and an awful lot of countries all over the world, all that stuff is so far out of Johnny's control. He thinks maybe try not to lose sight of the fact that, in reality, it just comes down to a conspiracy to murder charge being tried at the Old Bailey.

Friday, 24th May, Johnny is woken again by a knock on the cell door, and an officer's voice reminds him that he is due back in court again later that day. Johnny has now gotten into a routine, and after a slow start, he is up doing his daily disciplines, having cereal and coffee and getting his suit on, ready to be taken to court. He arrives in good time. Mrs Canon pops into his cell and confirms that she has the papers and evidence from his phone that he has specifically asked her to get from the Crown Prosecution Service. Just before 10 am, Johnny is taken up to Court 1.

The judge's clerk left the court to let Judge Turpin know everyone was in court. Judge Turpin entered, and everyone stood before the judge before he indicated that everyone should sit down. Judge Turpin then asks Mr Smythe if he is ready to continue; Mr Smythe indicates he is. The judge indicates to his clerk to get the jury. The jury walks in and takes their regular seats. Mr Smythe calls Lucy Bale to the stand. She takes the oath with the bible in her right hand. Johnny feels quite nervous and has a mix of emotions he can't explain because he has read Lucy's statement and known her a very long time, albeit on and off. He realises that if Lucy's evidence is believed and her interpretation of what took place between the pair of them, he may well be convicted. He is fully aware of the reality of which the evidence was obtained, but will the jury understand the significance of the events which led to the admission in his voice? Or will they just hear a defendant who admitted a crime? Johnny knew he could not argue with the words. It was all going to come down to interpretation and context in the actual moment of the words being spoken, as well as the way the words were being presented by the prosecutor, Charles Smythe.

Her evidence is going to be explosive and very contentious. Mr Smythe calls her to the stand and gets her to introduce herself. She replies in a very low feminine voice, almost like a vulnerable child rather than a grown-up woman. Is she shy and nervous, Johnny wonders, or is she merely acting for her audience? It is hard to tell; on balance, Johnny realises that if he is convicted, she will probably have interviews, book deals and a whole host of possibilities to become famous and rich.

She looks like a film star who is about to give her acceptance speech at the Oscars for best actress award. Her hair and makeup were perfect. Her nails had been done. She was wearing a Sosandar women's button detail mini-tailored dress, which was a perfect fit. Bubba had always prided herself on her appearance and thought she was every man's dream. She certainly gave that appearance today at first glance. She knew by now she was going to be on the front page of every newspaper in the morning and looked like she was trying to outdo Kate Middleton, Johnny thought. Mr Smythe then asks her, 'Is it true that during a lot of the time she refers to herself as Bubba as a kind of nickname/term of endearment, and that in many of the exchanges between her and the defendant, the identity of Bubba is in effect, her?' She confirms this is true, and it is a name she likes to go by and often refers to herself as.

The prosecutor then gets her to clarify that the name is in no way an alias or meant in any way to be misleading about her true identity. He then asks her to go into her background about where she first met the defendant, how they got on, and then the long period between them meeting again, purely by chance, at the Harvester restaurant in Ashford. She then talked about the book 'The Butler Did It'. She said she has misgivings about Johnny and could not quite put her finger on it, but although she liked him on the surface, she always felt there was a dark side to him that she wanted to explore. When asked to elaborate on what she had just said, she said it was just a feeling she had. She could not explain it, maybe it was simply her woman's intuition!

They then went through certain WhatsApp messages and texts from a 150-page bundle of messages that they had exchanged on the social media platform Messenger. They were all in the jury bundle, so Mr Smythe would just indicate page numbers and ask Lucy to read out certain messages. He then asked Lucy about how their friendship had rekindled and how she saw the relationship. She said they were both single and started hanging out. Johnny had said he wanted a film made and told her he thought she would make a great leading lady when the film was made. She said she had felt flattered and, of course, she would be happy to try acting because she thought she could play the role very well, and she felt her appearance would add to the character that Johnny was suggesting.

She then felt that Johnny wanted to write a new novel which was based on her, which would certainly be an interesting project to explore and be part of. In her evidence in chief, she was keen to portray herself as some kind of innocent virgin who really was being led by Johnny Butler and just following his wishes. She certainly liked the idea of portraying 'butter would not melt in her mouth'. She accepted the frequency of messages had been very intense, and very quickly, a physical aspect of their relationship had developed. Mr Smythe asked her how she thought the relationship changed at a certain point. She acknowledged that she felt she had been seduced by Johnny and his charm, his way with words, and maybe she had just got carried away with some of his promises about the future.

She then thought that, as a result of sleeping together, their relationship had a new dynamic. She had thought originally that they were casual and exclusive. That was the term she used. After lunch, Mr Smythe continues questioning Bubba. She then explained she got the feeling Johnny may well be having the same type of relationship with other women. She said she thought he was always chatting to other women and offering them roles in the film and characters being written about them. She thought he was using his newfound success and career more as a dating app, a bit like Tinder, just promising multiple women fame and success and seducing them. She felt he was nothing more than a total womaniser after a while. She had started to check his phone and email to see if she was right or mistaken about her beliefs.

Then she started recording some meetings between them. Then, after a period, she had taken her evidence to the police because of what had been said in one conversation. She had been interviewed, given her statement and agreed she would be happy to testify in court if need be. Mr. Smythe asked her a few more questions about her relationship with Johnny and the fact that she felt betrayed by Johnny.

Then, he plays the recording of a conversation that had taken place between her and Johnny Butler. The conversation goes Johnny: 'I think you are a real man, not like most of the men I know who are pretending and fake. You are a real man. Did you really arrange a contract killer to murder Mikey?' Johnny replies, 'You bet I did. I got him whacked in 1999'. The tape ends. The clock had just turned 4.05 pm. Mr Smythe had played it to perfection. He looks at the clock, then looks at the jury, then turns to the judge and says, 'I have no further questions for this witness' Your Honour. The very last words the jury had heard were an admission by Johnny Butler that he had committed the crime for which he was on trial.

The judge asked Johnny Butler if he would like to cross-examine Lucy Bale. Johnny indicates that he would like to cross-examine Miss Bale about her evidence. Judge Turpin then decided that the court would adjourn for the day. He then explained to the jury that Monday, 27th May, was a bank holiday, and the court would not sit on Monday. The court will resume on Tuesday at 10 am. Judge Turpin issues his daily directions and legal instructions to the jury before sending them home for the day. After the jury leaves, he asks Mr Smythe when he thinks he may be presenting his last witness for the prosecution. Mr Smythe smiles and says, 'Miss Lucy Bale will be my last witness.' Judge Turpin then asks Johnny how long his cross-examination may last. Johnny looks at Judge Turpin and says, 'I would like to reserve my position dependent upon the answers I receive to the question I have.' Judge Turpin raises his head and says, 'Yes, of course Mr Butler.' He then stands and leaves the courtroom.

Johnny had overlooked the fact that Monday was a bank holiday. Johnny is being taken down. He smiles at Mrs Canon and says, 'Hope you enjoy your weekend, Mrs Canon, and I look forward to seeing you again on Tuesday.' She smiles back. The court security officer takes Johnny down. When he gets downstairs, he is told that the transport has broken down and a replacement is being sent. He is locked in the cell and offered a microwave meal while he waits. After the day he has had a microwave chicken meal, it will not solve all his problems, but it will at least take his hunger away. The meal is edible. Johnny lays down on the blue mattress, which is on top of the concrete single slab.

He starts to admire Mr Charles Smythe KC slightly more than he had before. Johnny realised he had built the case up slowly all week, and then the last evidence that the jury would get to hear before the weekend, which was an extended weekend, was a confession by Johnny that he did indeed commit the crime. Mr Smythe had certainly presented his case well without any drama and then, bang gave the jury the whole case in one simple voice recording, which was confirmed as the defendant in his voice. It's a total masterstroke! Then Johnny realised that the tape was now in evidence and had been played in court to the jury. What on earth were the press and TV companies going to report about Friday's proceedings in the courtroom and, in particular, Bubba's testimony and the tape's contents? Johnny realised he had until Tuesday morning to move on from Friday and prepare for cross-examining Lucy Bale.

The only comfort Johnny felt he could take from the case was that he had known what was coming in reality. It just seemed a lot worse when he heard it in the courtroom. At that moment he thought about Elizabeth Butler and wondered how she and her broken leg were doing. At least on the upside, it was as Mrs Butler had gauged from very early on all about Bubba. 'All about Bubba, it certainly was.' That was for sure. The whole case was about Bubba's evidence, but it was a lot more about Bubba than people realised. Johnny realised he would need to separate Bubba and her evidence, make them two separate entities and show the jury how her evidence was all about her with no concern for the truth or reality. He was done for if he could not break her down and, metaphorically speaking, would be sent to the gallows!

His cell door opens a bit later, and he is told his transport is now here. He is led out to the vehicle. The officer takes off the handcuffs connecting him and the officer, and he is placed in a cubicle on his own in the back of the truck. He realises that the drive back to HMP Wandsworth is a lot quicker than usual. It is now later in the evening, and the rush hour traffic has finished by now, he guesses. The gates are opened at the prison entrance. The vehicle drives into the holding area and is checked before being allowed to drive into the prison and the reception area, where prisoners are processed. Johnny is led into the reception, and his handcuffs are now removed. He is met by a rather large female officer who smiles at Johnny and says, 'So the Butler Really Did it then, Johnny.' Johnny laughs and says, 'Watch this space'. It has now become a joke; everywhere he goes in the prison, he is having his leg pulled by prisoners and officers. It was all over the news and media about the confession, and no one was interested in anything Johnny said. Still, that is life and prison life, for sure. Johnny couldn't afford to let any of the remarks or jokes about him get to him. It was a phase. Maybe as the weekend passed, it would fizzle out a little, but at the same time, Johnny did think some of the comments and jokes were quite funny. At least he had not lost his sense of humour.

Saturday morning, Johnny wakes up later without a bang on his cell. So, Saturday morning and canteen day. Canteen day was probably the best day and atmosphere in prison in general. Prisoners get their purchases of tobacco, phone cards and food purchases, including sweets, treats and drinks. Johnny remembered being on remand at HMP Elmley, and one week, the company making up the canteen packs, which are effectively clear bags so contents can be seen and checked before the bags are opened, which avoids a whole host of short claims no doubt delivered the canteen bags but left them unattended for a brief period. Some prisoners saw the opportunity and helped themselves to about 50 or so bags full of goodies, including tobacco. By the time the alarm had been raised, it was way too late. The bags were in circulation, open and emptied. Then no one could prove anything. They had locked the wings down and searched every cell but never caught the culprits.

That was not the case today. the canteen was issued, and

most prisoners were in a good mood, puffing away like chimneys or eating sugary sweets to get high and hyper. Johnny ventures out on the landing and sees some newspaper headlines. He doesn't bother reading any of the articles. No point whatsoever. He was living through the events they were reporting about. Later on, after lunch, he starts walking around the yard on his own. After a while, he kept passing a younger group of lads whom he had spoken to a little, and as he passed them, they would sing, 'There is only one Johnny Butler.' He liked that song or chant. Maybe that was just the lift he needed to face the music again on Tuesday Morning. Saturday evening already. Johnny got his head down early.

Sunday morning, there's not much going on. After lunch, Johnny notices Columbo is on TV. Johnny grew up watching Peter Falk as Columbo and loved him. He was a shrewd, intelligent character who appeared to bumble about, but he got the job done. Johnny always remembered him for saying, 'There's just one more thing.' That was just before he was about to solve the case and unravel a whole tissue of evidence or inconsistencies which would catch the culprit out with their fanciful version of reality and crack the case.

Johnny watches Columbo and cannot remember the particular case which is on TV. He thoroughly enjoyed watching the program and realised Columbo was always ahead of the game. He just never let on until the end. As always, Columbo did it his way and solved the case. Monday morning, Johnny is up early enough. He has an A4 pad and decides to make some notes and comments to remind him for Tuesday in court.

On Tuesday, 28th May, Johnny is woken by the officer reminding him that he is in court again. He now has his routine and is ready for the prison transport in good time. He is put in a cell and Mrs Canon pops in just for a chat and to let him know where all the documents are that relate to all interactions between Bubba and him. Just before 10 am, Johnny is taken up to Court 1 and handcuffed to a different court security officer. Mr Smythe KC is already in court talking to some of his colleagues. The clerk lets the judge know everyone is in court, and Judge Turpin enters. The judge asked Mr Smythe and Johnny Butler if they would like to raise any outstanding matters.

No one has anything to add. The judge asks for the jury who all file in again and take their seats. The judge asks for Miss Lucy Bale. Bubba enters in a lapel long-sleeved double-breasted blazer dress with all the matching accessories. Johnny thought that she looked very elegant and wanted and needed to look the part for the court and, more particularly, the photographers and film crews outside the court. Still, he could not deny she looked stunning.

Johnny starts gently asking her about her background. Then moves on to her character. He asks her about the honesty of her evidence and, in particular, the presentation of her evidence. He then asks her if she feels she has missed anything and offers the chance to correct anything if she likes. Lucy confirms that she has been honest throughout and was honest with the police from the outset. She confirms that she has not misled the police or court in any way. Then Johnny asks her if she has any other agenda other than being honest and assisting the jury in seeing the truth.

She looks shocked by the question. 'No, of course not', in her sweet angelic voice. Johnny then goes over the relationship they had again. He suggests that due to her previous relationship with Zac, she had become accustomed to the high life and having money to throw around like water. As a result of losing that life, she had become desperate to become cash-rich again. She denied it. Johnny then asked her if, as a result of her insecurities, maybe she needed to become famous at all costs, regardless of how she achieved that. 'No', she answered. He then asked her if she saw Johnny and the book as her vehicle to fame and riches. 'No,' she replied. Johnny then asked if she had received any financial offers as a result of her giving evidence in the case.

Mr Smythe objected to that line of questioning. He argued that any offers she had since received were irrelevant because they may have come as a result of the situation that she had found herself in. They could not be held against her if any existed. The judge agreed with Mr Smythe and said Lucy Bale had made it clear in her evidence she was just reporting facts that had happened at a previous time and could not foresee or be accountable for events since that. He told Johnny to move on.

Johnny then starts going through the WhatsApp messages and the social media messages. A lot of them were Bubba promising Johnny sexual heaven and promising to fulfil all his sexual fantasies. She came across as a woman hell-bent on finding fame in books and, in particular, in films. Then, after a few more, it was very clear to everyone in the court that maybe the very well-dressed, elegant, softly spoken witness had a different side to her character or maybe a few sides to her character.

The messages indicated that Johnny had not seduced her. She had been the architect of the sexual relationship which they had. Johnny then asked her if she thought she was grasping. 'No, not at all' she replies. Johnny, by now, knows he can't do much more. He can't keep talking about two people acting out in the bedroom and promising to fulfil each other's fantasies and decides to move on. Johnny then asks for the voice recording to be played again for her and the jury. After listening, Johnny asks her how the recording came into existence. She replies that from time to time, she recorded conversations between them. He asked why. She replies, 'No real reason, sometimes I did'. Johnny then asks where are the rest? She replies, 'I deleted them. The only reason I kept this one was because of what you said. Then Johnny asks where the rest of the conversation is. Why only this segment in what may have been a much longer conversation? She replied she had confronted him about one specific issue, the murder in 1999 and recorded it as proof. It was just a hunch she had and wanted clarity!

Johnny then asked her if they had made videos of when they were in bed together playing games, including role play, so that they could watch them later for sexual pleasure. She replies, 'No, never'. Then Johnny smiles at her and says 'just one more thing' and asks for a video which was on his phone when it was seized to be played in court. The judge sends the jury to lunch and asks about the video. Johnny explains it was on his mobile phone when the police seized it. The judge asks about the contents of the video. Johnny describes it as an adult video made between the witness and himself. Mr Smythe suggests to the judge that it is merely an attempt by the defendant to somehow blacken the character of Lucy Bale and embarrass her in front of the jury. The judge says the matter will be resolved after lunch.

After lunch, the debate continues; Johnny argues that not admitting the tape into evidence would create a total imbalance in the proceedings. Johnny has said it is the heart of his defence, and after listening to Lucy Bale testify, he is entitled to put it to her in cross-examination and let the jury hear it and understand it. Judge Turpin allows the tape into evidence based on the seriousness of the allegation and after listening to both arguments. The judge asks for the court to be set up to allow the jury, as well as the court, to watch and listen to the video. There is a brief delay, and the judge asks for the jury back.

The video is played. It is a role-play sexual fantasy between Bubba and Johnny, which lasts about 17 minutes. Bubba is dressed as a female cop with the outfit, handcuffs and all the matching accessories. Johnny is dressed as a gangster, and after she starts questioning him, the video plays out in a fashion where she succumbs to Johnny sexually. Just before that, the conversation goes Johnny: 'I think you are a real man, not like most of the men I know who are pretending and fake. Did you really arrange a contract killer to murder Mikey?' Johnny replies, 'You bet I did. I got him whacked in 1999'. Johnny stops the tape and replays that fraction again for everyone to hear and see.

The tape plays out with full-blown sex and her screaming at him, 'I love it. I love you, Johnny.' The tape finishes, and Johnny turns to Bubba, who has just watched and listened to the tape. He asks her, 'It is true, isn't it? You took the voice recording from that sex tape, which was a role-play between a gangster and a female cop that we played out merely as a sexual fantasy.' She replies, 'No, that was a separate occasion'. That was a different time. He then asked her why she said they had never made sexual videos as a couple. She replied, 'I forgot about that'.

The date on the tape was a couple of months before she gave her statement to the police. Johnny asked her 'why would you wait two months or more to tell the police about the admission and the information on the tape. She looks lost. He then asks her again, why not tell the police straight away. She replied that she was under a lot of pressure and stress and not coping well at the time! She was confused.

Johnny then asks her 'Why you felt the need to go through his phone and emails without his permission, as she admitted she had in her statement and direct testimony. She replies that she was looking for more evidence. He then asks her, 'Were you looking for evidence of his womanising and philandering or evidence of a crime? She replies, 'About the murder, obviously'.

Johnny takes a step back and composes his next question to Lucy Bale. He says, 'Isn't the truth of the whole matter that after meeting up again and reading the book, you saw this as an opportunity to change your life forever? You loved the idea of being in a film and having a novel written about you. You wanted fame and riches. You would have done anything to achieve that. Then, as a result of your insecurities and the relationship not going how you wanted it to, you became suspicious about other women and realised that just maybe you were going to lose out on everything you craved so much. As a direct result of your fears, you took the opportunity to pursue fame and fortune by becoming the star witness, which you clearly knew would be in 'The Trial of the Century'. You then misrepresented reality by telling a tissue of lies to the police and this court. You thought you had it all worked out, but you forgot about sharing the video with me. She bursts into tears and screams, 'No, that is not true'. Johnny then accuses her of lying. She denies it. Johnny looks at the clock and then looks at Judge Turpin. I have no more questions for this witness, Your Honour. Judge Turpin looks at Miss Bale, then turns to Mr Smythe and asks if he has any further questions for the witness. No, your honour. The judge turns to Lucy Bale and says, 'The witness is excused'.

Mr Smythe then says he wants to present a piece of evidence that the defendant has not agreed upon in advance. The judge looks at the jury and sends them home for the day, reminding them of their duties and giving his instructions not to discuss the case at all. After the jury leaves, Mr Smythe explains to Judge Turpin that he wants to put Johnny Butler's previous convictions into evidence. Mr. Smythe handed the judge's clerk a copy of the criminal convictions, who handed it to the judge. The Judge glanced at the list and appeared to read it to himself. He then asks Johnny why it should not be allowed.

Johnny argues that the convictions were after the allegation before the court today and were not evidence of his previous character at the time of the allegation before the court. Mr Smythe reiterates his desire to have them put to the jury as they are relevant to the character of the man who is on trial today. Judge Turpin says he will rule on the matter first thing in the morning before the jury returns. The court is adjourned for the day. Johnny is led away and taken back to HMP Wandsworth. He reflects on the way back; he did his job to the best of his ability. He had given the jury a realistic and plausible alternative they could hang their hat on, that was for sure! On entering the prison reception, Johnny was greeted by the same officer he had been on Friday, who smiled and said, 'The plot thickens, Johnny'. My God, Johnny realised they were all following the trial daily. Johnny gets back to his cell, changes out of his suit, and grabs some nibbles from his cupboard before grabbing a shower before the end of the association.

On Wednesday, 29th May, Johnny was up early and awake when his cell door was knocked. He gets ready and is driven in prison transport from HMP Wandsworth to the Old Bailey. Just before 10 am, he is back in court. The clerk lets Judge Turpin know, and soon after, Judge Turpin enters. He says that in light of the arguments the previous day, he finds that the previous convictions are not relevant or admissible by the Crown unless the defendant, in his defence, suggests he is a person of good character. If this happens, he will allow the Crown to use the convictions to put before the defendant as evidence that he is not a person of good character. Mr Smythe then confirmed to Judge Turpin that this was the case for the prosecution. Judge Turpin then looks at Johnny and asks, 'Are you ready to present your defence?'. Johnny replies he has nothing further to add to his defence. He will argue his defence with a closing argument based on the witness's testimony and evidence presented by the Crown.

The Judge turns to Mr Smythe and asks are you ready with your closing argument? Charles Smythe indicates he will be by 11.30 am. The Judge then turns to Johnny and says, 'Mr Smythe will present his closing argument, which will be followed by your closing argument before I sum the case up for the jury and send the jury out after giving them the necessary legal directions with regards to the law. Johnny is taken back down to the cells. At 11.25 am, he is taken back up to court. The clerk lets the judge know. Judge Turpin enters. He asks the clerk to get the jury. The jury walks in and sits down. The judge then tells the jury the evidence and witnesses have all been heard now. The prosecution and defence will now make their closing arguments about the evidence and facts in the case.

Mr Smythe argues that the evidence in the court that has been presented paints a clear picture of events. There is no doubt that a man was murdered, and because of a lack of evidence, no arrests or convictions have ever been made due to the lack of evidence. Then, more recently, as a result of police hard work, diligence and determination, there were breakthroughs in the case, and witnesses came forward to cooperate and give evidence of the guilt of the defendant in this cold, calculated murder case. The facts presented in the case clearly show how and why the defendant committed the crime. It was an impressive speech, Johnny thought. He went through all the evidence and told the jury the police and crown had finally put all the pieces together in a complicated unsolved murder and invited them to convict Johnny Butler based on the evidence. Now, it's just 1 pm, and the judge sends the jury off for lunch before adjourning until after lunch.

2.15 pm Johnny is led back into court. The judge and then the jury returned for Johnny Butler's closing argument. Johnny stands up and looks at the jury. The last thing he is going to do is attack Charles Smythe KC. That would be pointless. He knew it wasn't personal and just about the facts. Johnny then addresses the jury and explains in his closing argument. Everyone agreed a brutal murder did take place, but there was insufficient evidence to charge anyone and take them to court and face trial. Then, in recent times, as a result of police work and anonymous tips, the case was reopened. Until now, there has been no evidence of any crime committed by Johnny Butler until Lucy Bale goes to the police. The whole crown prosecution case depends upon Lucy Bale.

To put it at its lowest point, if Lucy Bale did not go to the police, there would be no case at all, and none of us would be here today. There is no evidence of a contract killer, no record of a contract killer, no payments to a contract killer, and no evidence of contact with a contract killer whatsoever. He then goes on to argue that Lucy Bale wanted to live a better life; she wanted the so-called 'High Life', which she believed was very attractive and glamorous. She thought she had found that and was determined to get it with me. There is nothing wrong with that, he indicates; a man or woman pursuing a life they crave is not necessarily bad if that is what they want. Lucy Bale being in films and having a book written about her character does not make her unreliable or bad.

The whole problem started when Lucy believed everything was slipping away from her. She stopped trusting me, she just kept offering highly sexualised fantasy and fulfilment to keep me happy. That is supported in all the records of social media and WhatsApp messages. There is no evidence I seduced her. Of course, I was happy with that arrangement but not the architect of it. Nothing wrong with that. The real problem is she has presented evidence to the police and court which is misleading.

She has blatantly lied and taken on a new agenda which is about her becoming rich and famous in a highly controversial and attention-grabbing trial. She would dearly like to portray herself as a reliable witness. Still, no one who is of good character would dream of holding onto an admission of such a serious crime for a long period unless they had another agenda and options to consider. She was unreliable, and nothing she said could be relied upon, as was demonstrated in the court by the video of sexual role play.

He then asked the jury to return a not-guilty verdict based on the lack of reliable evidence presented in the case by any credible witness. He asked them to trust their gut instincts when considering Lucy Bale's evidence and ignore it and dismiss it. Johnny tells Judge Turpin he has finished, and the judge tells the jury he will start summing up the case to them at 10 am. He then sends the jury home and adjourns for the day. Johnny is taken down to the cells, where he will wait for his transport back to HMP Wandsworth.

On Thursday, 30th May, 09.30 am, Johnny is back in a cell below the Old Bailey, waiting to be taken to Court 1. At about 09.50 am, Johnny is taken up to court. Mr Smythe is, as always, in the court. The judge's clerk asks Mr Smythe and Johnny if they are ready. They indicate they are. The clerk lets the judge know. Judge Turpin entered shortly after and asked his clerk to get the jury. The jury enters and takes their seats. The judge then explained to the jury he would now sum up the case for them. Judge Turpin starts with the first witnesses and goes through what all the witnesses have said in their evidence, including the witness statements that were read out in court. He is very experienced in such matters and Johnny thinks he has a skill in delivering a summary which contains little or no emotion.

He could be reading a recipe from a cookbook rather than summing up a conspiracy to murder case. The judge takes about 2 hours to summarise all his notes. He didn't take a break at all; he did take a swig from what looked like a glass of water on a few occasions before finishing. He then says to the jury that after lunch, he will give them instructions before sending them out to deliberate.

At 2 pm, everyone is back in court. Judge Turpin gives the jury instructions. Effectively they were charges or directions, a set of legal guidelines given by the judge to a jury in a court of law. They are an important procedural step in a trial by jury and, as such, are a cornerstone of the criminal process in many common law countries. He made it crystal clear if they had reasonable doubt, their duty was to find the defendant not guilty, and if they had no reasonable doubt, they should find the defendant guilty. He made it clear they should deliberate with care and thought about the case. They were clearly necessary principles to uphold their duty as a jury. Then, the judge explained to the jury that they now needed to go and discuss the case and evidence between them before reaching their verdict. Judge Turpin emphasised there was no time frame for a verdict. He would allow them as long as necessary to reach their verdict.

He reminded them they should take lunch, a break in the morning as well as the afternoon as normal, and they would be fed as usual. He finished by saying he would like the verdict to be unanimous. Then he sent them out. What would their verdict be? Judge Turpin then turned to Mr Smythe and Johnny and let them both know his clerk would be keeping in regular contact with the jury room in case they required any further assistance from the court about the evidence or guidance in their duties. He will also let the judge know when they have reached their verdict. At such times Mr Smythe and Johnny would be informed and brought back into court. Judge Turpin rises and leaves the court.

Johnny is led away as he passes Mrs Canon on the way out; he says, 'Thanks for what you did for me'. She smiles back and replies, 'Good luck, Mr Butler'. Johnny is taken back down to the cells and offered a coffee while he waits. Later that day, at 4.30 pm, the jury was sent home, and the court adjourned for the day. Shortly after, Johnny is back on his way to HMP Wandsworth. It's certainly got real now, that was for sure! The jury could come back at any time.

The press was in a total frenzy now. Everyone knew the jury was out in the trial of the century and considering their verdict. Did the Butler Do It or not? was the only question being asked by everyone. The trial they thought on balance had lived up to the hype, in particular by Johnny defending himself due to the unforeseen circumstances about Mrs Elizabeth Butler KC. Mr Charles Smythe KC and Johnny Butler were being billed as David and Goliath.

All the serious commentators said you could never second guess a jury as they had listened to everything in court since day 1. Then the next question flying about was, 'How long for a verdict? How long would the jury be out? That was anyone's guess. Johnny gets back to his cell and goes through his usual routine before being locked in for the night.

Friday, 31st May, Johnny wakes up and goes through his daily routine before being taken back to the Old Bailey. The jury continues their deliberations, and Johnny continues to wait downstairs in a cell. It is just a waiting game now. It seems like hours and hours later, his cell door opens, and a custody officer tells him it is lunchtime and asks him what he would like. Johnny selects the minced beef and vegetables, coffee and fruit. At about 2 pm, the officer comes back for the empty packaging and cutlery and lets Johnny know it is now 2 pm and the court is back in session or more to the point the jury is deliberating again.

A couple of hours go by, and his cell door opens again, maybe a drink to keep him going, or his prison transport is ready to take him back to HMP Wandsworth. The officer tells him the jury has reached a verdict, and everyone is due back in court. Johnny is led up to Court 1. Judge Turpin had previously advised that now Johnny had finished his defence, he would stand in the dock for the verdict when the jury came in.

Mr Smythe is at his bench. The clerk indicates he will let the judge know. Judge Turpin entered and let everyone know the jury had indicated that they had reached a unanimous verdict. The judge asks the clerk to get the jury. A few minutes later, the jury walked in and took their seats. The judge then asks the jury if they have reached a verdict that they have all agreed upon. The foreperson says they have.

The clerk then reads out the one charge against Johnny Butler for conspiring in the murder of Mikey in 1999. Johnny can't hear what the clerk is reading out as his mind is all over the place! The foreperson answers. We find the defendant 'Not Guilty'. Johnny is shaken, and his legs wobble. It's all over. Johnny manages to compose himself a little now with a glass of water.

The journey of a young wayward lad becoming an organised crime figure before becoming a published author and then successfully defending himself in the trial of the century. It had certainly been an interesting journey, that was for sure. He had no regrets and wouldn't change a thing. He then stands in the dock and thinks to himself it's true: 'The Butler Really Did It'.

THE END

ABOUT THE AUTHOR

The Butler Really Did It is the author's second novel.
It is the sequel to *The Butler Did It*.
The author is enjoying his writing and exploring his new career.

Printed in Great Britain
by Amazon

40592523R00129